I0699736

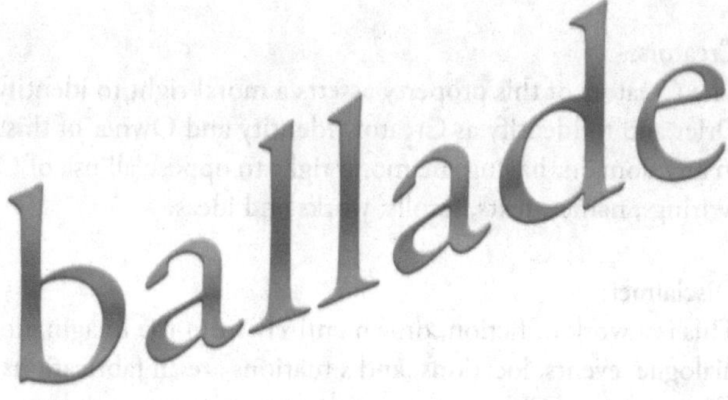

Book One

Four Tales
Inspired by Classic Ballads
of Long Ago

Realized by Terry Ulick

Ballade Book One

ISBN: 979-8-9880490-8-1

Published by:

Wherever Books LLC
A Division of Renegade Company LLC
Littleton, CO 80127
www.whereverbooks.com

Wherever Books and Renegade Company are registered trademarks
of Renegade Company, LLC

Roku Channel:
Wherever Books
Fantasy Realized
Dream Traveller

Trigger Warning

If you are sensitive to obscene language, graphic descriptions of explicit sex acts, use of language describing bodies that is not anatomical and is degrading, dirty dialogue between despicable and disgusting characters, please do not read any further. This book will upset you and you will be offended.

If you are suffering from any form of physical, mental, verbal, or sexual abuse, or suffer PTSD from such abuse or other types of violence or harm, please, shut this book. It will trigger you throughout.

If you have religious beliefs based on the teachings in the Bible, either one or both Testaments, this book contains concepts and references to religion, clergy, and Christian teachings that will upset and offend you. This is not a book about the *Bible* or of religious teachings and creates its own narrative of God, Angels, and demons. It will upset you and offend you. It is suggested you stop reading now.

Terry Ulick
Author

FOLK BALLADS
REALIZED
US * UK

Table of Contents

Introduction

When I was a young girl, I used to seek pleasure. When I was a young girl, I used to drink ale. Right out of the alehouse, and down to the jailhouse, right out of the jailhouse, and down to my grave.

"Turn the dial. We're tired of that one."

Static and buzzing, snippets of talk, a few blaring hog future reports, then a rock station!

My mother was a tailor, she sewed those old blue jeans. My father was a gamblin' man, way down, in New Orleans…

Riding past the tower the signal was loud and strong, after *House of the Rising Sun* came a song that made me think of life beyond this one.

I'm just a poor wayfaring stranger, while journeying through this Land of woe But there's no sickness toil or danger, n that bright world to which I go. I'm going there to see my Mother/, she said she'd/he said he'd meet me when I would come. I'm just a-going over Jordan. I'm just a-going over home. I'm just a-going over Jordan. I'm just a-going over home.

All too soon it was that Angelic voice singing,

Are you going to Scarborough Faire, parsley, sage, rosemary and thyme. Remember me to one who lives there. She once was a true love of mine…

Driving past the city, the signals faded and I kept turning the dial for something, anything. Heading into the rural south brought the songs I had been hoping to hear.

Now everybody knows the reason for the fall. When woman cheated man down in Paradise's Hall. That woman cheated me, and took me for a ride. And like the weary fox, I need a place to hide. She took all the love that a poor boy could give her, her hair shone like gold in the hot morning sun. She took all the love that the poor boy could give her, and left me to die like a fox on the run…

And then magic. A voice from six centuries back that told of a woman I loved who was but a wisp of air. A vision. A ghost. For a moment, I was taken out of the endless ride in the car my family lived in…

My true love said to me, my mother won't mind. And my father won't slight you, for your lack of kind. And she took my hand from me, and this she did say, it will not be long love, till our wedding day.

My fate was sealed. I was not of this time or place. I was a prisoner of the 20th century, of a culture that could only offer,

She bop a lub ah, she's my baby, she bop a lub ah, she's all mine…

It wasn't that I didn't like Elvis or pop music. I liked that as well. It just didn't take me to the places I was from. My home. The place I longed to be. I always knew I was not of this time or place. I had been punished by some dark sorcerer and fated to be enslaved in the backroads of the wasteland all feared, the barren culture seen only in crystals of beauties wearing silks and satins with eyes that stole your soul and made them young forever. I had been a peasant living in a clearing in the woods of warring tribes of Scotland, a place invaded by another clan and I boldly made my stand.

Making a stand against naked men painted in their clan colors may not have been the wisest move, but, what was a young warrior intent only on protecting the virtue of his lovely maid to do? Run? Hand her over to them without taking a few of the heathens down? Never!

More unkind than such death was to be held captive by a band of ne'er-do-wells running from the law in the 1960s. I had always been an outlaw throughout time. I had to face it. That had long been my fate, and the life of an outlaw is full of bawdy tales, and for me many maidens fair who were maidens no longer after a visit from me in their hovel. I was the highwayman at times, an errant knight when I wished, or a defiant rebel when the maids were keen on such. Whether it meant wearing armor or kilt, finery or running naked through the heather, it was always in pursuit of the sweetest maidens. There is no greater battle than one for love. Of that, I was sure. I know it was why I had died many times and in endless places in the days before the Amerikees, the sad migration to a new land that held no honor or majesty. Taking maiden pride was my duty, my rakish looks and charm my greatest weapon, foolish nobleman or sheriffs dispatched as the only way to liberate their women to my arms.

As relentless as I was in pursuit of maidens fair, I had run afoul of wizards and witches, and too often was in the keep, chained for my wickedness of loving the fair sex. My punishment was to be cast five hundred years hence, held prisoner in a cage called a 62 Oldsmobile that was a carriage without horses to pull it. And most cruel, tortured by hearing ballads sung of my many conquests, those tender loves I rambled the English backroads to find. The prison I was in had a evil device full of lights and glyphs that lit the cage, most cunning, that played madrigals to remind me of loves lost and my capture. What a cruel fate I was given, say I.

All my deeds were ever in the name of love. My crime was love savage and untamed with beauties inspired by what I offered.

Then my sentence for such. In this heartless land, to go into the Piggly Wiggly and ask if there was any rotting fruit they'd spare a starving lad most in need of sustenance. Then to find some hellhole called a motel where many had been loved, but the remains of their loving covered the bedding and vile carpet.

Even the most defiant outlaw deserved no such fate. But, there it was. The land of plenty was plenty of nothing. Lacking what any lover needed, there were no castles to storm, no steeds to ride, no marauders to challenge. Endless wasteland was all that lay ahead. No fiefdoms, no missions, no bounty, and no towers with a beauty to free. The torture was what the lurking soothsayers whispered to lords and dukes. It was the fate of the boldest wayward knight who sought the brides of such foul royalty wishing only to show them I was their true love. Yet, with my fate sealed ever so, I would break my chains, run from this land of peasants too fearful to rise up angry. I would lead a crusade most holy and true.

Alas, it was no longer such a time. I am prisoner bound by time and space, a spell cast that has no end. Time is the worst of enemies. There is no return, no way home, no battle to wage that can undo that which has been done.

So, here I sit, paying my due, thinking of loves most wondrous and kind. Reminded that I was the one who fought too bravely and loved too many. That, fellow wanderer, is the worst offense of any. To love. But is there a more noble pursuit? I think not. I gladly payed the fare to travel that road. To be a prisoner of love is the badge of honor few are given.

I had to stand my trial, I had to make my plea. They placed me in a criminal box, and sore commenced on me. Deprived me of my liberty, deprived me of my rest. Now go my lovely Flora, the lily of the West.

Here, in the box that is a dungeon cold and dark, I write tales that true are bawdy and not for the faint of heart. Know they tell only of what I have endured, of loves lost, of times now gone. They are ballades sung now by beatniks and hippies and minstrels wandering street fairs or playing in what are called coffee shops. None know battle or have rescued a damsel for the only reward expected… a night in her embrace. No, they sing of a time, but are not of that time.

I am.

What follows are tomes I have scribbled to speak of my adventures through many lives. They are all true, and still sung of as ballades. Only I know what they sing of, and of what such ditties reveal. They chronicle my loves and my battles waged for honor and freedom. I hope they inspire. There is no honor in this land. There is no magic, no glory. Just a prisoner who can tell tales that reveal a life worth living.

A life where love is the only thing worth living and dying for.

I am a mere wisp of a time long past. Listen carefully, for every song sung now comes from deeds of ones like me long ago. All tell my tale, and all are a story worth hearing.

The wayward love of many maidens most loving and kind,
Terry Ulick

The Faire

Full Song Name: She Moved Through the Faire

My young love said to me, "My mother won't mind
And my father won't slight you for your lack of kind"
And she stepped away from me and this she did say:
It will not be long, love, till our wedding day"

As she stepped away from me and she moved through the fair
And fondly I watched her move here and move there
And then she turned homeward with one star awake
Like the swan in the evening moves over the lake

The people were saying, no two e'er were wed
But one had a sorrow that never was said
And I smiled as she passed with her goods and her gear,
And that was the last that I saw of my dear.

Last night she came to me, my dead love came in
So softly she came that her feet made no din
As she laid her hand on me and this she did say
"It will not be long, love, 'til our wedding day"

My True Love Came To Me

Watching through the window of the small hovel left to them by their parents, it was a reminder both were taken by plague. Sad as the memory be, the twin sisters were aroused watching a stately man ride by on a fine stallion. Nothing between them was said for it was not needed.

Riding slowly by their window, the man was surely of status most noble and such men were rare to their small village. Growing dark early as it be past solstice, each knew it be likely the man would need lodging and sup for the night. It was certain he was headed to the lone business of the village, an inn. They ran from the window, grabbing aprons, making sure of their beauty, then ran from their home to the inn. They were maids when there be guests there and worked only for fare left for their service.

Knowing the only hope of finding love and husband would be the blessing they prayed for; a noble man finding his way to them with God's blessing. Both were aroused as each be sure this be the man they prayed for. Both be beauties, and lovely maidens such as they be rare, if any, in such isolated villages. Truly it would be the man's pleasure to cast eye their way. Smart they were, understanding the value of fair countenance, and most valuable they be virgin maids. There be no doubt they offered any man value equal to his wealth and honor — if any he had. Fair of skin, without blemish, slim, shaped as angels in paintings, each graced with lush brown hair down beyond their waists tied in braids, having faces most fair and lovely. Thankful for such gifts, they understood they be treasures, more lovely than any they had ever seen, even maids touted be beauties only as they be royalty. They had seen many such matrons at faires and festivals, but none beautiful as they. At such places noblemen were quick to offer them a bed, but neither be fools to lose maiden virtue to men who saw them but commoners. Nay. Such sought commoners only steal their prize, not marry. That be no bargain, and both denied all such offers.

Finding a man of honor who would value them as equal be worth all endurance of time. Now eighteen, in their prime, they looked much younger which was God's kindness as courting began earnest when twelve. Knowing age be not an issue as they be prize, the challenge was they be twins. Identical in every detail, each beautiful as the other. How could any man decide between them, or more vexing, tell them apart?

Knowing how different each was from the other in manner and belief, amazed they were as each had the same ideal in matters of husband. The fear be when a such a man crossed their path they would lavish him too much and confuse any man's wits to win his hand. Agreeing to ne'er battle or fight, such man would have to decide between the two or forgo such gift they be. Wishing only man of honor having wish of true love, he must put forth the answer.

Though each was equal in beauty, each was opposite in manner. The man would need to choose by what they were, not how they looked. It be true most men be simple in nature and be foolish, caring only for beauty. With them, they would only give time to man who would value them first by character. That would define the man beyond his mantle. It would reveal his true nature.

Fille and Fi knew they were two sides of one coin. Together bound, but each looked in a different direction. It twas accepted and could only be what it was. Having different values had not been important in daily matters but would be a challenge — for a man.

Fi knew her nature was such a man may think her less the prize than Fille. She was of heart, wanting only love true. Being sensible, caring, and aware of her feelings, she truly thought those her only offerings. Love was of the heart, nothing more.

Knowing Fi inward by nature, Fille understood that what be inside be virtue over time, but a man first saw what was before his eyes, and yea, valued what he be offered and in need of. Being baser in their nature, men admired a maid free with affection willing to offer body with heart. They had desire she understood — to be loved for their manhood, knowing such act would give her pleasure same. Knowing a man would place high value on her embrace, giving such kindness when Fi would not be a mighty advantage. She was ready to give a wee bit of bodily love before marriage to show the right man what pleasure waited with her as bride.

Discussing their manner many times, Fi held fast any good man would only value a maid who valued herself. Attempting to get Fille to understand any whore or wench gave such treasures away, thus good for a tryst, she maid not be one to marry. She told women did such for coppers, or the devil in them, and Fille would not be prize if free with virtue. Fille would scoff at her notions. There was no changing her mind on the matter. Fi hoped when a good man came passing, he would ask not for such sins; that he would value virtue above carnal lust. Fretting a man may use Fille then discard her as whore, that worry held fast in her thoughts. When the time came, she prayed God protect her sister from such use.

It was in their talks the sisters devised a compromise. A man, knowing not which be which, could be tested. Fille could talk of making love one day. Fi could talk of chastity the next. They would find out what manner of man he be speaking of both. The matter of deception was of no matter. The character of the man was. Fi would need be sure such man would not take bodily pleasure only because it be offered. Fille would learn if he be a match for her desires and not timid in such ways. Each would test what the other could not, finding which one the man be suited for.

Riding had always been a pleasure to Cadoc. On his steed he was free to go anywhere. A stout stallion was all he needed to pursue demons or escape when there be too many. With just his sword, saddle, and pack he was a free man, not beholding to any lord or manor — not even the King. He was a knight not of King, but Rome. He be emissary of the church, free from honor to any kingdom, beholding only to Cross and Eucharist. Known by tale and legend, he be the only one of his kind. The church had no intent using treasure for rulers and houses that rose then fell. It answered only to God, not to man. Churches and abbeys were fortified mightier than castles as the Church often defied foolish orders from a kingdom and was always prepared to defeat any man thinking himself more important than the will and word of the Creator. The Church paid no tax, gave no bounty, and gave no heed to any save the Pope.

Church was none concerned with the politic of the land. It paid heed of Lucifer and his minions. Such were ever present and knocked their gates in many guises and forms. The demons turned the weak against God to worship Satan, and those following darkness were dealt with. Accepting that heathens existed, their souls lost, the Church knew those souls had lost faith and folly be their only path. Twas the job of priests to show the way, and that had always been and would always be. Those taken by the demons were used to attack and corrupt values. Those lost souls waged battle against the righteous seeking the destruction of all that be holy.

Riding tall in his saddle, Cadoc was the knight from Rome. He alone be appointed by the Pope, thus sanctioned to fight the devil himself and all his minions. Through the ages, Popes had tried legions. Armies. Evangelicals. Being mortal, men fell to temptation. Wine, women, coins, perversions of every manner corrupted such congregations. It came to pass that one beyond temptation was groomed from birth and appointed by Pope the knight of Christ. This warrior was free to do with demons as he saw just. With demons never human, he mastered the ritual to cast them to hell. For those possessed, he was master of the Rite, expelling demon spirit from humans possessed. He knew such labor held peril as many who did such work had fallen into possession themselves. He had been tried by demons countless times, and none had ability to penetrate his defense as it not be metal. He wore divine armor. A relic of the Christ. A small pendant holding a thorn from His crown while hanging for man's sins on the cross. Cadoc had protection from Satan himself.

Riding into the village of the sisters, he smiled at the irony of the village name. Thorntree. He new not long ago village be named Roseville, having lush gardens growing the fragrant flowers used for masses, funerals, celebrations and in houses of nobles. One year a demon arrived guised as wealthy lord who bought all land rights from the owners of rose farms. Once done, all beautiful roses began to fall from their stems. Within a year, naught a rose grew no matter what be done to cure the blight. All that be left were branches and stems, them covered only in thorns. The dark lord, true demon, saw his work complete and thus left, saying to all town be named Thorntree hence. It was true. Roses never returned, and once glorious Roseville lay a ruin of but a few hovels and one roadhouse serving as inn. As Cadoc approached, it twas a reminder of ways the demon spoiled all good, leaving but ruin and decay in his passage.

Only a few peasants lived there after. Being on the King's highway, he gathered the roadhouse remained important for travelers, and those in lonely hovels likely worked the inn. It twas late in day, and he decided to sup and stay the night in the village of thorns. He thus decided to study the plants. Taste the soil. Take some cuttings to monks who worked plants to health. What had been done, Christ could undo. His battle was not only with demons, but with the destruction they left to make all suffer. The thorn trees were proof of such. He would bring roses back to tell the devil, again, evil had no power here nor any other place.

Approaching the inn, he smiled as the establishment had a well-kept sign hanging with its name: The Rose. He thought it a good omen that at least one rose remained. Little did he expect to meet two more in the form of maids most beautiful.

Resisting temptation was a quality Cadoc possessed since birth. An orphan child, he was found on hard stone steps of an ale house in the dirty city outside the walls of the Vatican. An elder priest walked by, saw a baby naked without swaddling, calm without whimpering or crying. As the concerned priest approached the child, the babe bore a look of warning that shook the old man. Seeing such a look of threat he thought it must be a demon child, born of unholy union. Thinking so, he was compelled that the devil be driven from the babe. Taking his shawl, he wrapped him tightly knowing not what powers he held. Making haste to the basilica, he rushed to find both a senior Bishop and a resident exorcist. Presenting the babe and his account of finding him, the exorcist took him and held him in his lap, sitting in front of the Christ statue. He too was an old man, near ninety, but vital still.

Knowing even if just newly born, if so possessed, the demon within could not tolerate the Christ statue or his prayers for all evil to be away. The child had large, intense eyes and stared at the Christ without fear — he appeared most enamored of Him. As prayer was read, the babe whimpered gently, the first sounds he made. The exorcist asked an attendant for holy water and oils. Once given the sacramental announcements, he doused water and oil on the infant. The little one smiled and cuddled. Finally, he took a small crucifix from his pocket and placed it in the boy's hands. Rather than repel the cross, the boy hugged it over his heart. The exorcist got up and holding the child tenderly declared no demon be in him. Be it miracle, the infant was filled only with love most true for God. The exorcist called a gathering of papal teachers and clergy, suggesting the babe be ward of the church as the child possessed love of God all could see.

Long called only "the child," the infant was kindly named Cadoc by the elder Bishop from Wales. Growing in the care of the church, he learned prayers to cast out demons, save the lost, and with help of guards, to do battle with sword and cross. He did well in studies, devoting much of his study time to the art of battle. He learned the skills of weaponry, riding the largest stallions, and mastered the ultimate battle: Exorcism. He was skilled in both the holy rituals and the art of battle to strike demons down. All such skills came to him as if he were a flower growing in the Sun. By manhood, he was both disciplined and savage when called for battle. He could spot a demon or its prey when none other could. When fully grown and mighty, he was called for audience with the pontiff and was appointed the protector of all that was holy as the Knight of the Church. His appointment was to be warrior against any working for Satan. He was truly the sword of the church, soon sent forth to find the trail of the dark lord himself. The Pope often warned him of women as he worried a temptress could offer deception such to fall man mighty as he.

It was with such caution of women he rode into Thorntree.

Riding to stables behind the lone inn, Cadoc found an older man grooming the one horse there. Looking at empty stalls, it had room for at least a dozen horses but his would be the only other this night. Dismounting, the man stood waiting. Cadoc removed his weapons and kit, then the man took the reins without speaking. Nodding, Cadoc knew the man would take decent care of his fine stallion. The stable was clean, the oats and hay fermented not, and a wall was lined with brushes and blankets. He finished looking about, hoping his lodgings would be kept so well. The man hobbled his stallion and finally spoke, saying he'd be most willing to carry his gear. Cadoc nodded with appreciation and gave the man his kit, but not his weapons. He was led to the door in front and the man led him up stairs as the building had a second floor for rooming. Following him, Cadoc had no need to ask of the room given. The place was well cared for and clean. After a long ride, his thoughts were on a meal and how soon he could rest.

Cadoc put weapons down and asked the man to tell keep of the inn he would appreciate a hearty meal in short order. The man nodded but said there be no keep to tell. He was proprietor, but winked and said he would tell his missus there be hungry man waiting. Turning, he pointed to a jug of water and basin, and some cloths for drying. With that, he turned, and Cadoc had the room to himself, glad to rest before dining.

The room was in good repair, the bed decent and the pillows filled with down. It was clean and had a table and chair with oil lamp. He saw nay hint of other guests, so worried naught of securing weapons but kept a long blade on his belt as was his habit. He knew not what demon may be lurking as evil visited at unexpected times and in forms deceiving to any. The blade was made so that it formed a cross when hung on his belt or held out. It had been blessed by the pontiff himself as a symbol of the Christ.

Resisting temptation to lay down for a short time, he thought best not to and decided to wash the dust of the road away then read letters from various abbots he would be visiting in the days ahead on his visit to the land. Sitting at table, it had a decent window and noticing movement, he stared out to see who could be going about in such a lonely hamlet. From a small cottage there was a brief blur of fabric. He considered there would be a maid serving his meal and attending him, but of interest was he thought he saw two different blurs, each of its own speed and haste. He had to rub his eyes as they may still have dust of the road. That, or he was seeing double. All would be revealed when he ate but he was strangely aroused by the presence. Though knight of the church, he was no priest and hoped one day to wed a maiden fair.

He heard the door downstairs open and shut, then sounds of plates, cutlery and glasses clinking. The wee staff were hard at work. Looking forward to learning the circumstance, he knew it would be but a short wait. He organized his letters and planned a route when there was a light tap at his door.

Getting up to answer, he found himself pulling at his garments and glancing in the small mirror hanging over the basin, checking his appearance. Opening the door, he marveled for standing there, with gentle smile, was a maid. He was taken with her that instant. Everything he saw pleased him. Her shining brown hair, her lovely lips, the bloom on her cheeks, but most of all her eyes. The windows to her soul were a glimpse of pleasure. Her smile was delight. Her dress was cut to show the fine form it covered. His only thought was that she be the most beautiful woman he had yet to see.

She was no timid servant in manner. She appeared confident yet gentle and mannered. She was looking into his eyes since he opened the door and her gaze had him entranced. He bowed slightly, and she curtsied at the same moment. Like lad meeting his first lass, he stood staring in awe, though hoping it did not show. Skilled as he be keeping his manner constant, he knew she understood his true reaction. She gave slight pause, then spoke with a voice he imagined only an angel could have.

"Kind sir, we have readied your table, and your sup be ready soon. There be wine and ale waiting. I will be attending your meal. It be fine carving of local ham, fresh carrots and potato, all such roasted with ham. To start, our best cheese, and for pudding, egg bread baked with cider and spices then covered with sweet cream. Be there anything else you desire?"

His immediate impulse was to tell her that spending time with her was all he truly desired but kept his wits. He smiled at her, maid looking into his gaze yet keeping her manner respectful.

"That sounds most delicious. I can smell most of it, here, in hall. But there be something more. Sweet, fragrant."

He leaned forward a bit. He laughed.

"Why, of course, it be scent of you!"

She nodded gently. "It be rosewater, kind sir. I be glad it pleases."

He put his hand to his chin. "The scent of roses in a village where none grow. That is a pleasant gift. I have done all that need be done. I shall be down presently and my appetite for good things, we'll, it be quite strong."

She made a sweet curtsy and turned to head back down the stairs when he called out to her.

"Your name, fine miss?"

She turned enough to face him and told him she be Fille. He nodded.

"Of French descent. But no accent?"

Shaking her head politely, she had a look of sadness. "Me mum, she came from France and wished to carry on her joy of such lovely names there. She was most precious to me, and a beauty that ne'er have I seen equaled."

Nodding, Cadoc decided to find out a more of the mother and compliment the lass. "Matched, then? She may be of mind you have surpassed her."

Smiling gently, she nodded. "I think hearing such from grand man would please her kind sir, but both me mum and dad were taken by the disease. They suffer no more and are in the grace of God now." Without waiting for a reply, her emotions swelled inside her causing her to turn and head down the stairs. Cadoc understood, knowing plague to be more than rats, it be the delight of the dark lord to bring suffering to good people. It be a sad world he travelled, and darkness fell too often. He pondered what horror would be devised next to take joy from all.

He headed down the stairs hoping to find better news of other matters.

The maid was at table with basket of hot bread, slicing it in preparation of his arrival. Looking at her fine form, he said, kindly, "Thou work most quick. You just descended." The girl put the knife down and curtsied with astonishing grace. Looking up at him, as he was at least five hands taller than her small frame, her eyes were the same color but in manner, they were most different.

"Kind sir. I be Fi. You were speaking to my dear sister, Fille. We be twins and most difficult for any to tell one from other."

Standing with his arms crossed, the lovely lass in front of him, he nodded with a look of fascination.

"It be like one person with two names. You are exact in appearance and dress. Though so alike in appearance, you surely be quite different in manner and person. It is intriguing to me. Different, yet identical. Let us leave it there, and I will appreciate you both all the more for it. That bread be calling to me!"

She moved round the table and bid him sit. Nodding, he went to a chair, but kneeled first in prayer of thanks. He kissed the linen on the table, then sat. Looking about, Fi had left and he was glad of the bread. It was rich with yeast with crisp crust. The butter was creamy and rich of fat. Tasting it, with first bite he considered it better than bread he tasted even in Rome where bread was considered art.

Though there was a pitcher of brown ale, he had no like of drink. With potable water at times spreading sickness, tasting the ale it was heady and too strong to quench his thirst. The keep came to ask if his lodging was in need of other comforts. Telling the keep it be more than expected, he begged a large pitcher of boiled water for his meal and the night. The man said he himself had taken to drinking only from his own well which he was certain of, but still boiled all for cooking or drink. Cadoc smiled, said that he had no need of ale, though it be fine, and would like only water as he ate. Getting a nod, the keep turned and went behind his counter and brought forth a pitcher with lid, then pored water. Nodding, he said the meal be near ready and left.

Admiring the water, it was clear and much needed after his long ride. With barely a sound, as promised and told by the look of passion in her eyes, it twas Fille with large tray holding a plate filled with ham, generous portions and bowls of extra vegetables, gravy and ground dark mustard. The smell overtook him. He loved ham, and the tray was filled with a fine one. Taking care to set it down gently without spill, Fille smiled as she took her tray. Nodding his thanks, she smiled and turned with a flourish of her finery.

Thinking, he realized he had good lodging, delicious food, and maids belonging in castle, not as servants. He was taking his time as it was hard to find such fare. He would tell the keep at breakfast ham, cheese and bread for his ride would be most appreciated. He looked up, and the demur Fi was standing quietly gazing at him, shy in her manner. He smiled slightly as his mouth was filled with ham. She smiled too, and asked if he would like more of any, and if he liked pudding hot from oven, or rested a while. Having swallowed his food, he asked her which way she thought best. She almost seemed embarrassed and flush from her reply.

"Perhaps it be only me, but I think things best are ones we wait for."

In his training, he certainly knew how to read all signs of veiled messages. The lass was saying to him she had waited a long time for a good man, but she would have naught else. Nodding, he was gentle, yet sincere.

"Fi, ya be wise on that count. Not just pudding, but all things of value. I respect and share that mind. Many maids with naught your beauty and manner are married at twelve. You be, what, in your late teens? It be only a good man be worth the waiting, I venture."

He was looking in her eyes, and they were exceedingly kind. Keeping his stare, he felt they were mystical and thus a question formed in him. They brought out feelings from deep in him ne'er known before. She tilted her head down and gave the slightest nod.

"I can say naught else, kind sir. You understand my meaning. Yea, I know it not proper, but I need to let you know you seem the man I long dream of. The one, that, aye, I have been waiting for, fearing would never meet. Kind sir, I am not bold like Fille. This be hard for me to share. I pray you understand and tolerate my bold declaration."

Cadoc sat, filled with emotion. This beautiful maiden, one he sensed to be pure of heart and body, which was his skill to know, was saying he appeared to her as premonition. More than a dream for maiden do not wait for dreams at her age and living is such a desolate place. Like his dream of a maiden pure and loving, she had the same sense true of him. Taking chances of any sort was not prudent in hunt for demons, but this lass be Angel on Earth. He was a confident man, and he told her that after finishing his meal he desired a walk with her. He explained he too had such visions, and his vision was standing in front of him.

Looking relieved and glad she spoke her feelings, she assured him she hoped such would happen. She said she understood, ever so. With an expression beautiful, she looked into his eyes.

"Me thinks the pudding of sweet cream you wait for be ready and will be with you presently, most delicious."

They both smiled in understanding. In short time, she returned. Cadoc admired her graceful manner carrying but small tray with crock and jug of cream. Placing it before him, she came close to his side, expertly turned the quite warm crock upside down and gave it a simple tap. The pudding stayed on its plate as she lifted the crock, which she set down to the side. Lifting the cream, held it perched for pouring but looked in his eyes waiting approval. Taking his knife, he deftly sliced the mound top to bottom and the two halves each fell to their side. Knowing his choice, with a gentle pour she coated the halves with a delicate weave. Looking at her work, she nodded approval, leaned over and in a soft whisper so close to his ear he could feel her breath, told him straight, "When you taste this, think of me."

Turning as she stood back up, she left the pitcher but took only a few steps, turned back to him, with chin down and her eyes looking up into his, said, "I pray it truly be your taste." She turned and was gone.

Having dealt with many under spells and those taken by demons, he knew the message she gave was pure, only desire and hope, not some gesture to deceive or trick him. Seeing her so close, smelling her, feeling her breath warm and soft, his heart began to race. Such had never happened even when facing the evilest of vixens, or fights with monstrous henchman of the dark lord. The maid had aroused fires of passion and ignited desire he knew ne'er before. Eating pudding, he realized every bite was taste of her. The cream her offering, surely symbol of her womanhood. Savoring it, he be filled with delight eating it thus, both a delicacy and taste of the maid in his mind. He found himself in a state of what he intuitively knew was pure lust. Animal desire. He had eaten much, but now beyond hunger, only Fi could fill his need.

Stopping for a moment to gather thoughts, he understood all that had been unleashed had been held back by his teachings and duty. This day was to honor himself as a man, not noble knight. He was, like Christ, a man. Just a man. He cast away restraint to free his true self — and knew Fi wished to give her true self in return. Putting things right in his mind, he looked at the plate, thought of the message to let each bite remind him of her, smiling, as the cream could never be rich and silky as her fair skin. He then was in awe that though Fille looked just as beautiful, meeting Fi had revealed her inner beauty and he could scarce remember what Fille be like.

Knowing she would be waiting, for her protection and his, he rushed up the stairs and gathered his blessed sword and holstered it to his side. Looking in the mirror, he rinsed all supper from his face and was sure he looked powerful as his passion. Saying a simple prayer for understanding and of thanks, he left the room to meet the Fi — and with God's grace be with her.

Fi trembled as understood true the words she had whispered, and message given. Knowing each defied her caution in presenting herself as gift from God to be respected and courted properly, something in Cadoc assured her most certain he did respect her and would court truly. Inside her heart, she knew she would encounter such man but once in her life. She had blessed knowing, a voice from her Angel, that Cadoc be destined for her. No caution be needed. Telling her thoughts, hopes and dreams be most important, as was telling him being near him had given her inspiration from the Divine to make her feelings known. If not, the love given for each other could be lost forever. She trembled more, worrying if her simple words could offer the true importance of what she felt.

Although deep in thought, she heard his footsteps on the stones that led to a lone tree with a beautiful bench crafted by her father not long before he grew ill. He had given it to her, saying, "This be place where love shall join you." Each day hence she tended it. Doing such, it grew more beautiful with age. She had rushed to the bench, turned, and stood in front of it. With apron off, she knew she would please as her dress be true a beautiful thing made for this day by her mother. Azure blue, embroidered by hand with white thread making sweet pea vines and leaves, she felt as a blooming flower poised thus on those vines. Her hair was pulled back on each side, now off her cheeks, showing her face with shy honesty for his approval. Her cheeks were blush with excitement, her lips were slight red naturally. Holding herself with grace, she stood with a gentle wind sending the long hair cascading down her back and her long dress to sway and follow its will. Most enthralling, she felt passion embracing her all round, and was sure Cadoc would see such passion in her above all.

Being true to his manner as knight, he approached with a certainty that was comforting and reassuring. He said naught, reached her and stood in front of her, gazing into her eyes for a long moment. He lifted his left hand and held it out for her to take as she sat on the bench. He smiled as he bowed, examining the tree then bench. He spoke with soft manner.

"In this barren place, I find beautiful tree, bench most pleasing, and beautiful flower gracing it. How gifted I feel for such vision." She patted the bench close by her side, and Cadoc sat, close, facing her as she already turned to face him.

"My father, before he died…" They both crossed themselves. "Made this as a gift to be used by Fille or me the day we met man worthy of our love. I have kept it with care, but today is first time ever I sit on it. You be first man to sit here. I must reveal something you may think a young maid's dream…" Cadoc reached to put both her hands in his. "I assure I will accept your words as truth. Please, tell."

Holding her gaze into his eyes, she smiled. "Then, yea, I will tell you my thoughts before you left the inn to meet me here. I have long held I must remain virtuous in all things. That should a man show attention, I must maintain honor. That he should court me with like honor. Not for my beauty, but for my heart, and, yea, my respect. My virtue and love are my only true possessions and I vowed never give them to any but one worthy. Knowing most certain he would cherish them. I am not chattel or a possession and must never be treated so."

Looking at him, his sincerity radiated out as he said with voice from his heart, "Dear Fi. I true appreciate what say you. In every way I see myself standing in that very light. I would not wish a love who was other. But I interrupted you. I be most sorry. Please, I beg, continue."

She nodded, knowing he was not being impolite and was most glad of what he said.

"Your words be of great comfort to me, so worry not. I long for such. Today, since you arrived, I had a feeling that could no be denied. I thought I was just smitten by your countenance. The dreams I have had of such a man, his arrival, for so long. The need for love. I admit that all was, and is, inside me, but only one true would have led me to this bench. I had wondrous visit from my holy guardian. She filled me with message most Divine. To let maiden dreams be away, tell loving man he has opened doors to my love. Not by manner or appearance but true, as meant to be. It be will of God that we met. She be most certain it be my choice, my will, that will make it so and thus please God, and yea, each other. It was then I told my sister I had been gifted so and said words to you in a way I had no idea I could do. That I wished to meet you here. On this special bench. All has but one purpose. One message. For me, it is my message to you. It be my hope you too have the same message for this maid."

Wind blew and it washed over them gently. He had not let go her hands, and his expression grew with eyes that opened a window to his soul.

"Blessed is God and his Angels. They give us so much. Most can not see such, but true of heart can. I too was overwhelmed with an understanding that I have ne'er had. Much as yours. I was blessed with certainty that I must let you know I had abandoned all hope of love. I found no interest in ladies high or low in my travels. Today, that be gone. I knew my life had changed forever, and I would be naught without you as my love. That my life would mean nothing without you by my side. My love. My intended. It was so powerful that I knew it was the will of God, and as with you, also the choice was mine to make. That is why I am here with you on this bench. I look at you and I see my hopes and dreams. Where I had nothing, now I am full. Same like pudding you brought, there is none more needed. You have brought me all, and I know true I be but pudding, and you be crème. Two, becoming one."

Fi fell into his arms as he wrapped them round her and she sobbed tears of joy and thanks, and he did so with her.

As they clung to each other, Cadoc sensed a presence quite familiar. A demon. He whispered in her ear he sensed evil approaching. To fear not. He was knight of the church and had no fear of demons.

Battling demons when not yet a man, Cadoc had been taught much by the priests of Rome as they knew he was destined to battle such in his future appointment as Knight of the Church. Speaking to those closest and most experienced, the pontiff decided the boy had the calling. God had divined him as His warrior. His training began in earnest when he was ten, the lad already fluent in many languages including Latin.

Before his training had begun, Cadoc could not help but notice demonic possession of maids was greater than sires. Although elder priests explained with proof none maids were more vulnerable to possession, Cadoc argued it be not so. Thinking it only priests had high opinions of men as did the whole of the church, often he asked why Mary had not given in to temptation such? What of nuns, women of family and truly most of all rank? He saw and knew maids strong in will and spirit, some more than any man of calling. It came to pass his thoughts were shared with the pontiff, and he was called to meet and speak of such things.

Sitting in his private quarters, the Pope bid him relax and take refreshment. Cadoc was not in fear of reprimand or correction. He knew only what he saw and all read in scripture. The old man sat nodding. He was quiet as they both drank tea. After enjoying a few bites of a beautiful cake, he looked at Cadoc and smiled gently.

"My dear child. I am but steward. I can only speak for God. Over time I have learned He is much a mystery. When I understood you were to fight vile devil, I worried. You have no calling to take vows, and you sought no training. But, it be so, none be needed. God has given you sight and strength. That, son, is not in question nor shall ever be. When I heard tell of you questioning the teaching maids possessed in greater number than men, it was then I fully understood why you were chosen. It is a point of which I agree. I say to you, have you an opinion of your own?"

Eating more cake and sipping tea, he relaxed, looking at Cadoc with great interest. Cadoc nodded and leaned forward. He did not have to consider the answer.

"It be no matter of who be possessed more. It be of those strong enough to seek our help. Men, this be certain, be too proud to admit weakness and that is folly. Pride such allows surrender to demon. They be foolish, ashamed of their weakness, thus seek no pastor. It be same for those none possessed. Men fight, proud they be as they form armies while maids be wise to talk of things first. Maids be more aware of changes in themselves. The folly of pride is ignored by clergy I fear. If maids be strong, that deserves study. It be good and none to be ignored. My question had purpose, and tutors heard not my concern. It is an important one."

Still nodding gently, the old man sat with his eyes closed and was deep in thought. He kept them closed as he asked what that concern may be. Cadoc was sipping some tea.

"It be what all cleric must understand, but, nay, do not. Maids have power of beauty. Most be mothers and wives. If possessed, I think it be harder to know it. The demon may have them as always in manner whilst doing evil work. Such, loved and minding young, demon reaches strong, bringing all who love or depend on possessed maid to ways of evil. There be times, many, maid possessed be hard to know. Being such, in my eyes, she be most powerful once possessed. She has hold hearts of children and men, and yea, her carnal power fells even mighty men. I fear we spend much effort on men and pay little worry to maids. Truth be both powerful villains when in demon servitude."

Opening his eyes, the old man smiled and put his hands together.

"My child, what you speak be truth. Man has most might of body, woman might of mind, persuasion with words, and offering of body. It be why I warn you of woman. The demon uses maids in ways most vicious, yes, to beguile men smitten with live or lust. What is important, young knight, is you know such. I can only advise you take only what you know, from God, be wise from the old men teaching you. They have not the grave duty you have been given, so know they mean no wrong. They be limited in experience but strong and resist temptation. My advice be to continue following your mind. It is power you have been burdened with. It be wisdom true and will of God."

Certain of his message, pontiff crossed himself, chanting blessing for Cadoc's safety. Inside him, the thought be demons would curse such blessing when facing the warrior to come.

Fi watched Cadoc change from man of love to man of battle and it shocked her. In an instant, Cadoc had risen from bench, his sword drawn and raised. He was majestic in manner and fearsome in figure to any, yet seeing him such excited her most unexpectedly.

Walking towards them from inn was wee lad, naught but ten. With his hand out, he looked innocent, meekly asking for coppers. Fi was stunned at Cadoc's alarm with such mere child. As his sword was drawn, Cadoc began shouting prayer in Latin as powerful in manner as his sword was mighty. The lad stopped and cowered as if being lashed. Cadoc continued his prayer and advanced to wee thing. Skin on lad started to change, and there be foul stench in air. In brief moment, lad transformed into a creature most hideous. It grew none in stature, yet loomed large in threat. Features much like lizard formed, teeth grew to fangs, eyes were red flames and hands shaped to claws sharp. It slithered and hissed as it became serpent yet still man.

Rushing the vile beast, Cadoc was not taken by the change from child to creature. He swung his sword to pin demon against wall of inn. If creature sought move to escape, it would be impaled by its own force. It stayed motionless, but seethed hisses and snarls, speaking a language most strange.

With nay book nor Bible, Cadoc began chanting ancient prayers in Latin. Doing such the creature moaned in agony. None able to hear prayers more, it shouted pain, then smoke, green in cast, issued from mouth and nose. Such horror did not stop Cadoc saying prayer with more passion, then shouting it with might. With warning none, the thing plunged forward on to mighty blade pressed to its chest, laughing as it did so. The blade went clean through its chest, then most upsetting the creature looked joyous and let itself sink slowly down, using resistance none, slicing its form in half as it sank until blade reached its head, then face, laughing while split by sword. Once head be opened such, putrid cloud of sickly green mist erupted from within creature. Watching in dismay, Fi saw whole of its remains become but cloud, slowly sent away by gentle wind blowing.

Fi looked at the only thing left, the large sword still pressed to wall. It was shining with nay trace of violence against creature. Cadoc pulled it from wall, seeing it clean put it back in sheath, crossed himself in short prayer, turned and went back to bench looking calm and with nay bother. Fi was in state of shock and dismay, grabbing hold of him as he sat.

"I thank the Lord you are unscathed. I was frightened that… that… thing would do you harm. Cadoc, I saw but child coming. You knew that no be human. How? How could you know?"

Sobbing with both fright and relief, she took a delicate cloth from her sleeve to wipe her tears. Cadoc gave her time to gather peace, gently rubbing her cheek as she reached up with her hand to hold it in place.

"Fi, truth be only fear I had was thought if demon had come when I was no here. It true be on unholy mission. Yea. To see who be here, or, and this I worry much, to meet someone. Nay, thing did no expect me here or would not have approached. Had you seen it prior? I mean in child-like form it showed first?"

Shaking her head, she said nay. She promised to ask her sister Fille and inn keep as well. With his mantle calm, she too calmed her worry, then asked how he knew it be villain, and was he not frightened?

Smiling, he understood he must be quite a mystery having fear none of such being. It be matter she knew not such attacks be common during his travels. He thought a while how to best explain his manner.

"Dear Fi, I know demon looked frightening. All demons look such. They take various forms, as did this one. It be my lot to see true form, such, and I have duty to stop them. That be my mission. I fight demon, any, that torment this land. I have such gift, though it be burden times most. Truth be I be chosen one, yea, by God, who be given such burden. That be why church made me knight. I can see devil within, and I have no fear of them. Cry no more, the devil is a deceiver, ever. They seek not to harm our bodies as they desire most to steal our souls. That be their mission. That demon, it was set to steal yours. That is a great concern. Most come because they hear a call. Someone be calling to them, yea, seeking them for evil purpose. I know that not be so with you, but someone could have called to have you oppressed. Have you enemies? A man you denied who was spurned? Any of that sort?"

Her eyes showed surprise at such mention. Then a look of fear. Her face showed dismay.

"Why, none. If so, not intended or that I would know. We have but few guests, and yea, Fille and I visit towns and Faires when we can, so it may be from such journeys, but nothing that I can think of. You worry me, such."

Nodding, Cadoc understood but needed to see her reaction. Such a call may have went forth, and he needed be sure. She had reacted and that caused him worry. Denying any man be turned that way was not true. He smiled. Perhaps embarrassing moment and none more. Taking her hand, he decided that such travail best be left behind. He had wish none to scare her further. Looking, he could see she was still shaken by sight of foul event.

"Fi, I want you know, that twas no person. I seized it in a fury so it could no come close to you. My sword is blessed by God, through his servant the Pope, and it has power to send demons back to hell. I am protected from harm. I am protected by our Lord, Christ."

Reaching under his garments at the neck, he pulled a chain. With it came a beautiful solid globe of crystal. She was dazzled by it. Though small it radiated power and glowed its own light. In the middle there was an object all too familiar to her. It surrounded the land around them in abundance. He asked if she knew what be in the globe.

"Why, yes. Tis what this village be now named. A thorn. A rose thorn."

Holding it to the sky, he kissed it. He held it to her mouth, and realizing what he had done, kissed it as well.

"Your kiss will help protect you, and me. Yea, it be thorn of rose. It true be beyond sacred. This thorn is from the crown worn by Christ when he hung upon the cross. It is coated in His blood."

Astounded, looking at it, she had heard of relics from Saints, but from Christ? She knew not any such things existed. She stared at it, then at Cadoc.

"Blessed be this thorn, and blessed be thou. I am beyond words. It be as if Christ is here. With us, now."

Putting the relic back under his garments, he nodded.

"That is so. He is. When I battle a demon, it be that He is there as well. That gives me power no demon can face. It is why I fear none. The day it was placed upon me, I was born anew. I felt the power it had, and I felt protected and without fear. I have been given the gift, and I use it."

Cadoc sat on the bench, looking solemn. The presence of such creatures was not mischief. It was intent. Knowing his presence was not anticipated the demon had shown such intent on one of the few in the abandoned village. He thought on it while holding Fi's hand. She was still trembling despite his assurance of protection. He decided he must address the matter with haste.

"Fi, we have found each other this day. The demon was looking for one as well. It had little chance of knowing of my presence. I doubt it would have come if so. I worry it appeared to find one living here."

Feeling a shudder run through the lass, she was wide of eye and deep in worry.

"There are but few here, though. The keep, a groundsman living on a farm not near, Fille and me. But dear Cadoc, it approached me. This has me with fear. I know you be here, but ye are a knight with duty. You can't stay, surely."

Thinking while rubbing the relic through his vestment, he nodded.

"Yea, that be so. The thing was headed to you, but we must consider that you are identical in look and voice to your sister. May it be he thought you Fille?"

She turned her head to the Inn, staring at it. Her lips quivered and tears rolled down her cheeks. Still crying, she turned to face the knight in despair.

"Cadoc, that frightens me so. But it be most possible. Fille and I look the same, but of belief and manner we are opposite. She has a wild nature and feels trapped here. She says that it is loveless I'll be as I won't give my chastity to capture a man, where she would. In matters most serious, where uh stand back, she runs ahead. Now, I worry she has done something… well, something sinful. I have given no quarter or need to evil, but as you say, it may be I was taken for my sister. Cadoc, either is terrifying to me. We may be different, but I love her and have great worries of her. Please, I know you intended but stay a night. Could you stay a wee bit longer till this matter be known and we be safe?"

Looking at her face, there could only be but one answer. He would stay. It was his charge to send demons back to the fires, and it would be his call to battle regardless. He gave a gentle smile, squeezed her hand, and assured her with just his gaze and manner. She leaned forward falling into his mighty arms, crying more but from relief. No words were needed, she understood, and he was glad of her response. When she was able to rise to look at him again, he had things he felt needed be done, and must be.

"Fi, the Inn has three rooms upstairs. I can't watch the Inn and you house, close as it is. To protect you both, until I gain hand in this, you two must stay in the empty rooms where I can guard you. Tell your sister of matters. You may learn something by her reaction and manner. Gather all your needs, and quick. It grows dark and the hour of demons is upon us. Go now with haste. I will be standing watch until you both are safe in the rooms. Now, no words about it. Go. And I love you. Let that be the light that guides you."

She threw herself on him, rising to kiss him with all her passion, then she was away.

And Fondly I Watched Her

Cursing the devil with a fury never reached prior, Cadoc realized darkness was upon him by attack of his love. He intended no quarter, no caution if any dark one came near. He would attack with the might of Christ and the power of his body and weapons. Considering the intruder had been a sorry, weak creature, it may have been wandering looking for any tasty morsel such as a damsel. Such mattered not. It be vile, it be destroyed, and his prayer was that it be alone and of no mission.

He patrolled the grounds for signs or hints of more such, knowing he would hear screams from the sisters if anything approached. While rounding the inn from the far side, he heard opening of a shuttered window then saw Fi lean out, calling to him they were safe inside. He showed his relief and said to secure their doors, he had more to do. Nodding, the shudder closed, and he heard the bolt securing it. He decided it be time to visit their hovel, looking for charms or items that would be like beacons to the night creatures. From the early days of his training, he learned that demons are invited by ones suffering a loss of faith. They have no power against true faith in God. He learned that a simple item, prayed to as surrogate to Satan could summon his minions. Such charms were like lamps in the dark, guiding the creatures to find souls to steal. He realized the child form of the minion now smote seemed to be headed to Fi, but in tracking the course, learned it was on a direct path to the hovel the sisters lived in. It appeared now it was making passage and acting as beggar child to pass.

The hovel was small and kept well. It was spotless and had the touch of the maiden to it. It was under a thatched roof, made from stone in good repair, and had smells and hints of recent repairs. Twas a simple arrangement of one large room with a good-sized hearth for warmth and cooking, table with four crafted chairs, a good number of books including a Bible, and stout beams holding the roof high. At back, there were two decent rooms. One must have been that of the parents, the other for the daughters. With the parents gone, it was clear each sister now had a room of her own. Much could be learned from their hasty departure at his heed. It had grown so dark he found a lamp and started its flame. He kept alert for any calls or screams and began the task of finding any object that could call evil their way.

With care and patience, he examined each maid's room and belongings. They hadn't much, but what they possessed was well made and kept. He grew aroused touching the lace and intimate undergarments and felt the same examining brushes for hair and fine powders. Knowing such be intimate, he reminded himself even a bodice or ribbon could be a cursed item. All seemed innocent and he sensed no peril from garb or finery. Looking at the few books in the room, he saw the difference of the two. Fi was fond of romantic yarns and tales. Fille had some books of strange publication that spoke of bawdy acts of fornication. They had illustrations that were not expected in any book for a maiden fair, but he understood that such books were common and filled lonely nights when real passion would be preferred. Tawdry, they were only such and held no call for evil.

Owning so little, possessions were prized shown by their care and placement. All were sentimental and what a maid would treasure. He looked under quilts, the beds, under objects laying on tables. He was thorough and did such in the large room. Flipping through pages of books, in pots, in the larder. All seemed ordinary and common. He found a wooden box, made with care and detail. Inside were drawings and stories written by the girls when quite young children. It was in the trove, the things kept dear by their mother, he found a drawing that felt as fire in his hand. It was much like the others, but he knew it was more than it appeared to be. The paper used had a lighter cast, smelling different. The drawing was a child's, but he knew it be done but a short time ago. It was placed with the others and fit well, but it twas not from childhood. It was a crude rendering of two young girls kneeling as if in prayer. Each was kneeling in the direction opposite of the other. They were back-to-back.

Cadoc took the drawing and lamp to the large table and sat. One girl faced toward the Sun in the sky. The other to Moon above. One praying to light of day, the other to symbol of night. It had childish quality and could be just imagination about their morning prayer, and those of night. Being new, he saw it as a message that while one prayed to God, the other to the dark of night when the devil has his minions at work. The most concern was that it was of prayer. A drawing of God facing the devil was common as children learned they were against each other. This showed, quite clever, an overture and devotion to darkness. He saw it as call to be visited by the dark lord. He rolled it up to have it in his possession when he returned to the inn. He finished his search and found none else that would be a beacon, and he had finished his task and found what may be calling to the dark ones. He decided to do one more round of the grounds and return to the inn. He also decided to not reveal his find. Such would only be denied and could expose his knowledge.

All seemed quiet round the inn. He checked his horse, and the stallion was calm enough though glad for company. Walking to the door of the inn, it was bolted, and he be glad of the caution. Knocking, he called out to the keep that it was calm, and he was back for the night. It was with a look of relief he was greeted by the man. Cadoc was offered some fare after his doings, and he accepted a green apple which he knew his horse would enjoy if he had no hunger later. Asking of the inn and upstairs, the keep had nothing to reveal, and was sure all was bolted and time normal for all to bed down. Cadoc nodded in agreement and thanked the man once more for his fine care, saying he could but only guess what wonders breakfast would bring. The keep smiled, saying he need but wait, and well worth it.

Glad that naught else was dwelling near, he headed up the stairs and was heavy in heart as he had the childlike drawing in his vest. If a minion or demon came, it would find him holding it, not a maid. Knowing too well that it may well be some game or flight of fancy done recently, his keen sense of things such told him it may well be beacon and a danger to all.

If it were calling out, he was glad it be with him as he would make quick business of any seeking it.

His room was nicely lit, the comforter turned down, and on the pillow was a note in fine hand. This caused a smile to see it laying thus. Picking it up, it had a sweet scent of rosewater, and was wonderful to smell. The words moved him as none had before. It was how he felt as well, as it but said,

"Thank you for saving me. I am for you, and you are for me."

There was a small drawing of a bird with wings looking like an angel as well, then simply an "F" under it. He felt his inside swell and his heart beat fast. He be impressed with the candor and certainly of the message. For all that happened that day, he knew it be God's will he arrived when needed.

Taking off his sword, then his garments, he stood naked in front of the small mirror and basin. He washed off what dust had gathered and felt clean and with a head full of thoughts, all of Fi. Stepping back, he examined his form. He was in fine shape with muscles everywhere from his training and continued practice of strength building taught to him by Roman soldiers. He was covered in scars. His training days had cut him many times, and battles with evil ones also had dealt some deep cuts. Looking, he thought them badges of experience and wore them proudly. A true fighter would be less so without such. He hoped that Fi would understand that most were from practice, and few from actual battles. He studied his face, and it was that of a true man. Strong features and brown from riding in the Sun. He had gray eyes, a strong brow, good smile, and ruddy cheeks. His neck was thick and matched his form. His hair was dark brown, but the Sun had lightened it in places, it having various shades almost blonde to deep brown. He grew it long, pulled back into a braid half down his back. Many had warned him that hair such was easy to grab in close contact and he would be best to keep hair short. Cadoc said that if such length were good for Christ, he was worried not.

He had a bed shirt but preferred to sleep naked as there was a small stove with glowing embers that made the room warm enough. After kneeling for his prayers and the safety of all this night, he got in the bed and under the soft down of the quilt. He started think of what Fi would look like in front of her mirror naked and it was a pleasing yet arousing visage. She was his ideal. She was a good head shorter than he, thin of frame. Her finery could not hide her shape which was made of pleasing curves. She had a small waist, and breasts none too large, which was pleasing in his mind. Her face was as a painting of angels he had viewed in Rome. Oval, large cheekbones, lips just as they should be, and very long brown hair combed back and off her lovely face. Most beautiful were her eyes, brown to match her hair, and they were windows to her heart and soul. She but looked at him and the rest of her faded away. He had no doubt she was the most beautiful maid he had seen, and she glowed from within, making such beauty even more wonderful to him.

It was as he thought of her so, there was the lightest tap at the door. Then it opened and the room, lit only by the embers, showed the fine form of his young maid. She said not a word and made no sound as she went to his bed. She was in a white night dress, and he could see her slight form within as she approached, lit from behind by the glow of yon stove. She held her finger to her lips to let him know no words were needed. He was surprised by such visit but could not send her away. He was in awe as she pulled at her shirt, up and off, revealing the very form he had imagined and pulled the quilt so to join him in his bed.

He was trapped in conflict. There was not more he could want, but it be not expected. He could not refuse her lonely heart as his was lonely and longed for her. Two destined for each other were not in sin and had already become one in the eyes of God, he was sure.

She moved his arm to rest her head on his broad chest. Her body wrapped around him, her breasts, as he imagined them, soft against his side, and her long leg rising upon top of him, moving gently up and down his stomach, making his already enlarged member grow larger and harder. Her leg slid down and touched him there, which was beyond any such dreams thus far. Rubbing him with her leg, slowly her hand worked its way down and caressed his shaft. She started stroking it up and down, then kissing his chest with wet, soft licks of her tongue. Her head moved to join her hand.

He found in the pleasure of her actions he was rubbing her without knowing he had started doing so. Down her back to the smooth curve of her smooth bottom, then his hand in the wet, hot place between her legs.

He had waited long for such, n'er taking a maid as he wanted only his love for this gift. He was pure and was surrendering his manhood for the first time. He felt like he would explode as he had done in dreams, understanding what gift a man gave to his bride, and that it be how they would create children as well.

Her head kept its path true and with gentle movement, suddenly he be in her mouth, her head going up and down. It was naught like anything he had ever imagined. It was the most wonderful feeling he had ever. It was just the knowing where he was. Inside of her. In her sweet mouth, those lips wrapped round him, her tongue licking and all with such passion. It be more than he could bear and without expectation he erupted his white juice in her mouth. It gushed for a very long time, over and over. He felt not a drop roll down onto him. Her mouth was wrapped tightly around the top, and she swallowed it all as if a feast. And he knew it was.

When the last bit had been taken by her, she lay there with her head on his hip, admiring it. He was still rubbing new parts of her. He was growing large and hard again. Once more, she began licks and kisses, bringing him to full size. Then, a sight most beautiful. She lifted fully up, moved to get on top of him with legs on each side, and he could see the beauty of his dream there in front of him. Hair down cascading over perfect breasts, soft skin pale in the glow, legs long to hold her just above his shaft, and a look on her face that was pure passion. She took one hand, held him, and rubbed him between her legs where it be hot and wet, then guided him up inside her as she slid down onto him. It was beyond all ken. He was in her most sacred place, and it wrapped around him then began, as her head had done, sliding up, then down. He could see her beautiful body as it did so, and that added to the unbridled pleasure of her love making. Her hips rocked and began moving in a small circle as she moved up and down. It was more than fantasy; this is what men craved and would do all to have. Her mouth open, she leaned down while still riding him and put her tongue in his mouth, filling him with her spit. It was then he erupted again. This time, even more explosive. She went upright, feeling the gush inside of her and she too erupted in her own manner. She was in spasms and quivers and her head was thrown back as she moaned in delight. He saw that such, she was more beautiful than was possible to fathom.

When she finished quivering, she gently raised up and off him, then put him back in her mouth, sucking off his juices and hers, leaving him smooth and clean. She approached him crawling in the bed on hands and knees and put her mouth over his ear.

"Does thou think Fi could give you such?"

In his shock, she had slipped off the bed, grabbing her garment, and quietly left with a noiseless close of the door.

Laying there, Cadoc was in shock and panic. It had been Fille, and he had been deceived beyond measure. Not only had he made a grave error, but he also betrayed Fi and then the most horrific realization: He had saved his manhood for his true love, and it was gone. He no longer had the most precious gift he owned to give to Fi. He was more devastated than if a demon had possessed him.

Then, even worse. He realized he had been.

He reached, in a panic, to the bed table where the note had been, and the childish drawing. The note was there. The drawing was gone. She had taken it with her.

And This She Did Say

That night offered no rest to the defeated warrior. His life had changed, and he was a different man. He had been deceived. His only solace was he was sure, beyond all measure, that he thought she had been Fi.

He realized, for the first time, how the devil actually spun his weave. He was the master of deception and knowing what any needed most. The pathetic little demon he smote came not to seize the maids or any other. It had been sent to create fear and need for comforting. There were no demons coming. It had already done its deed. It made him need to protect and make his love safe. In his arms, with him, she would be such. In the dark, with no words and the two maids so alike, he fell prey to the worst the demon could devise. He was trained to stop anything such, and he had been slayed without a fight. His blood boiled and he knew that was exactly what Satan wished. To cause such pain. To betray his true love, to live in fear and shame.

He suddenly remembered being in his last battle with the Roman soldiers. He was taught to remain calm, fight the battle, and be true. He had been bested and in his heart, there had been no betrayal. He would need to be a man of honor and tell Fi of the deception and the devastation it had wreaked for both. He felt such grief for Fi. She would hear that her sister had stolen her prize and served the dark lord. She too had been betrayed as he had not thought, ever, that it be her sister. He thought only it be his love. He would tell that it changed naught of his love of her but understood if she turned away though that would let the devil have his plunder. He would also explain that he had new understanding of how cruel and ruthless the demon was, and now knew the true depths of harm he caused to even the purest of hearts.

With thoughts racing as swift as his stallion, he heard quiet steps on the stairs and knew dawn had broken and the day was starting. He decided that if it be Fi, he would beg her be to the bench and let breakfast wait.

He hurried to wash and dress, using his sharp knife to shave, and made haste down the stairs. He first encountered the keep but needing to be sure of who he would be speaking with asked if Fille was helping in the cooking. The man shook his head. "Nay, she be late as often she be. That be Fi, working with smile for your eats."

Cadoc explained that it would be fine if breakfast be late as he needed to talk to Fi, now, if that be acceptable. The man nodded, saying he be their guest and protector, and he could have his request, surely. Cadoc said he would be on the bench, and to please send Fi to his company.

It was a beautiful dawn, and he had no worry of more creatures appearing. He only sought to tell Fi of his despair, the vile event, and of his heart. At that moment, Fi came walking to him, smiling in the first rays of light most happy. She had an apron on and a white dress clean and flattering. He rose as she approached, holding out both hands to her. She looked a bit surprised at his serious manner and hugged him asking why he looked so. He bade her to sit with him for he had hard words to hear that must be said. She sat, looking at him with concern, holding his hands. She told him that no matter how hard to hear, she will listen with understanding and trust in him.

He reached in his vest and took out the note from his pillow. She blushed and looked at him wondering if that be his concern. He looked at it and smiled.

"When I read your note, I was elated as ne'er before. It twas my dream, in my hands, and what I have saved my self for and no other. This, dear Fi, you must accept as if from God himself.'

She nodded, smiled, but still looked unsure. He took a breath and kept his eyes fixed on hers.

"There has been deception here. Just hours ago. It be the worst I've ever encountered. I am supposed to protect all from such, but I find myself a victim of it. I have no words for my humiliation and what damage it has done. I know naught else but to tell all, and to do right. I beg that you hear all, then we can both see what the road ahead will be. If you can sit by me, here, and be naught afraid, I would be most thankful."

She still held his hands, and gently nodded. Her eyes fixed on his, he understood she would not run from the truth and hear the events through. He squeezed her hands and began.

"I surveyed all places and hoped not to find demons. The truth is that demons show up because they have been summoned. I knew that was why one appeared. I went to your house and looked through all there for any beacon. They are hard to know, but I have that skill. I can see you are surprised I would think so, but please, I thought nothing more that something, even gotten innocently, called that creature here last night. Oh, Fi, with heavy heart it was so. I found your childhood drawings. One stood out to me. A drawing of two identical girls kneeling on the ground, back-to-back. One facing Sun, one facing Moon."

Fi looked at him with dismay. He paused. She looked confused. "Cadoc, I made none such. I would know. Those were precious to me mum and we looked at them many a time. Not since she passed on, but I know every drawing and none such as that be there."

He nodded. "Yea. That is why it called to me. It showed a girl facing the light of God, and one facing the night when demons are at play. It was different and certainly recent of origin. I realized it must be the beacon called the demon. I ne'er thought you put it there. I couldn't be sure if Fille did either. I took it and said to myself, if this is the call, come hither and meet me. I put it in my vest, checked round the inn, saw all was peace, and went up to bed where I found your letter of love. I got into bed dreaming of your grace, and of your beauty. You are who I've waited for. You, and none other."

Cadoc then told her of the events following, and how with her letter and their desire for each other, on his stead and before God, he thought it be her. It had been the hardest thing he had to admit in his life. Fi kept calm and mannered, but Cadoc could see the sorrow in her eyes. He left no detail amiss and stopped after telling what Fille said as she left his room. He was crying through most of the telling, and hid naught his sadness.

Sitting, the day so calm and beautiful, he knew all he could do was hear her speak of the events and what it meant to their love. She turned her head away, and kept one hand in his, the other to use her cloth to dry her tears. She raised that hand to let him know she was in thought, and to but wait. Cadoc wanted to wrap himself round her and tell her that he was now lost, and she was the only soul could guide him home. He waited, and after a final wiping of tears, she turned back and looked at him. There was lilt in her posture, and her eyes we moist with the tears that remained. To his relief, she had not run away, and she did not appear angry. She looked sad, and he felt her sadness, and his. Finally, she looked him in his eyes and spoke tenderly.

"Dear Cadoc. What a cruel deception you have been given. I know your honor and position were also cruelly harmed. I knew you be brave but telling this to me makes you braver than all else you have done. I understand that telling me thus took a true man. A man of honor. I believe you thought it me and know it has robbed you of the most precious gift ya had. Your honor. My being the first you give your chastity to as mine to you. Oh, what a sad thing. How can any do such? Cadoc, I do know the answer. It is what I have always feared, and it has happened. Fille has told me she would give her body to gain a man. She gave her body, but now uh see that you are right. She has given in to the dark one. That she is not who I thought. Yea, you are expert at such deception and with our talk, my note, the demon coming my way, how could you not be blind as we are identical?"

She moved to him and caressed him. She was sobbing, and he felt her love, stronger than the day past. He was crying and she felt good to hold once again. She stopped, sat up, looked at him again and had a look most somber. He was worried, but all he could do was hear her words next.

"I value your strength in telling all and have something to say that is hard to tell ya. But, I must. Last night, as ya undressed and imagined me and it went to visions of me naked, I must tell that I was doing the same. In bed, my thoughts wandered to you coming to me, naked and mighty. Then kissing me and being in my bed. I was aroused and began rubbing my, well, my privates. I imagined all the things described! I was doing those very things and it excited me so. It's as if Fille was reading my fantasy and doing that which uh thought. I had the very same spasm of great excitement. Then, I felt that soon enough we would do such, and it was more than the fantasy of this maid, it was a vision of us pleasing each other as man and bride. Do ya understand that it's what I wanted to get up and do? That Fille did what uh was none able to do though I longed for it so?"

Her face had a look of desperation to be understood. She was looking up at him and clearly, she had revealed her deepest truth. He was moved and understood as he felt the same the night before.

"Fi, sweet flower, I understand. How could I not as I had the same need and thoughts? I am pleased that you thought such. That it was me that aroused that passion. Worry not. Fi, my question be just one. How can we be one when I have had knowledge of another? I no longer have my chastity…"

She lowered her head and looked at him with an expression of desire.

"Dear man. You have your chastity to me! That, in your heart and mine, was me. You have not slighted me! That was me. You wouldn't have done so if ya knew it be Fille. All is in place. I do not feel slighted or cheated. It was cruel, but ne'er about robbing me of anything sacred. If that be not so, then I be fool and you be demon, and that is not so. Worry not. When love we do, it will be sacred and pure. You were mine last night, and love, I am yours. Curse the devil, not ya love of me and my virtue."

In that moment, it was as if God had touched them both and answered all by making Fi show what love and understanding truly are. Cadoc was amazed, and his look of love showed her all she needed.

"Fi, God shines his light on you. You are beyond a blessing. You are a miracle for this weary knight. I have never met one with understanding so clear. You are right. I feel relief. I was deceived, but it truly was you in my mind and heart. I did no wrong. Wrong was done to me."

She nodded and then smiled. She reached up and they kissed, each of passion as if in prayer. She whispered that she was his, and he could have her fully and she longed for him inside of her. He wanted to take her that very moment to his room, but there be matters to settle first to make that a joyous moment.

"Fi. I would take you this very moment, but you know we have a matter than must be discharged. Your sister. She seems be in league with evil. By my oath to the thorn on my chest, this must be stopped. For God, and for any in her path. Fi, oh Fi, for us. She may harm us again."

With a fierce determination, he looked back at the inn. Fi nodded, sadly, but she was of like mind. Her fears had come, and they had come in the harshest manner.

"Cadoc, you have virtue and your duty calls. My heart is broken to be parted even for a moment. My parents, now my sister. Careful and strong your actions must be. If you are next, I will be alone. Make haste, worry not of me. What of Fille? Can she be saved?"

There was no hesitation in Cadoc's reply.

"It shall be done. I must find her, and without her knowing, take her to a most dedicated Bishop, here from Rome. He's placing a new abbot at the abbey in the town and there to bless the start of the Faire. He will exorcise all evil from her. If she has knowledge of my intent, she could call for demons, putting all in danger, most of all, you. I am going to ready my steed, gather my things, tell her I think it was she left the note last night, and I want to bring her with to my duties at the Faire. When you return to your room, I beg you do not tell of knowing her deed. Let her go. It be but a day's ride on my steed, and then I will return after Bishop takes her. Can ye do these things? For us?"

Hugging him she said of course. What he thought best is what she will do. She looked at him, turned and went to the inn. Fondly, he watched her, knowing what a brave lass she be, facing her sister so. He stood until she entered, then went round to saddle his steed, making sure all would be ready and room enough for two. He arranged tackle and gear and it would be sturdy for the distance and speed he would use. He entered the inn and told the keep of provisions needed, and that he would be back after going to the Faire. As he turned, Fille was walking down the stairs. Her eyes were on fire, and she hid not her lust and was looking for the same from him.

Understanding her message, he went to her and whispered that she need gather her finery for he was taking her to the Faire and there they would regale in each other, unbridled and free. She gave a look of aroused passion at his words, and with haste went back up the stairs. He knew she would change from the white dress both wore as house maids into a dress of beauty. He had left her with the command to meet him in the stable, then they would be away.

She Moved Here and Moved There

Cadoc knew she would not be long. He had food and water for the ride in his pack when she appeared. She was in a dress of deep red. Her hair was pulled back with a red ribbon tied with abandon and she looked much the seductress she was. She spoke not a word. She approached him and looking into his eyes, her hand rubbed his groin then she looked down at it with admiration. He said they had a long day's ride, and he mounted his horse, holding out his hand for her. She used both hers as he lifted her as if a feather and she was on his saddle, legs wrapped round him, not both to one side. Her arms went round him, and she put her face against his back. In full embrace, Cadoc gave a flick of the reins, and his mighty stallion began its run at a mighty pace.

He thought of Fi, thinking she be looking out the window watching them part, with Fille wrapped around him such. He hoped just as he was, she was in prayer for her sister.

The thunder of hooves and the fast pace made talk wait until a rest, and he be glad of it. He had no desire to discuss much, and the faster the pace, the better thought he. After a good distance, she shouted that she needed to answer nature's call and had thirst. Seeing a shady grove in the distance, he headed to it and slowed to a prance and held her as he slid her off the saddle. Swinging his leg back, he jumped off as well, and took the pack with food and water as she, without shame, lifted her dress and squatted to pass water. She had only a slip under her dress, and no more. He played his part and watched her, pretending to be excited by watching such a sight. He took a blanket from his pack and laid it on the ground, placing a canteen and some apples on it. He took one, gave it to his horse, then sat. She was drinking water, letting much fall from her mouth onto her breasts where the dress soaked the water, forming to her breasts and nipples. Taking a bite of apple, she held it out for him to eat from. He took a bite, and she took it back, licking where his mouth had bit.

Cadoc knew she would want to engage in more lustful acts, and he stood and said that a wonderful lodge awaited them, and if they dallied, they would delay that place of pleasure. She smiled and started gathering the supplies and in quick time they were back on the highway.

Alert for any traps or demon riders, he rode fast as possible. His mount had plenty of rest and oats and was used and practiced in such haste. Fille would ask to stop, each time tempting him in some manner. He kept to his story of a wonderful night ahead if they made town well before dark. She said the room would be there. In reply, shrugging, he said with the Faire about to begin, such could be given to one who did arrive with plenty of coins in his purse and he wished no such luck. She nodded in understanding and said then haste was in need. She wished for a grand bed, not the ones of straw as at the inn.

After a long day, certainly the longest Cadoc could recall, they made town and it was busy being prepared. Tents and poles were being placed, platforms built strong, and there was a smell of roasted boar in the air. Banners were already hung, and flags were waving in the wind. The festive event should bring joy to the two riders, and Cadoc knew he must act as if they were sights merry to him. He rode to an inn he stayed at in his travels and knew well the keep. He had been thinking of how best to handle what was to come. They both had eaten little, so he would talk to the keep while she gathered her things, then tell her to go to yon room while he fetched some hearty fare and sweets as they would need their strength. He also said that there would be a bath to prepare herself in beauty for him. His plan went well, and she agreed that she would like to bathe and be as fresh as the morning dew on a blooming flower and just as wet for him. He told her a maid would help as she was a guest, and he'd stable his stallion and find their eats. The maid came out to help her with the little she brought, and the attention was pleasing her.

Riding off once she had gone with the maid, Cadoc made haste to the abbey and all gave him berth as he was known there, and all knew to make way. He asked a monk of the Bishop and was led to him. He wasted no time to and told the man, who he knew well from Rome, of Fille and her need for driving the demon from her without delay. Knowing Cadoc to be in great favor with the pontiff, he did not question as no clergy, none but the Pope, could deny him any request. Reaching for his book of Rituals and the holy instruments needed, he was ready in minutes. Walking out of the abbey, Cadoc told a young brother to stable his steed, and as the two walked to the inn, Cadoc told that she had deceived him as the devil himself would do, been visited by a minion who he slayed, and of the charm calling for the darkness to fall on her. The Bishop nodded, understanding all and was familiar with such possession. They reached the inn, and once inside the keep told that Fille had finished her bath and was settling into the room. The Bishop explained he was to perform a ritual on the lass, and no matter what sounds or screams may be, no one was to enter. The keep gave them a sad nod and crossed himself.

The two men of the church readied themselves, and the Bishop had his cross in one hand, a bottle of holy water in the other. He nodded, and they entered. Expecting only Cadoc, she was naked, hence quickly covering herself with a sheet she had pushed down the bed. She had a look of confusion and looked hurt.

'I know ya be knight for the church, but this be not church business, surely.'

The Bishop began his prayers and she looked at him in wonderment. Cadoc watched, ready to help should it be requested. After the first prayer, the Bishop sprinkled holy water on her. There was no smell of burning flesh, no smoke rising. The two men looked at each other. After several rounds, Fille reclined as she had no idea of why such was being done. The Bishop asked her to repeat prayers as he spoke them. She had a bit of trouble as they were in Latin, but no resistance to them. The Bishop finally asked if she accepted the Lord, Jesus, as her savior. With a puzzled look, she said yea, she most certainly did.

Closing his prayer book, he made the sign of the cross and told Fille that Cadoc wanted to protect her from any harm after a demon showing itself at the inn. She smiled and said to them both "Ya could have just told me. I would have been dressed, properly, had I known."

The Bishop put his hand on Cadoc's shoulder and asked him to help him down the stairs. Cadoc said he'd be back after and went with the Bishop. As they headed out, the Bishop shook his head.

"I have not known ya to make one out to be possessed if not so. I see no sign of infestation in the lass. A sinner, that she be. Confession and some time with a pastor all what be needed. The demon appearing. A passing, perhaps nothing more. The charm. Perchance just some remembrance of childhood. I understand how it all went together such, but I think she just be a love-crazed maid. I hope to see ya soon, and it was best to be sure. This was no folly."

Watching the Bishop leave the inn, Cadoc now had a quandary. The lass was not doing the devils work, and she would be wanting lovemaking when he returned. That, he could not do. He decided he would need to explain that she be mistaken for Fi, and that he thought she was vexed by the demon so brought her to the Bishop to be sure. Knowing not what to expect, he decided they would need to return to her home.

Entering the room, she was still covered in the sheet, looking over his shoulder making sure the Bishop had left.

"That be quite a surprise to have me thus in front of a holy man. Ya could of warned me."

He nodded and explained he was very worried and could waste no time. She gave in and smiled. Then she threw off the sheet and knelt up telling him it be time for her thanks for his care.

As gently as he could, he explained his mistake, and that it was Fi who had his heart, and he genuinely thought she was being guided by dark forces. She looked at him with surprise.

"Aye, Fi has your heart, but ya had my body. And next, hers. That be very clever, in my thinking. And now, ya break my heart. It was no devil had my, it twas ya. Look at me! Ya would say no to lovin' such as this?"

Cadoc sat on the bed and hugged her. Only with care, not with passion. He explained that he had promised himself to Fi, and he was a man of honor. She scoffed at him.

"Ya be the only man with knowledge of this maid, that is what ya be. Ya have taken' me, and that means I be yours. Wife to ya, that's what I be. I could go to that Bishop and he would say same. Ya know that. Would ya take the last rose of summer and throw it by the side of the road? I have given ya my flower! Ya must care for it."

Fille was serious and about to weep. Cadoc was in a panic. She be right. Without the demon in her, she had given her honor to him, and expected him to return honor. He sat, and knew it was how she saw it, and at the same time had Fi expecting him to be his in marriage.

"Fille, I say honestly that I had knowledge of you, but it twas but a circumstance of folly. You and Fi are identical. I had just told her she be mine, and when ya came to me, with my heart and soul I swear to God,

I thought ya be Fi. Had I known it twas ya, I would have denied. I intended no wrong and would do no harm to ya. This, ya must accept. We be more than bodies. We are souls and have delicate hearts. Yea, I had your body, and you are beauty beyond measure, and gave loving so sweet it can not be described. But could ya be happy when my heart is with Fi? Knowing it be her I made my pledge to? At this very faire there are many good men who would give all for wife such as thee... I would never tell of my mistake, and a decision to reveal it be yours. I hope ya do, as that is right by the lad. Can ya forgive me this mistake? Know I will love you, forever, for the kindness of it?"

As he spoke, she had started crying and his heart was hurting watching her so. Slowly, she nodded.

"It must be. I want a man in love with me, not my sister. I understand now that ya thought it be she, now that I know all the matter. Dear Jesus, wha' be this lust in me? Hearing ya so true and caring, I wan' ya so much right now. Ya think, now tha' ya been in me, that a second go at me will do any hurt?"

She moved quickly and was up with her arms wrapped round him, crying and kissing his neck. He rubbed her arms and hugged her back. She was sincere, and he didn't sense she was tricking him. She had been waiting for love, just as Fi had, and was hurt because she wanted him so and craved the love making she was waiting for the long ride there. He reached to her ivory shoulders, then pushed her back a bit to look her in the eyes.

"A second go would be doing wrong. I know who I love, and I know who'll go with me. The Lord knows who I'll marry. Loving ya again would be a sin. For ya too. Ya be beautiful, very tender, and I know ya be full of desire. Fille, let it be for the one ya will marry. He will be so blessed as ya are, well, very special. Here I be, holding a beautiful, naked beauty, wanting to have her way with me. That be any man's dream. Most men would say I be fool for not having' ya, right now. Ya know most certain that we can no do so again. Now, put on your finery, and let's go hither to the Faire. We can sample the fine eats, and maybe you'll spot some handsome Johnny looking at ya."

She looked sad, still. She sat back onto her feet and looked down between her legs. She was beautiful to behold, and she was not ashamed being naked with him.

"I know ya be right. I'm no sinner, and I will always have the memory of ya inside me, here, and I guess that be better than naught. Well, laddie, if ya not be taking this pleasure, yea, the Faire it be. Will ya watch me dress myself? I do not fancy being alone right now. An', ya can tell me how pretty I look."

Cadoc nodded, saying he would not leave her by herself, and asked her to not try to tempt him. She looked at him for a long time, then nodded.

"We both know now how God made us, so no shame. I'll no tempt ya. Dear man, this maid just be denied, so my heart is tender. I have feelings for ya. Just stay with me and comfort me with smiles and ya words. No wrong in that."

She laid out her finery, studying each item. He was not familiar with just how many frilly things a maid wore. She slowly built layers of undergarments and Cadoc was getting aroused as some were mysteries and made her look even more exciting. She talked of them, and said they be all hand sewn, and treasures. At one point she held up a stern looking wrap that had long laces. She asked if he knew what it be. He shook his head, saying nay. She explained it be a corset, and it was to make her waist smaller and push her breasts in. She held it up against her chest and breasts, then held it up to view.

"I hope the day is far away when I'll be needing it. I think my waist be just right, and my breasts none too large. I bring it to remind myself how I none need it. If we be lovin' right now, uh think it would be exciting to wear. To have ya pull the laces e'er so tight with those mighty arms… No need for a look like that at me. I be no tempting ya. Just thinking it may be good for other things."

She asked him about what he must go through with his many articles of armor. That it must be far more than what she was putting on. That was a good change of topic as he was just a man, and her dressing be far more exciting than he anticipated.

"Yea, it be no simple thing. It takes a knave to don, and it be complicated and takes a long time. Under it all, there are full garments. Thick, as the metal is harsh against skin. Then chainmail o'er most of me, and it be heavy stuff. Then, every part of me has its own metal plate. They all need to be bound to me. Then, when all is placed, more chainmail on me head and throat, then the helmet. Then, I can barely move. There is a hoist that lifts me up on my steed. It be why he is huge. I weigh much, and I'm a heavy rider. I can barely see, so he uses his wits in battle to keep us safe. Most important, in battle, is to not fall off the steed. There be no way back up."

As he finished, she stood before him, fully clothed. She circled around for him to see all her finery. He nodded in approval, which made her smile. She gave him a quizzical look.

"I read that in battle, the clansmen get naked, paint themselves like savages, and have at it that way. I think that would be such a sight. Men of muscle, running naked, all wild like beasts. Are they no frightened? No protection from clubs or swords?'

Cadoc stood as she was ready. He nodded.

"In any battle, only a fool be not frightened. Ya either live or die. Ya face death each time and it weighs heavier than the armor ya wear. Yea, Scott's fight in the savage manner. Battles between clans are not for king or country. They be about feuds and deep-rooted hatred over insults or rape of a daughter. Those be real battles. They be blood feuds. They never end. The wounds, they go too far back. Enough of such. Ya be beautiful. Are ya ready to be seen with scoundrel refused to bed ya?"

Giving him a push with one hand, and blushing a bit, she curtsied and smiled. Cadoc opened the door and said although the Faire didn't start till the morning, it seems most things were prepared and a good time to find some fine cooking.

As they left, the town was active with final preparations, but all stopped to admire the beautiful maid and the grand man she walked with. Although still in his riding clothes, no finery, he was obviously someone of high standing. He held Fille's hand, knowing that would help her get over his turning her down when she was wanting him with all her passion. She said she had been to the Faire with Fi since they were wee high, and they stopped all they passed being twins, and rare beauties, but this was far better. Being admired for being with such a handsome Johnny and all could tell she walked with someone of high degree. Cadoc laughed, saying he was just a humble servant and had little but title. Fille stopped right there and looked him in his eyes with true love and passion.

"Ya have might. Ya have honor. Ya had me. Nothing of ya be little. I be witness to that."

She smiled at him and turned. He was amazed at how he felt. Most people stopped and watched him pass out of fear. He was well known for battling demons in these parts and others. Today, he was being watched for he was with the most beautiful maid anywhere who certainly was no demon. They envied both of them but knew not the trials and ordeal they had just encountered. Fille lifted her head and was breathing deep. He knew why. There was a saddle of beef roasting, and they looked at each other, both nodding.

Cadoc saw a table had been made for eating next to the tent with the beef. He escorted her to the bench, and said it was time for some decent fare. She nodded with a beautiful smile. A bawdy woman came and welcomed them, asking what their pleasure be. Cadoc laughed and said many things were, but right now, a selection of all they were making. The woman understood and told them they would not be disappointed.

People passing by nodded or waved, and it was a happy day. He thought of how it was originally to be. He was thankful Fille was just in need of passion and love, and not in league with the devil. As they waited, he asked her about the drawing he had found. She was truly surprised at his concern.

"That be the cause of your worries? It be just a wee way to pass time, and remember me poor mum. I remember when we were wee, mum loved our drawings. We still have paper and chalk she bought us one year. We had both finished visiting her grave and were praying there. Fi prayed that she feel the warmth of the Father, I prayed her rest and peace. The drawing was of what each one be praying for. Fi loves the Sun, I love the moon and stars. It went well, so I put it with the others. It also saddened me, I couldn't bring my heart to show it to Fi and make her cry."

Cadoc felt relief, and foolish as well. He was so used to omens and signs of evil, he had read too much in its meaning. He asked if she was concerned that an evil creature had been outside of the inn. She nodded and said that she was most worried. It was that event that gave her the courage to visit him that night. The world be a place of danger for a lass, and she thought how something could happen to her before she had ever had the loving, or love, of a good man.

The woman appeared with platters of roasted vegetables, hot rolls, fresh butter, beautifully carved beef running red with juices, and hearty gravy. She told them there would be pudding to follow, so leave room. Cadoc knew that the young maid could not fit much in her small waist, but he could so none would go to waste. It was delicious, even better than it smelled. He had never eaten with a maid at his side, and that made it even more delicious as watching her eat was a pleasure. She was enjoying it all. The food. The admiring looks. And being there with him. She had been a mystery just a day before, then he thought her possessed. She had been a passionate lover, and now like Fi, a sweet maiden who was showing her joy honest and true. An orphan living in a hovel, here with a good man, majestic in her beauty and she had put doing what was right above her carnal desires.

"I be proud to be here, with ya, grand knight. Ya know there is only one thing that would please me more. And I am not speaking of more pleasing each other as hot as that fire still burns in me. I speak of a true love. A man that be mine alone. Ya have given me hope that will be, and I thank thou for it. Oh, I can smell pudding coming…"

With a happy smile, the woman put a crusty fruit pudding in front of them to be shared. As back in the inn, she brought sweet cream and left them to it. Fille lifted the pitcher of cream and poured some on it. She used her spoon and scooped some pudding and cream then lifted it to Cadoc's mouth. He smiled and opened his mouth as she fed him. She blushed, telling him more.

"The first bite be only for ya. Just as thou had the first of me."

A wave of enchantment washed over him. It be true. She had given him things he knew nothing of prior. Now, with love and kindness, she gave him even more with her simple gesture. He realized that as with Fi, he loved Fille. It frightened him as he knew that the truth be each had his heart. He had a sudden fear he was being tested by God — or tempted by the devil. No, he stopped and realized he was not being tested. This was life. He has met two maidens fair. Each had beauty inside and out. Each was good, each was kind. So alike, but each different.

He found himself thinking of being inside of Fille's mouth as she took a spoon of pudding and thought how he would be happy there at that moment. Such a thought shocked him. But it be true. Her mouth was sweeter than any cream, and he felt loved and safe in it. He wanted to tell her of his thought but dared not. Then he looked at her perfect form. He knew what she looked like naked. Far more beautiful than with clothes. He looked at every curve, every shape, and how could such beauty exist? It was beyond imagination. She fed him another spoonful, and she put the spoon in the cream and opened her mouth, putting the white cream in it, closing her eyes from the pleasure it gave her. He knew she was thinking of when he filled her mouth with his cream. They were both thinking of their passion. He was praying for strength. He wanted to take her back to the inn and have her again.

She saw the look on his face. He was staring at her, and she was worried for him. She had been struggling with her lust, wanting to tell him she ached for his touch. He had been so kind and loving to her, that to bed him again would be far more passionate than the first time. She put her hand to his cheek, and he leaned into it.

"Dear man, something is going on inside. Ya can tell me anything. I am but a little thing but may be able to calm your worries."

Cadoc took his had and put it over the one on his cheek. He looked at her and could not deny the truth inside.

"Fille. I am faced with something new. It be most powerful, and I don't think it can be denied. Being here with you, watching you, I realize that I want ya again. To be in ya. All the things I said just a short time back we could never do again, I want to do right now. It be wrong, but it be all I can think of. Ya are wonderful. I am in awe of ya. I am not married. I am free to love."

Fille gently closed her eyes and looked upwards. He knew she was saying a prayer of thanks, and knew what he saw true. All she was. She opened them slowly, looking right into his, stood slowly, then took his hand. He rose, took a handful of coins from his pocket, put them on the table and she led him back to the inn, saying nothing but with the squeeze of her hands on his, and the swaying of her hips as she walked.

She Put Her Hand O'er Me

There was no limit to the passion each showed that night. The first night had been instinct and the first time for both. That night, they each knew the things that pleased, and took their time to revel in the magic of it. No thing was left undone. They let free their love and passion as one thing and had confidence and a lust that was pure and unbridled. Cadoc filled her with his body and heart. She gave every part of herself to him, and inside her he felt her love and desire. Over and over, they learned to be as one as they both erupted in ways their bodies had never known. Things had reached a point where just a look, a simple kiss, a sigh would send them into a spasm of delight. The world was only in each other. None else existed. There were only stars and the sky outside the walls. They were the only two God had created, and he had given them this joy.

Finally, after exhaustion took hold, they found equal passion laying just holding each other. That was serenity. Cadoc held her and realized that aye, he loved Fi, but Fille had done what Fi could not. Fille came to him and showed she was his, body and soul. Fi had talked of love. He was sure she would be his. Fille used no words. She did not warn him of Fi or try to dissuade him. She entered his room and showed she was his. There was an honesty in doing thus. She never said she was Fi. The sisters had known that the man would need choose between the love each would show. Fi promised to show her heart, and not let her body be the reason for his love. Fille knew that we are both mind and body, and that showing him love with hers was revealing all to him. He felt such intense love, which included love of her body, watching her fully clothed, eating and feeding him a spoon of pudding, that he could not deny she had given herself to him with no demands. She gave him her most precious gift, and he could none refuse it.

He knew she was still awake, and as he had been thinking, his eyes had been closed. He opened them and she was looking into his, smiling contentedly. He saw the need to tell her of his love. She had won his heart.

"Fille. Ya have touched my heart. Not just with your body, but in your kindness and your goodness. I love ya with all I be. I am yours. Will ya be mine. My bride, and my wife?"

Her expression was as if the gates of Heaven had opened, and he saw eternity. He knew now why he fought evil. So people could experience this. Real love from the Divine. To see the expression she had at that moment. Love, honest and real. The most precious gift God has ever given. The one Satan fought to deny all souls by corrupting us.

She nodded ever so slightly, her face showing her love.

"Dear love, I am already yours. All of me is what I gave ya, and I knew that only love would be what guided ya. Yea, your wife I am, and shall always be. And married we shall be on our wedding day. It won't be long. We have but ask the Bishop, and bride I shall be."

He nodded, and with all things right, they fell asleep in each other's arms.

No greater shock could there have been to both than the thunderous crash of the door shattered to splinters when each was asleep in each other's arms. Prepared always for any attack, Cadoc reached for his sword, but it was gone. He grabbed at his relic of the Christ thorn, and it vanished from his hand. Fille was crying out in terror.

Standing at the foot of their bed was a moor, dressed in black and frightening to behold. He was tall, thin, dark as night of skin and hair, and was growling and hissing. Steam was rising from him, and he filled the room with darkness and heat as if a fire raged. Fille was grasping at Cadoc. She managed, in her fear, to say, "That be the lord who turned the roses to thorns!"

Cadoc shouted out to her, "That be no lord. That be the devil!"

The demon stood there, then nodded.

"One needn't be Knight of the Church to know that. I summoned you here. I need the thorn you wear. I am turning the world to thorns. You... You sad creature, have the one from the crown. But, I waited until you had the last true rose. She now becomes the thorn I'll wear round my neck. I've come for both."

Fille screamed out. "I said no before, and I say no now. I am his rose, and always shall be."

The dark one laughed as Cadoc jumped from the bed, grabbing the crucifix the Bishop left from his visit earlier, and lunged at the demon with it. With demonic power, the devil waved his hand. The cross flew from Cadoc's hand and it landed on Fille's naked breasts. Not stopping his attempt, he continued to lunge at the evil one. The devil raised his hand and Cadoc rose in the air, trying any way to escape the force holding him. The demon looked at him and in his eyes were the fires of hell.

"I'm not here for you, knight. You've have sinned, and you are corrupt. I wish you to live with the truth you defiled this virgin, not even yours bound in your marriage ritual. Know she was mine to spoil. Think of that as you pray. You defiled Satan's bitch. You spit at the commandments of your God. That is why you live. To suffer as I do. As all do."

At that moment Fille cried out and both looked at her. She screamed, "I

am his wife forever…" as she plunged the crucifix into her breast, into her heart.

Satan let out a cry that shook the town.

He looked at Cadoc. He was beyond wrath and vile.

"She is already with my Father. She will never be mine, but knight, my solace is she will never be yours. She will never be yours for she is where sinners like you are not allowed to enter. Suffer, knight. And know even in paradise, she will be suffering you."

In that moment, Cadoc fell to the floor and Satan had vanished. He ran to the bed, and Fille lay there, dead, covered in blood. The crucifix had been a dagger in her heart. He ran to get the Bishop and to have her prayed over, and to seek confession and absolution for his sins. His tears would not stop, and the Bishop could provide no comfort until he heard his confession and gave him God's forgiveness, his greatest gift to his children.

No Two Shall E'er be Wed

Cadoc told all to God and begged forgiveness. The Bishop said he had sinned greatly, but with penance, he was forgiven. He was told penance was to tell Fi all he had told God and be truthful evermore, to never betray nor lie again.

He made arrangements to have Fille's mass and burial once he returned with Fi. The Bishop said that was an honorable gift and right to do. He was given his steed and rode at full pace to the cursed town of thorns. He did not stop until he reached her small house. He went inside, but she was not there. He ran to the inn and heard the keep and his wife talking and went to them.

"Fi! Where is Fi?"

They looked at each other with a strange expression, then the keep put his hand on Cadoc's shoulder and led him to the table where Fi had served him and bade him to catch his breath and sit. Cadoc was still in a panic and asked for her again. The keep looked at him and spoke gently.

"Lad, she went with you to the Faire."

Cadoc stared at him in total dismay.

"Why do you say so? You know it was Fille that I rode with. Fi stayed here. Why are you saying such?"

The keep's wife came out. He had not met her, but she was an older, kind-looking woman who had tears running down her cheeks.

"Something happened to Fille? You are so upset, what else could make you so?"

He told that he had fallen in love with her, had betrayed Fi, and that the demon who had killed all the roses had come for her, and his thorn from the crown Jesus died in. The demon demanded her, saying she was his bride and the last true rose. He explained that they had just vowed to marry, and that she would not be taken by the dark lord, stabbing herself in the heart with a crucifix.

The looks on the couple's faces were of horror, then tremendous sadness, and despair. They wept and wailed in pain. Understanding their need, Cadoc waited. The wife finally was able to look at him and speak.

"Poor man. Poor man. We know you suffer so. I must break a promise vowed I would ne'er break. It is needed now, for you. She will be understanding and no be upset. She loved you. Enough to die. For ya both."

Cadoc could only look in wonderment. He asked what promise must she break.

"It be hard to explain. I will do my best. There is no Fi and Fille. No sisters. You ne'er saw them together, for that could no be. Twas but one girl. Fille. When her parents died, something happened to her. She was hurt so, her poor mind had to find a way to deal with the pain. She became two different parts of herself. One be Fille, full of passion and fire. The other be Fi. Her mother's pet name for her. When she be Fi, she be calm and mannered, yea, and dedicated to others. Fi ever be part of Fille. They be the one hurt girl… We saw it happen, and one night I asked the Fi part about it, and she revealed that which I kept as a promise to never tell. Now, I be sadder than ever. That girl be saint and Angel, and she did the impossible. I see ya are in a state. Test your mind. Just accept she became two for real. She needed to. When you are ready, I'll tell the rest."

Cadoc knew people suffered from shocks so great their minds protected them in strange manners. He could only accept that it be so. He had not heard all, so he said he needed to and was ready for all. The woman nodded, and began.

"Her parents died when the black moor came to this village and began killing the roses. But, that's not all he killed. The people who grew them all died too. They had what we thought was plague, but twas only the rose farmers, and Fille's parents died. The plague would have took us all, but, nay. Just those with roses. And, as ya learned this day, Fille was the most beautiful rose of all. The evil man said she was to be his, and that was the day she became Fille and Fi. Not one rose. Two. Each not as precious as the one. She fought off that demon by changing thus. He was angered so, he vowed one day she would return to one true rose, and rode from down in a thunderous fury, changing town sign as it is today. A rose has ne'er grown here since that day, and we prayed none would. It would mean she had become the one rose again. Henry, show the man what ya found this morn."

The keep left the room and was back in a short time. He had a young, new rose blossom in his hand and laid it on the table. A rose had grown the day prior. They all stared at it. She struggled to continue.

"We knew what it meant. Fille had found thee. And as she moved through the Faire, she realized to love ya truthful, she, well, we are sure she made herself back to one, Fille again, to be true to ya. Ya loved both. She knew it was her that you loved but torn because ya couldn't love one part of her and no hurt the other. She knew ya fought the devil, and with you to protect her, she took the risk of being one true Fille, yea, for ya to love right. As the devil promised, he knew that day would come, and he would take her. That happened, but ya didn no know and were no prepared. She did the only thing she could. She denied the demon again, sending herself to God, where she waits for ya."

The story was so powerful Cadoc fell to his knees, vowing his love to her, and with an anger equal to that of the devil swore to hunt him down and hurt him. To destroy all who worshiped him. He had the Rose, not the dark lord. He would remind him each day she loved the Knight of God, not some vile fool cast from Heaven, none loved by any but the sick and demented.

He rose up and looked to be mightier and almost not human. He had a glow, and radiated power from the Divine. He held the rosebud. He said soon the whole village will be lush with her gift to their kindness. He invited them to the funeral, and though the Faire be going, she was happiest at the Faire that day with him. It be fitting that the Faire be the anniversary of her return and victory over Satan. She had died of love.

It Will Not Be Long

With the mass said, and Fille buried, Cadoc stayed to wander the Faire. He had the same room, and though sad she was not there to wander with him, he had her in his heart at all times, as he would forever.

The night before the Faire ended, he lay in bed, glad the Faire was near done for he would begin his campaign against the devil at its close. He vowed to stop Satan in every way possible. He had destroyed the roses. Cadoc would destroy his houses of sin and his servants. He would destroy black churches, find his minions and cast them back to hell.

It was the start of a new day, just turned 1600. He would insist the pontiff send excoriates with a powerful ritual to exorcise all those possessed. The battle had begun. He lay making his plans as he fell asleep where he had held Fille.

That night she came to him,

His dead love came in.

And softly she moved, though her feet made no din.

Softly, she laid her hand o'er him, and this she did say.

"It will not be long love, till our wedding day.

Fair and Tender Maidens

Come all ye fair and tender maidens
Take warning how you court your men
They're like a star on a summer's morning
First they'll appear and then they're gone

They'll tell to you some loving story
They'll tell to you such a beautiful lie
Then they'll go and court another
Leave you alone to pine and sigh

Do you remember our days of courting
Your head would lay upon my breast
You made me believe with all of your charm
That the sun rose in the West

I wish I was a little sparrow
And I had wings and I could fly
I'd fly away from my false true lover
And when he'd ask I would deny

But I am not a little sparrow
I have no wings nor can I fly
Straight way I'll go to some lonesome valley
Just to pass my troubles by

If I had known before I courted
that loving was such a terrible crime
I'd have locked my heart in a box of golden
and tied it up with a silver twine

Days of Courting

Knowing she had little chance of ever leaving the cabin and finding a life of her own, her father's death had left the care of her mother to her. What little hope she had of finding a better life and a true love had vanished in an instant of violence, killing her hopes just as a cruel fate had killed her father.

Looking out the front door, as she had since her earliest childhood memories, she could not fully understand why her parents, or anyone, chose to live in an isolated cabin far from towns or people. Looking down the dirt road, she shut her eyes and thought of how the bumpy, muddy road led nowhere. It did lead to a town if one considered it such. A general store, saloon, post office and a gathering of ne'er-do-well misfits was hardly a town, and no place for any of a decent kind. It had a name, Pinewood, and she guessed that said it all. The few buildings were made from wood, and they sat amongst the pines. Not much more could be said for Pinewood or those who dwelt there. It was a long journey, even with their cart and mule, and the road had perils. A young woman, alone, could be preyed upon by beasts, or worse by the toothless miscreants waiting to seize a woman and drag her to their holler to make her slave to their sick needs.

Carrying her father's ancient old musket rifle, it was loaded and ready to be cocked and fired when she ventured to Pinewood. Holding tight the rifle, though not the reins, the mule knew the way. It was the only road the poor beast had ever gone down, and sadly, she knew the same could be said for her.

Looking up at the sky, she hoped no rain was coming. Her mother needed supplies, so she had to face the journey and its sadness that day. Rain meant mud, and with the cart in poor repair and the mule quite old, she knew any number of ways rain could cause peril. Muddy, the road could break a wheel from sliding into a deep rut or let the wagon — and mule — slide off the road down into a holler. Having no wish to be stranded only to be found by some crazed hermit who would tie her up as his pet for perversions of all manner, she knew better than to head down if there was a cloud in the sky. She wanted the journey finished; there and back home before the sun went down. A prayer was the only help she would have apart from her stout hunting knife, a bag of powder and lead balls she had rolled into cartridges for the relic of a rifle she would have at the ready. She could only wonder why her dad prized a weapon used since the colonial days. Loading was slow. Against a modern repeating rifle, she knew to make the first shot count if used. Her father had taught her to quickly load, reload it, and keep it in repair, but it was still only good for one shot in a crisis. A rifle or shotgun with a load of shells was on her wishlist for hunting and protection.

Knowing how many things could go wrong with the musket, she spent a good deal of time making paper cartridges and testing it before she went on her hunt for animals. It wasn't of use with small critters like rabbits. The shot was a good size and the small animals would turn to a mist from the power of the shot. It was needed for mountain cats or larger predator types such as a raccoon. She now was the one getting furs to trade for more supplies and using traps to win skins and have meat to make a stew.

Going inside, she saw her mother was awake and attempting to raise herself up a bit in her bed. Her mother wasn't old, just having turned 38. She was strong, healthy and a beauty. As she was getting stronger, she decided to raise herself up to get out of bed, she saw her daughter was standing in wait but wished no help.

"I know you are here for me if I be needin' you. I know it be hard to watch me such. I am feeling strong today. Thought maybe I could make us some eats. That I can do, Anne, just give me time."

Listening to her mother's beautiful Irish brogue, she couldn't help but smile. Even with her mother feeling down, her sing-song accent made her feel good.

Going to the stove, Anne put some split logs in along with kindling to start it going. It was an old thing, but it never let them down. It was stronger than the mule and would last far longer. Such chores kept her mind off woes and there were plenty of worries along with chores and she had the burden of them all. More than anything they kept her from thinking of her loneliness and the shape her mother was in. Wandering, her mind started to think of what happened to her mom, and she shook her head to make such thoughts fly away. With the trip to town that day, she only needed thoughts of the road and what could happen on it.

Taking the long ride to the small white frame church the morning after her husband had been killed, Maggie gathered enough strength to tell the pastor her husband was dead. She sat crying and clutching his blood-stained handkerchief, asking the pastor to mention Kevin, her dead love, in his next service. She had no donation to offer other than the pan of biscuits she had brought. Telling him she and Anne had buried him a few hours back, she wanted no animals gnawing at his remains. Her daughter was working a cross of pine for a marker and saying prayers. The preacher was a good man, with wife and a daughter of his own, close in age to Anne. He said he hoped his family would be as strong and Christian if any such fate fell to him.

"My heart cries for both of you. I will remember Kevin at service, and in my every prayer. You have suffered a great loss, Maggie. My prayers will include you and Anne. Your family. Oh, and poor Anne. What a terrible thing. I have known Kevin since we came here. Please, I know this is the worst time to talk of such, but it helps say proper service to know how the Lord took him. I had no idea he was ill…"

Crying and sobbing, Maggie managed to say he wasn't ill.

"He had never been sick. Ever. He was killed… Murdered by some thief in the woods!"

Leaning over with head falling between her knees, she passed out. The pastor called for his wife, knowing he needed help. Working on church records in the next room with the door closed for privacy of any visiting, she came running, seeing Maggie on the floor.

"John, what happened? Did she look about to faint?" Kneeling, she felt the tears cried and thought she heard crying, which was not unusual from loved ones suffering a loss. Looking Maggie over, she ran and got a soft cloth soaked with cool water, then gently pressed it on Maggie's face and back of her neck. Her husband told her all he knew, and she nodded saying with all that, it was exhaustion. Maggie was in a sad state from the shock of Kevin's sudden death. The cool towel was working. Maggie began moving her head side-to-side and was coming around. She opened her eyes and took a deep breath. Slowly, she sat up, looking at both.

"I was wanting to get through this without falling apart. That cool water… that helps. I didn't know who else to tell. Thank you, both."

Helping her up, the pastor guided her back to the chair. Looking at her with kindness, he assured he would help any way he could. Gently, he said if she could manage, it would be good to share what happened to not be alone in her grief. She had calmed down, and slowly nodded.

"I came to tell you. It was unexpected in every way. Kevin was out gathering skins in the traps as he did most days. Those woods are dense, but he knew every hole and branch. A few days earlier he told me he worried a poacher be about as one trap that had sprung worried him. Bloody, but no animal. He said some stranger must have passed through and he took the catch for food. He didn't seem worried, but I was, some. It is just us and I worried on it for a while. He said no to my worry. He would check about and track the poacher."

Stopping for deep breaths, tears continued rolling down her face.

"The next day he left early in the evening as poachers like to thieve at night. I cautioned him be careful. He had that old rifle loaded, and the bag with cartridges. He held it up showing he was ready for trouble. That was the last I saw him alive. The night went on well past when he normally returned. I was sore afraid, pastor. I felt it in me. Something had happened. It was so dark. I was worried so I told Anne we needed to find him. She was scared too, but we each took a lantern and headed down the road. We were terrified. About a mile down, Anne screamed, and I stood still. I knew what her scream meant. She pointed to the edge of the road, and there was poor Kevin's hand. Just his hand, laying there from out under some bushes. I went to it, and it was white. White, white, white. And so cold. I knew he was dead. My first thought was a cat got at him. He had crawled to the road and if not, I do not think would have found him. That was him to the end. Doing things for us. It be strange at such a time. Both Anne and I knew he be gone, but you need be sure. We didn't cry, we did not say anything. We somehow knew to each take a side, reached in and using his arms, pulled him out…"

Stopping, she gasped for air, telling them she only needed to catch her breath. She looked determined. Then calm. She continued.

"Laying face down. He was face down. He was still. No breath. I reached at his shoulder to turn him up. Anne helped and we got him righted. It was no beast, not animal beast, did him in. His face was cut apart in the front. An ax I guessed. Hit full in the face with an ax. That poor man. He was killed. There is no surviving such. Anne got sick and turned to not get any spew on him. I lifted his poor head and put him on my legs as I sat with him. I stroked his poor head. I looked at Anne as she got done heaving so. I told her we could no leave him, to go get the cart. She ran to the cabin and was back soon. She had put blankets in the cart, and I can no remember just how, but we got him in. There was no else to do but bury him. I plan to get a casket for him and put him right. Anne gathered some canvas he used. I got his best clothes, and we dressed him. I washed all the blood I could off him and took gauze and wrapped it round his head to keep it clean. It took most of the night, but we dug a good grave deep as Anne in our shady grove out back. We wrapped him with canvas and tied it with care, then put him in the ground with the dirt over him. I knew I had to keep going or I would be dead from grief before I took care of him right. I told Anne I was off to see you for a service and she should make him a cross…"

Finishing, she fainted again. The pastor and his wife were in tears and knew this time she had fainted from grief. Carrying her to their parlor couch, he laid her there for the rest she needed.

Watching her mother closely, Anne knew her wanting to cook breakfast was a sign of recovery. Although her movements were unsteady, it was clear she was determined to do the job. Anne helped in the same way as before all had happened, setting out plates and getting coffee ground and butter for bread. She went and got eggs from the few hens they kept and smiled when her mother looked at her now and then.

Knowing all was done, she sat down as her mother filled their plates. Letting her do things as she used to, she nodded with thanks as her mother put her plate in front of her. It looked wonderful because her mother made it. It was the first time she had cooked anything since she had taken to her bed six months prior.

While they ate, Anne said they were sore low on supplies, and glad she was up and feeling a bit better as she would not worry so going to the general store. A look of fright showed clearly on her mother's face. Anne knew it would upset her but knew that she had to get supplies and there was no rain on the wind. Taking deep breaths, her mother calmed down and with a stern look, told her only if she loaded the rifle and had it on her lap ready to shoot any that appeared from any direction. Anne nodded with assurance. Her mother told her, "No matter who, shoot, load again, and make sure the job be done. Then, ride on."

Anne knew better than to do other. She agreed it would be done such, then her mother relaxed and finished her coffee.

Looking determined, Maggie said not to worry. "I will do cleaning and dishes. You best go. Get the supplies. Be on your way". She stopped and looked at Anne. She was thinking hard, and Anne stood and waited. Her mother asked her how much money they had, and if they had enough money for a casket.

Anne nodded her head.

"We have enough for things as I've been tending the traps with some success. I've saved casket money. Well, from that little bag of gold coins. It's hidden where we hide things."

Her mother looked comforted.

"Don't take money with you. Go quick then as I want you to stop by the Doughty barn. The dad and his boy work wood. They make coffins for all hereabouts and saw your dad at services enough so will know well what size. Ask only the cost. Then on your way. Get you going, darlin'. Have that gun in hand, always."

Filling the cart with pelts had been done earlier, and she had food for the day. The last task was hitching the mule to the cart. She worried each time the mule pulled the cart. He was old and she was worried he could collapse if there was any struggle or too heavy a load. He seemed to enjoy the journey and took his time along the ride. Much as she worried about the mule, she worried more about her mother being left home. She seemed on the mend and cooking was a good sign. Trying not to think about what happened to her, she went in, made sure she was ready for the day, then said with all finished she was on her way. Her mom held out her arms and they hugged. Anne watched as her mother sat on the bed, reached under her pillow, and pulled out the long dagger she kept for protection, laying it by her right hand. It had been given to her a few years before meeting Kevin by her parents and was a family heirloom most precious to her. Like her, it was from Ireland where they had migrated from and had a finely honed blade with handle made of pure silver. It was detailed with a Celtic snake winding round the handle, giving it a good grip and stern message of its threat.

Riding to the ramshackle town was a bumpy ride. She wished the cart was a carriage that had springs under the seat to keep her from almost being thrown off with every rut or bump. After the long ride down, she faced the ride back up and there was no way to enjoy her day away from the cabin in such conveyance. As she rode, she sang songs her father taught her. Her favorite was, *I'll Fly Away*, which he would play on his fiddle and her mother would sing. Thinking of her dad in his grave, the night they laid him down, after saying prayers she leaned over him and said his favorite line from the gospel tune.

When this weary life of mine is o'er, I'll fly away

The two had little chance to mourn what happened to him, but those words set the tears flowing. One day, husband and father, that night dead in his grave. It felt like nothing else; no way she could imagine life without him. After they ran out of energy and tears, they went back into the house. Asking her mother what had happened to him, Maggie was calm. First, she said she was going to the church past the town and ask the preacher to say service for his journey home. She would also ask him if any miscreants were known to be about. She repeated, as when she found her husband on the ground, it was no animal attack. Only a sick bastard would split his face with an ax that way. If she heard news of any about who could do such to a decent man, she would take the old musket and track him. She planned on doing justice if she could.

Being glad the small town was in sight it, stopped Anne from thinking of the horrible events she had been dwelling on. Approaching the dilapidated buildings, she held tight her rifle letting all know she would tolerate no sass. The town was rife with drunks and sick men waiting for women to pass by and offer them some cash or whatever they had for a visit to the stable to lie in the hay. Without her father, she was taking no chances and all too willing to fire at any who approached. Her message was sent as none came near. Getting off the cart she held tight the knife and gun entering the general store along with pelts she had brought to sell or trade.

Having a list made getting supplies quick work, but the owner offered her far less than normal for the furs. She lifted the gun.

"Don't think I heard you right. What was the offer?"

All the men there knew she was doing her father's work, causing the bearded store owner to fear she may be ready to let loose on anybody. He decided to offer her the same sum he would to any other trapper. He told her he'd even load her cart, which he did as she stood back, rifle at the ready. She told him she had no wish to be impolite and hoped next time he would do best to be honest. Nodding, the man said it was just a simple adding mistake. She backed out and was glad she held her own. Knowing inside she would have fired on him, she was glad there was some sense in the man, even though just fear.

Riding on level ground at a good pace, she was soon at the farm with spare house turned sawmill and lumber supply company. She was able to relax and lower her gun. The family were church goers known by her father and were no threat to her. The father was a handsome man, and it had been a

few years since they had seen each other. Coming out to greet her from the barn, he waved a hello and held the harness for her to climb off the wagon.

"Anne, all at church have prayed for you and your mother. I guessed when ready you'd be needing a coffin for your dad. If too long passed, I would have come up to bring one. I have it made. My family and I want to give it out of remembrance of your dad. He was one good man in a sad place, and kind to all."

Getting off the cart as he spoke, she was in tears.

"That is the first kindness we have had since… well since things happened. I am overwhelmed and I know mom will be shocked. Thank you. This is a light in such darkness. Dad always said all from church were good people. Now I know why."

Stretching his arms out, she went to him and they hugged each other. It felt good and reminded her of hugs she had been given by her father. He backed up and looked at her.

"You we're still quite a young one last time I saw you. You're all grown-up now. Just like my little Howie. You're the same age if I remember right. He's grown into a fine young man. Works hard and knows his wood. I know you had a long ride, and the road back ahead isn't any shorter. I'm sure you must need lunch, so please, join us. Howie just went in, and I was headed there too when you rode up. How would you like that?"

She felt appreciation and told him so, but she wanted to be home soon as she could as her mother was waiting on her. He sadly nodded his head.

"Terrible thing losing your loved one. What a sad world. It will take time. But I'll send Howie out with a treat for you and your mother. He'll make plans with you to bring the coffin up, and he'll do all the work. I heard the news from the pastor. You did it once. Not right to do it again."

Nodding, she hugged him once more and said his kindness was much appreciated. He gave her a sad smile and nod then headed to the well-kept and whitewashed house as she climbed back in the cart. At the same moment the door opened, and she was amazed at how much Howie had grown — and how handsome he had become. He was carrying a pan the cake was baked in covered with cheese-cloth tied with string. He too had a look of surprise seeing her. He stood looking up at her, just amazed.

"Anne, I am sorry for your poor father. Most sincerely. I will pay my sympathies to your mother when I visit. It was good my ma just finished this fine cake. I know none better. I think I best set it on the seat for you. I can say this... I still see the little girl I used to see at service, but what a beauty you've become. My dad said I wouldn't recognize you, but I do. He says I've changed much as well. I can not see it, but I am taller."

Smiling, she nodded. "He said you've become a fine young man, and you have. I'd still recognize you as well. Hard work and good folks have favored you. Your dad said you were going to bring the casket for my father and would do the digging and such. Howie, please know this… I want to be there doing it with you. For my dad. It is important that I take care of him. I could use some help with a better marker, though. I only managed two slats tied together to make a cross. Not right, if you know what I mean."

He stared at her. He nodded sincerely.

"I understand and would ask the same. You will be the last to touch or hold him. I wouldn't expect other. We will make it a respectful resting place. I tell you what. I'll cut a real marker from hard oak wood and lacquer it. I'll bring chisels. You and your mom, think of the words you want on it, and a fitting marker it will be. My dad said this Saturday would be a good day for me to do all. Only if that is the day you would like. If you need more time for it, that will be what I'll do."

She reached down with her hand, and he gave her his.

"Saturday will be most kind. It will be an important day. And a fine marker... Much more than we could ever hope for. I'm sure my mother will wish to make you her best cooking. I've fresh supplies. Please, thank your mother for her gift. Carrot cake is our favorite. To all of you, for your kindness. We wrote no epitaph nor have words as we were not expecting such a marker but will work on some. I will see you then. I pray it not rain. If so, please, delay. I will understand. I must head back. This old guy is slow going down, even slower going up. It is hard to say goodbye after such warm hellos."

Taking the harness, he turned the mule around saying he would be there early. Looking, he also said he was glad she had the old gun. Giving the mule light taps on his rump, she was on her way home, rifle in her lap, smile on her face.

A Chain Five Miles Long

Knowing her mother was making the long journey to the pastor, Anne sat on the porch then fell asleep. It lasted only a short time as she was anxious for her mom to return. She admired that after such a horror, she was strong enough to make the journey to have service said for her dad. Her mother had lived hard and was an inspiration to her. She sat on the porch rocker thinking of the life her mother had led and how cruel fate had been.

Starving when a young girl in Ireland, losing her only family, she was able to find a loving man who thought it best they should wed and move to the new country. He managed to get labor on a freighter and the two came to Amerikee.

Looking for work, with none to be found in the cities full of immigrants poor as they, he heard that there was open land in the Blue Mountains, and there they could settle and build a home. They soon learned that others had such plans, but most gave up just a short time after leaving as the journey was hard. They passed dark cabin windows with rifles pointed at them making sure they stole no crops. They made their way through hastily built towns full of violence and drunkards. Both agreed a good place would be one where all such depravity ended. It would be a place where none other wished to live. Kevin said up in the mountains farming was not easy or even possible, and people tended to want something without doing such hard work. He was right. In the heavily wooded mountains, few settled, and fewer bothered to climb, keeping to valleys and along rivers.

Finding a small clearing down an old explorer path, it had room enough for a cabin. The work would be hard, but it would be their own. Starting by living under canvas they carried for a tent, they survived on small animals Kevin trapped or shot. Saving the skins, he would hike the long journey to the general store down in the valley and sell them. Using the money for tools, soon he was cutting trees and building a cabin. Getting good at trapping and finding it paid well, he was able to get an old cart and a decent mule. Being resourceful, he found homesteads that had been abandoned and scavenged things left behind, including a stove, more tools and even clothes.

Finishing the cabin took near a year, and they were both content with the home. Maggie had Anne later that same year. Slowly, the small family had enough comfort and Kevin was a skilled trapper. He made friends with the few good families in the valley, and they settled down knowing the days ahead were better than those behind.

The full push westward by immigrants and religious zealots soon reached the valley. All too soon they learned many traveling west were misfits not able to behave decently in settled towns. Outcasts, often forced to leave by order of law or a mob, such looked for desolate places where they could live wicked without fear of reprisal. Most were passing through, but while there did plenty of harm. Theft, rape, shootings, and drunken rages became common. Good folk had little choice but to carry arms and stay to their homes ready for any sort of misfit sneaking about.

Anne grew up hearing her parents speak of people harmed by the constant arrival of such strangers and were glad of their remote cabin. Her dad said most of the misfits were too lazy to make the climb, and that was their best protection. He was right. Occasionally some scavenger would wander up, only to be shot at by her dad. He took no chances and although firing only warning shots, his message was heard. Always on guard, knowing there were dangers about, the family called little attention to themselves in town. Maggie and Anne would dress like travelers and not appear to be the attractive women they were. Rape was one of the most common crimes by strangers who often would kill the ravaged women, then run off never to be found.

Thinking of her mother, Anne was amazed that after such a hard life she was still beautiful and strong. A delicate-looking woman, thin, she wore her hair pulled back in a bun, reaching her waist when let down. She had beautiful green eyes, light reddish brown hair, high cheekbones, and a pleasing figure. Anne had grown up wondering how she could ever be pretty as her mom, but she had grown to be a beauty as well. Like her mother she was fine-featured, but had pleasing dark brown hair, a nicely shaped body, and deep brown eyes. She looked like her mother, with the colors of her dad's hair and eyes.

Thinking of what had happened to her mother on the way back from the church had been so painful she had shut it away. Doing chores and tending to her mom, she managed to keep the horrific thoughts from her mind. It was becoming harder to do. Forcing her thoughts to their life ahead helped. Looking to where her dad was buried, she understood she one day would end up in a grave. It was only by the strength of her mother she was not completely alone. Her mother was the only family she had now.

Riding home from the church, Maggie was having trouble staying awake. Feeling a sense of relief having made the arrangements for a proper service, she longed to sleep, but feared facing her bed. Her sweet man slept alone in his grave, and she was alone. The thought sent a shudder down her body as the mule plodded along. No Kevin. It was not real. She must be having a nightmare. If she could just wake up.

Instead, she nodded off while the mule kept heading home.

She woke with a start, realizing some villain had killed her husband. She needed to find him. Shoot him. Leave him for buzzards and vermin to eat away. Then just as quick, she nodded off for more sleep.

She woke again with a start. Yes, a nightmare. She was dreaming of the villain who killed Kevin. She could see his face. Ugly. Scarred. Laughing. A ratty beard. Having only two teeth on the bottom. Dirty. He stank. He had a rope. She couldn't move her arms. She was grabbing for the rifle. She still couldn't move her arms. The face laughed more. She started to scream. She felt cloth being pushed into her mouth. She needed to wake up. Now! She saw the butt of the old rifle. It was being swung and it hit the side of her head. Then peace. Black comforted her. No face. Nothing.

Aching, her head felt damp. She was nauseous and everything was blurry. She tried to call for Anne, but her mouth was filled with something. Thrashing about, she felt a hard pain in her ribs. She heard a voice.

"That won't help you girlie. No siree. You be good. Do what I say. I'm your husband now. That I made sure of. Yes, you are my pretty gal now. And you done got you a good man to love ya all up."

She blacked out.

Finally, coming out of a deep sleep, exhausted by all that had happened, she was fully awake and instantly realized the strange dreams had not been dreams at all. She was naked in a poorly made shack outside of a cave hiding the entrance. Her hands were bound with rope, as were her ankles. She had been secured with a metal collar with a ring used on barn animals connected to a stake in the ground with a long chain. Her mouth was gagged, with a fire nearby keeping her warm. She felt sticky and she realized she had been masturbated on, and she was sore in all her holes and knew she had been raped while unconscious. Her jaw was hurting, and she remembered she had been struck very hard.

Terrified, she tried at her bindings. They were expertly tied. She heard many reports of women being abducted by depraved men living in caves or hollers and kept captive as slaves, often murdered if they fought back or cried out for help. The realization Kevin had been murdered just to get her shot through her mind. She realized whoever had her was Kevin's killer. He would do the same to her if she made any foolish moves. Her blood was raging through her, and she wanted to flee but was trapped like the animals they caught for their income and food.

As hours went by, she was praying the villain wasn't going after Anne. The chain was long enough to let her crawl and look around. Anything she could use to possibly free herself was beyond the range of the chain. She was sickened when she saw an ax, far from her, with blood and bits of flesh and what she knew were brains from her dead husband. The sight brought no tears. It enraged her. Running through her mind was the man who did that would die by her own hands. She started planning. She was smart and knew it would take time, but she would find a way. Thinking if she eventually seemed to enjoy being his slave, he would give her some freedom to pleasure him and do chores such as cook. One way or another, no matter what, she must endure. That would be how she would split his face with that ax.

Hearing the crunching sound of footsteps on twigs and dried leaves, she lay back down pretending to still be asleep.

It was the man. He was not concerned about her, knowing she was securely bound. She heard his footsteps approach her, and he stood there, obviously looking at her. He mumbled a, "Still out, darlin'? Let's get you up..." Then the rustling of his clothes. Unexpectedly, she felt a hot stream of urine hit her face, his way to wake her. Shaking her head, gasping, he stood by her and was laughing.

"Nothin' like a good piss first you get up. I knew that would help you greet the day." Sitting up, she shook the urine off her face and hair best she could and looked up at him. He was smiling and obviously pleased with himself. Her hands, though tied, were in front of her, not behind her back. He turned, got a dirty rag and threw it on her lap. She used it to wipe herself. She worked her face, then other parts covered in his crusty semen.

He went, sat, then using a large knife skinned a squirrel he had caught and made quick work of it. Driving an iron rod through it he placed it over the fire. There was a tin pot he pored water in, then coffee from a tin, adding the pan to the fire. Unexpectedly, he went to her and with an open palm, slapped her hard on her face. He looked at her, then did it again. Standing back a bit, he smiled his sick grin.

"Enjoy that? I sure hope so, 'cause I sure did. Get used to it. I'll have you begging and thanking me for such kind acts… Well, compared to some things I might enjoy more. Say… How's your sweet bottom? It was damn tight. It was good, though. Better than some damn sheep or cow."

He moved away. Getting a tin cup, he pored hot coffee in it. Sitting on a log, he stared at her while drinking his coffee.

"You are one beautiful thing, that I shall say. Ne'er had me none prettier.

Not even when I paid whores. I was out hunting rabbit when I came cross your humble abode and saw you and your mister. Knew right then I would want you be my wife. Just had to clear the way, ya understand. No need for your man interfering in our business, so I gave him a surprise with that ax over there. Now, it's just us two in our little love nest. All fixed up for you too. I've been shittin' outside and all to make it homey. Just do what I say like a good wife, and you'll be happy and much appreciated."

Every word sent chills down her spine. The man was evil — and insane. At the same time, she felt relief as never in her life. Somehow, he had not seen Anne. She almost started laughing as the man missed the real prize. He was also making it clear he was a coward. He only caught a glimpse of her and Kevin, leaving for fear of being shot. Anne would be tied up with her if she had been seen.

Meekly, telling him she was a bit cold, she said she would like her clothes to get warm. Laughing hard at her he stared in disbelief. "You ain't needin' no clothes, darlin'. We don't need none in the way of lovin'. Clothes! I like you jus' like God made you. Those nice jugs. That sweet ass. It would be a sin to hide those. Adam an' Eve didn't have no damn clothes. I live by the good book, and you are a one fine roll, so, here, this will warm ya up…"

He had found a blanket stained with his excrement and urine and threw it on her. Managing to pull it over herself, she was barely able to keep from retching at the smell. Taking the squirrel off the fire he mumbled, "I takes care of the missus" or something close to that. Opening a dented old tin, he walked over to her and poured out stale crackers for her to eat. Sitting back on the log, eating the squirrel including most of the bones, grease ran down his matted beard and he didn't bother to wipe it off. Watching his habits closely, he did what she knew would come next as she had seen several crock jugs, which meant hard liquor. Picking some bones from his beard, he got a jug and started in on the liquor. Stopping as if remembering something, he took a tin cup and weaved to an open barrel filled with water, scum floating on top, dipped the cup in it and brought rancid water to her.

"Them crackers sure are dry. We don't want that mouth hole all dry now, do we?" He was completely serious. Shaking with understanding that when he looked at her, he didn't see a human being. She wasn't someone to talk to or even know her name. She was just three holes to go at when he pleased. She was only holes.

Thoughts, fears, panic, emotions, sorrow, and terror swirled in her head. She was in a state of pure panic. Anyone, even Kevin, facing such a creature was doomed. She understood how a smart, brave man such as Kevin didn't stand a chance against the cowardly monster. Nobody could undo the bonds he tied. Not a strong man. Nobody.

Drinking more, he got uglier. He got quiet. Sitting, drinking more, staring at her. Already in a state of terror, seeing him that quiet ignited mortal fear in her. She knew it would be bad. It ended up worse than she could ever imagine.

Without any warning, Anne's life changed forever. In their remote location her parents were the center of her life. Now, alone, waiting for her mother to return from the church she had the impulse to go out back to the woodpile and ask her dad how long it would take mom to get home. Shuddering and then experiencing reality, she stopped and stood with fear. Her dad was no longer there to ask. He was gone from this life. She would never be able to turn to him again. Feelings of fear washed over her, then through her. She dropped to her knees and cried for a long time.

Suddenly, as if it were her father speaking to her, an innate understanding filled her. His body was gone, but his good sense and wisdom remained in her. At any time she could think of what he would say or do in any situation. His example and good sense would always be with her. She could pray for his inspiration at any time. Understanding he was still there with her, inside, gave her comfort. She stood up and smiled at that comforting thought. She asked herself what her dad would do if his wife had gone to town and was so late in returning.

Instantly she knew he would go down the road to look for her. Wheels on the cart could have fallen off. Animals could have scared the mule and the cart was stuck or turned over. All things were possible, but it was possible she just needed rest and took some at the parsonage. Regardless of the possibilities, though she was tired and still in a state of despair, she knew she had to be sure her mother was safe.

Her mother had the old rifle. Having just her hunting knife and legs to carry her, she filled a canteen with water. Hoping to hear the cart before she went too far, she determined if needed she would head to the church and find out if she was there, or if she made it that far. Knowing it could be a long journey, she packed some jerky and bread to have with her. Going back to the fresh mound of earth where her dad was at rest, she told him she'd be back with mom soon as she could. Speaking out loud she hoped he heard her. Crossing herself, she turned and was on her way.

It was still light out. Calm with little wind and a blue sky. Walking down the middle of the narrow road she avoided the cart tracks which had formed through the years. Wearing overalls instead of a dress, she had worn them when digging the grave. Searching was no occasion for a pretty dress anyway she thought as she walked. Her mind began to wander, thinking of rides down to town with her parents and playing on the road when little with her dad. Shaking them off, she knew those thoughts were distractions. She needed to be alert. To listen for a mountain cat or any number of dangers. Having only gone about half an hour, she saw something that shocked her. The mule and the cart were up ahead. The cart was not moving.

Standing looking at it, her first thought was relief as it appeared her mother was almost home and stopped to relieve herself in the bushes off the side of the road. Walking fast, in no time she reached the cart, rubbing the mule's cheek. Calling out to her mom, she expected to hear her call back. Calling louder, still no reply. Shaking, she knew something bad had happened. With no answer from her mother, that could only be because she could not reply. Looking in the wagon, there was the old rifle and the munition bag. Those were not things her mother would leave unattended. That created more concern. Standing behind the cart, thinking, she knew she must remain calm. Her only thoughts had to be finding her mom.

From her earliest years, she grew up going trapping and hunting with her dad. He was expert at tracking animals. Anne watched him look for broken branches, twigs snapped on the ground, and indents on grasses. All were signs of recent passage or flight, the map to where an animal went. Deciding to track her mother using skills learned from her dad, she went to the cart, took the musket, made sure it was loaded, then took the munition bag which held cartridges, extra gunpowder, and large bullet-shaped lead balls. Taking a long drink of water, she started round the wagon and began tracking.

It had not rained the past few days. The road was dusty, but it would show tracks as her mom had not been gone long and there had been no strong wind or rain since. The cart had stopped not far from where they had found her dad. Forcing that thought away, all she needed was to concentrate on tracking her.

Starting, she carefully looked in the cart. Examining the bench, she saw the first important sign and it shook her. There were brown droplets on the seat. Knowing the bench well, she knew those drops were blood soaked into the wood. Blood dries brown in a small amount of time. Shaking again, something caused her mother to bleed. Not much, but it happened. A large animal attack would have caused much more blood. It was not sign of an animal attack. Her mother had been cut… or hit. Becoming very alert, she suddenly knew inside it was a sign of being struck. There was no time for prayers or worry. She started following the signs.

Kneeling on the right side of the wagon, she studied the dirt on the road. Nodding, she could see much of the dirt disrupted. There had been shuffling about. Looking where the shuffle marks led, it was to the bushes. Heart racing, she could feel it in her chest. Moving slowly, studying the bushes, quite a few branches were bent enough to indicate there had been passage through them. The ancient woods hosted a benefit for tracking. Endless years of pine needles and pine cones covered the ground. They were old and most were brittle. New steps left impressions and showed the trail. If her mother had been abducted and dragged or carried, it would be revealed by the forest floor.

Her suspicion was right. Past the bushes were clear indents. Boot-shaped, large, also deep to indicate her mother was being carried. None made by her mother, they were clearly made by a large man. Seeing no animal tracks, the rifle at the ready, she carefully followed the tracks, one by one. Showing no indication of stopping or of her mother's feet, it seemed the man had a clear destination and had no need to rest. Upsetting, it meant he had held her with no desire to stop and put her down. Had her mother been awake, there would be signs of a struggle, and the tracks showed no such signs. No stopping or resting.

Looking for every possible clue was made harder with rocky areas where the tracks did not show. Following their very purposeful direction, they started again after the rocky terrain was passed where the ground was again covered in rot. Assuming that the man was not too far from the road, moving carefully she realized he could be on watch or hidden off to the side. She knew the area well but had not been there in the last year. Stopping, she worked on remembering what was ahead. Gradually remembering the woods ahead led to a small holler — a valley leading to a creek none too large — it was an area with a few caves. None contained gold or valuable minerals. Realizing with water and caves, it was a likely spot for an interloper to set camp. It was the type of area an escape convict or villain would hide.

Over the years, she heard many stories her dad told her mom of women found raped and abused, some dead, brutalized by sex-crazed misfits. The very thought made her sick as she understood that was the only reason to abduct her mother. Maggie was a beautiful woman, and that day a beautiful woman tired and distracted by the death of her husband. It would have been easy for a villain to lay in wait and jump from the bushes to strike her. Carrying her to some cave in the holler, the man would feel free to do his sick work. The thought was sickening but the only one making sense. The wagon, the blood, the deep boot prints, the trail. All telling her a tale horrific. Stopping for water and thinking what best done when she found her mother, she thought only of what her father would do. Although she was small and young, she was a good shot with the musket, and she would survey the situation with care before acting. Thinking of going back to get the mule and ride to town for help, she quickly dismissed the thought. Her mother could be killed in the time that would take. Her only hope was to surprise the villain and fire true. If he had her mother, then he was deserving of a bullet and must be stopped.

Walking slowly, the trail was easy to follow. After a short time, she heard the gentle sounds of the creek, which had no name she knew of. Starting to shake again, at this point anything could be danger. She started slowly going step-by-step, listening carefully for any sounds — especially voices — from that point on. Taking pauses between each step, she was trembling but doing things as her father would. He used to tell her the art of tracking was to not be noticed or the hunt would be alerted and run away. Wearing dark clothing, she would be hard to see against the dark of the trees.

Reaching a crest above the slight valley, crouching behind a growth of bushes she gently pulled them slightly apart to see the valley floor. Smelling a tinge of burnt animal, it was a clear sign of food cooking. She was close. Looking for smoke from a campfire, none was visible. Listening carefully, she was patient. Everything indicated there was a camp in the holler. If it was the one with her mother, at some moment there would be sounds or words spoken.

Shocking her after a long wait, there was the terrible sound of pain. A wailing. Being hurt. Instantly she knew it was her mother. She had heard her wailing in anguish so recently at her reaction to her husband's death, Anne was sure it was her. Such screaming meant she was being harmed. Immediately she had the impulse to jump up and run to save her. Controlling her reaction as she had done so far, it was as if her dad was there by her side, telling her stay calm, not alert the man to her presence, find where they were, then approach with no sound and survey how best to down the man to save her mother. Guided so, she still needed to act without delay. Her mother was at risk of being killed.

Tender Maidens

Getting as close as possible without being heard, the painful screams from her mother stabbed her heart. Freeing her from whatever was being done meant Anne had to move forward with measured steps down a hill, careful to not send branches or rocks tumbling. Knowing she would only have one clean shot as the musket only fired one round then needed reloading, she determined her aim would be true. She would down the man with the one shot. Knowing it meant being close as possible, she accepted that she could not be afraid of the man — or what she would see. Her advantage was that her mother was making loud wails and the man would be focused on her mother — not what was happening outside.

Slowly moving closer, things looked worse than seen from afar. The man had built a crude shack at the entrance to a cave. It wasn't large, and she guessed it was there to keep rain, wind, and wild beasts out. It meant she'd have to either shoot through the small cut-out opening of the crude door or opening boldly to enter not knowing what to expect. Stopping to study the entrance, she decided to crawl to the door staying low as possible. She wanted to get a look at the layout inside. Thinking it through, that was her best chance. Not far from it, all depended on the musket firing with the cocking of the hammer. She had loaded it many times and knew how to shoot with dead aim. Suddenly alarmed, she checked it before moving to the door as it was strapped on her back while climbing down. Examining it, she almost gasped. The powder was solid in the pan, the firing cap secure, but she panicked that the lead ball and padding had fallen out somewhere during her descent. Staring in disbelief, she needed to check as it could have slipped out during her descent. No lead ball in the barrel was a frightening thought. Using the ramrod, she sighed relief as the ball and padding were in place, but she still forced it out. Reaching into the bag, she picked out a large bullet style ball, put it in the barrel, then wadded it and tamped it down with the ramrod. Pulling the hammer back getting it ready to fire, it made a click she worried was loud as a whip. Shaking her head in frustration she was angry at having a gun in favor hundreds of years ago.

Knowing the ammunition fixed, her knife on her side and easy to pull for use, she listened closely to the wailing and screaming of her mother. It had a pattern, and she knew the creature was going at her with a rhythm she would use for her timing. She would peer in during a scream and then enter during one. Timing was essential and the sound would hide any sound of her entrance. She knew the man would be fully absorbed in his sick torture.

Taking longer than hoped, she finally stood outside the door. She would not be able to use the rifle when she peered in. Positioning it such where she could grab it fast if he came running at her was all that could be done.

Screaming was occurring faster, meaning she had to act quickly. If her mother passed out, there would be no sound to cover her.

Knowing the moment upon her, looking through the small window in the door was just enough to see inside. All she saw was horrific. Naked, the monster had both hands held up and out to his side as he was pulling her mother's hair, using it like reins on a horse, pulling her head back and up. There was a rough-cut table and her mother's legs were tied by the ankles to it. She couldn't see more of her than her hair in his fists and her legs apart as he had her bent over the table. Although the man had his back to her, she heard a sick gurgling sound he made while thrusting his hips back and forth. What he was doing was obvious and she understood why her mother was screaming in pain with each thrust.

Taking only a few seconds to decide what to do, she knew she could down the man and he wouldn't know what hit him. With the screams, his perverse noise making, the panting he was emitting, she knew he would never hear her. Holding his hands as they were, his back fully to the door, he wouldn't see her. The table was only about eight feet from the door which was in her favor. Most important, her mother's upper body was flat on the table, only her head tilted up from hair being pulled. She knew the one shot had to do the deed completely. Shooting into his back, he may have enough strength to turn and go at her or pull her mother's head back as he reeled which could kill her. It had to be the back of his head.

Without any more thinking, she stood tall, put the butt of the rifle against her shoulder, moved fully into the doorway, pushed the door open gently with the rifle barrel, walked to where the muzzle was a foot behind his head, then squeezed the trigger slowly to not change her aim with a hard pull.

Never closing her eyes, she felt the recoil against her right shoulder, smelling the powder, seeing the flash at the muzzle, she saw the round hole in the back of the monster's head. He never knew she was there.

Frightening her, the man stood upright for what seemed like an hour. All was happening out of real time though it was only a few seconds. Expecting him to fly forward, his head few back towards her instead. Slowly, his knees buckled, and he went down, falling backwards with his upper half landing at her feet. His face was gone. All she could see was blood, veins, and parts she guessed were what brains remained.

It was then she understood why her dad liked the musket. With a large pack of powder, and a ball larger than most bullets, it unleashed hell on what it hit. In the right hands it had immense power.

Her mother lay whimpering and was in bad shape. Her back had much of the man's face splattered over it, including two rotten teeth. Seeing her hands were bound to the other two legs of the table, her hair was wet from blood spray. Leaning over to her mother's ear she said all was okay, it was Anne. Telling her she had stopped the man; he could not hurt her ever again. Maggie didn't seem to know she was there. She didn't look at her; she just whimpered and was shaking. Getting out her knife, Anne got busy cutting the ropes, gently rubbing wrists and ankles. They were torn and bloody. Seeing the metal collar, she reached into the man's pocket and found the key, then took it off her. Not wishing to move her yet, she leaned over and said she was going to wash her some. Maggie kept whimpering. Anne was aware she couldn't deal with things at that moment, and best not to force her to do anything. The man had done the last of that, ever.

Seeing the barrel of water, taking the ladle she removed as much scum as she could from the surface. Finding a pail, she had a hard time finding any cloths that were close to clean. Deciding to take the one blanket and wash as much out of it as possible, it was all she could think of. Wetting then wringing the thing, it would have to do. Cutting it into eight squares, putting four to dry next to the fire she had the others wet to wipe the spatter that covered her mother away, then clean cuts and wounds. Filling the pail, she used the ladle to rinse the teeth, bone, brains and blood from Maggie's back and hair. Gently pouring the water, the splatter fell to the floor. It was all fresh and rinsed off easily. Tending to the wounds, there were many. Finally, washing her mother's face, she remained strong. She hardly recognized the battered, swollen, and discolored skin as her mom's.

Carefully drying her with the warm blanket parts, she scouted for her mother's clothes. They were under the mound of filthy rags the man wore. They had some blood from the first blow made at the wagon, but they were not torn apart. Deciding all she could do is gently move her mother off the table, she wanted to see if her mother could stand. Helping her up, her mother clung to the edges of the table, afraid to move from it. Anne was patient, then said something that reached her somehow. Telling her they needed to finish her husband's grave, she said he was there all alone and needed her. Maggie opened her eyes, looked at her, and gave a little nod.

With Anne gently helping, she got to her feet while holding the edge of the table. Not for fear, but for support. Anne next helped put her clothes on. Maggie was still shaking but stopped whimpering. Then, she finally saw the man on the ground. She held out her hand, still in spasms, and pointed. Looking at Anne, somehow, she muttered she wanted her dagger. She had it with her on her ride, but it wasn't in the cart. It was valuable and Anne was sure the monster had taken it and hidden it from her. Helping Maggie lean against the table she told her she would find it.

The cave had little in it, but the dagger was not in plain sight. Thinking the man had a place for valuables, under a pile of wood for the fire was a small chest. She knew it was the keep. There was no lock, and opening it she found the silver dagger, and something most valuable. He had a large caliber Army revolver and ammunition. He also had a small pouch of gold coins. There was a folding knife and a few letters. Behind the chest there was a leather pouch with a strap. She put all in the pouch, except the dagger, bringing it to her mother, putting into her right hand.

Looking at the dagger, her mother found enough strength to lower herself to kneel next to the dead man. Using both hands to hold the dagger, with power that shocked Anne, Maggie plunged the blade into the crater of the man's face over and over. Stopping when satisfied, she looked at his groin, then just as determined stabbed away, cutting his penis and testicles leaving only small bits and shreds. Showing no expression, she only looked serious. Holding the blade of the dagger up, looked at it, then mumbled *here* to Anne. Taking it, she rinsed it in the barrel then wiped it clean with one of the drier rags. Standing in front of her mother, she was sure to let her see her put it in the leather pouch, telling her if she wanted it, let her know.

It was going to be a hard walk back to the wagon. Her mother could barely walk, and the hill out of the holler was a hard climb. Holding her mother's hand, she said they needed to head home but they both could rest outside a while first. Nodding slightly, her mother started taking steps. Slow in pace, she seemed determined to head out. Anne led her to a large fallen log that was a good height to sit on. With her mother out of the cave, she felt the need to finish matters. Wishing for her mother to never see a trace of that nightmare ever again, she told Maggie she had to finish a few things while she rested. Going past the door and the dead man, she went to the wood pile and threw much of the wood on top of him, scattering the rest around the area. She had smelled kerosene while looking for the dagger. Following the scent, in a recess of the cave she found it. Dousing the man's body, then the floor, finding matches, she stood just inside the door, lit one and it landed on the man's face.

Going to sit with her mother, they both watched the fire. While they sat, Anne reloaded the musket, admiring it for the first time, then examining the heavy revolver. The man had either been in the army or stole it from a dead soldier. They would never know. They didn't know his name, but they knew he had killed Kevin and brutally raped Maggie. Recovering from the horrors seen, Anne sat and could only wonder why. Why her mom? There were prostitutes. There was every chance for him to get cleaned up, work and be a God-fearing man. There was no answer, and he had changed their world. Neither would ever be the same again.

Somehow, watching the fire and the assurance the man could do no more harm calmed her mother. As they sat the fire slowed and as there wasn't much in the cave, leaving embers and not much more. There would be bones and some metal, but no reason to stay. Getting up, Anne thought about the easiest path out of the holler, deciding not to go back to the cart. There was a gentle rise that would go almost directly to their cabin and may have been how her parents had been watched by the man without being noticed coming up the road.

Going slowly, it was still a difficult walk for Maggie. Anne noticed she had a determination that kept her going. If it had been flat, it would have been an easy walk, but it was all uphill. She planned to get her mom hot water for a good bath and get the mule and cart. Talking of little things and asking no questions as they walked, those would wait until a time when Maggie would bring it up herself.

Finally reaching the house, her mother said she wanted to sit with Kevin. Going first to the fresh grave. her mother finally broke down and cried laying on the soft dirt mound. Leaving her there, she started boiling water for the bath, and once the water was hot, went to Maggie saying she had the bath and clean nightdress ready, helping her get up and into the bath. Making simple sandwiches, she put them by her bed. Waiting until her mom was ready, helping her dry off, combing her hair to get all the tangles out, Anne got her settled in bed with the food. Knowing that was about as much as she could do, she said she needed to go get the cart and would be back very soon. Maggie made a stabbing motion. Anne got her silver dagger and put it by her side.

From that day on, Maggie slept only with the dagger, never another man.

Days of Courtin'

After her trip to town, Anne thought about the visit in a few days when Howie would bring the casket. Maggie thought it a kind act, happy to have a proper grave for Kevin with a decent marker which was not expected.

Anne was sure the visit would be more than the grave being righted. She was secretly excited as it meant a visit from a boy; one she liked. He hadn't hid attraction to her when they made the plans. She thought about what best to make for dinner as she promised one of her mother's meals. They worked on what best to make. There was a smoked ham in the shed, and both agreed it was the best choice. It would be a special day in many ways. Maggie knew Anne was looking forward to the young man's attention.

Having few dresses, Anne picked out clothes to work in for the burial, then washed and ironed her floral dress as it flattered her most. For a finishing touch she chose some ribbon to tie her hair. Doing the same for Maggie's best dress, sooner than it felt, it was Saturday morning.

Howie said he would arrive early. They got up with the dawn and started preparations for the special day. Anne went to their garden to pick fresh vegetables while Maggie made biscuits for breakfast. Glad of their early start, as promised, quite early, they heard the wagon coming. Both went and standing on the porch greeted Howie. Pulling a sturdy wagon was a beautiful horse, Howie smiling and waving as he pulled the reins, stopping in front of the porch. Getting off the wagon, he went to Maggie, took both her hands, saying his family was saddened by their loss and hoped when ready they would come for dinner. With sincerity he added if they needed any repairs both he and his dad would be there to help. Turning to both, he said if any repairs were needed right away, he brought his tools and some lumber. Anne told him she had been keeping up with things and appreciated the kind offer; at most she had some worry of the shed. Smiling at each other, she said they had biscuits and coffee ready if he would join them, causing a big smile to shine on his face.

Sitting at the table, he told of his family, new folks in the area, and inquired if all was going better for them. Neither mentioned the horrific man or that terrible day, summing things up saying it had been a time of adjusting to life without a father and husband. He nodded sadly with understanding.

Maggie said the proper burial would help to close that chapter in life and being grateful for such kind help.

Knowing Anne's excitement about the visit, she decided to gain understanding if such enthusiasm was shared by the young man, asking if he had courted any young ladies they may know. Being such a handsome bachelor, she thought he may. Making it sound polite and good conversation, it was a question only a woman such as Maggie could ask without seeming obvious in the inquiry. Looking a bit embarrassed, Howie sat shaking his head.

"That's a question my mother has asked of me as well. I keep explaining we live in an area with few families — with fewer daughters my age. I am not shy, and I would like to court, but the truth is no. I'm thinking you most perceptive as I wish your blessing, only if Anne be obliged, for her to join me at a pig roast at Mr. Donnelly's ranch. I would be most happy if you were to go — if you are up to it."

Looking apprehensive, he sat waiting to learn if he had asked properly as his parents had coached him how to. Anne lit up with a wonderful smile, looking at her mother. Maggie was having a good day and surprised Anne with her reply.

"Howie, I think you can see by the smile on her pretty face that Anne is hoping I will say yes. And I do. I hope you don't mind an extra load. I would love to go as well. I've been here only, and I think it's time I get out and leave worries behind. Goodness, I'll have some sewing to do! When is the pig roast?"

Smiling, obviously happy, he said it was three weeks away. Nodding, Maggie said that was time enough, and they would make some desserts with strawberries as they would be just ripe at that time. She sighed and sat forward in her chair, emotion radiating from her expression.

"Howie, my last visit down was the day we laid poor Kevin in the ground. It is time I start living again. Please, tell all I need no sympathy or condolences. I want you two to have a good time and I wish to meet with friends and enjoy the company."

Nodding, he assured her that he would let that be known. Looking relieved he confided he worried the whole ride up if it was the right time for such an invitation, but now glad he worked up courage to ask. Maggie smiled, then looked at Anne and back to him.

"You saw smiles, and only I have said yes, giving permission to take Anne. Dear boy, I think you need to ask Anne if she desires your company."

Showing a look of alarm, he sat upright, turning to face Anne who was waiting most patiently.

"Anne, having your mother's blessing, would you accompany me to the pig roast three weeks from now?'

Not wishing him to worry any more, she nodded, looking him in the eye saying she would be most pleased to accept his invitation. They all broke out in laughter, Maggie telling him he had done a fine job. Finishing their coffee Howie asked Anne if she was ready to honor her father. Standing up and taking a deep breath, said she was. Maggie told them both she'd put refreshments on the porch from time to time and be busy preparing a good lunch for later.

Leading the horse and wagon around to be close to the shady grove, he unhitched the horse, wiped him down and gave him a feed of oats, tying his reins to a railing. Taking two shovels that were excellent for the task out of the wagon, but leaving the coffin and wooden marker there, he figured seeing the coffin would raise emotions, so best left until needed.

Walking up to Anne, she was standing next to the cross she had made.

Nodding gently, handing her the shovel, she took the cross off the grave, setting it against a tree. Saying no words, just looking at each other, they both started digging. Keeping the same pace as Anne, he knew it was important for her to do the work fairly. The ground was not too packed, and digging was easier than expected. Asking how deep they managed to go. Anne said she thought only a few inches less than her height, so less than five feet. Knowing her father had only been covered with canvas, digging down to four feet he suggested stopping and using caution going deeper. Anne understood. Saying he had the right tools for this depth, he climbed out of the grave and went to the wagon.

Returning with two large hand trowels used for planting, they started gently removing smaller amounts of dirt. It was not long before Howie felt the trowel touch the body. Telling Anne that at this point it would be best to use their hands, he was correct. It took little hand digging to reveal the canvas. Anne looked with both sadness and affection. They had done a good job tying the canvas. Using the ropes the body was tied with, Howie gently lifted the body fully out of the dirt. He was thankful the canvas covered the man fully. The site of a corpse in the ground that long would be a disturbing one. Looking at Anne, he said it would be a good time to wash up and stop for lunch. Nodding, she watched him climb up, then he held out his hand from above, helping pull her up.

Getting lunch ready, Maggie felt proud of Anne doing such a painful task. She had not been able to visit them while doing the work. With all she had been through, it was best to keep more hurt at bay.

As she prepared the food, she spent time thinking it was now Anne's time for courtin' and realized how fortunate she had been with Kevin. Even poor as they were when they first met, Kevin could have looked for a young thing from a family with land or income. Smiling to herself she knew that he was a handsome a lad as any could be found, and resourceful. With his sincere manner and smarts, he could have courted a girl whose family could see his potential. She had even told him he could do better, but he looked at her with passion in his eyes and asked how could he possibly do better? It was a moment she would always cherish. That magic moment when she was willing to walk away from anything for his happiness. The look in his eyes told her that he had found it in her. With eyes wet with tears of joy and sorrow mixed, she wanted only that memory, not him in a half-done grave.

Her mind wandered to the days back on the farm. The one in Ireland where the crops died, and her father worked harder than any farmer near or far. Working hard until he died, he would only stop working if she brought him lunch. Looking at him on her visits, she saw what dead crops and lenders saying they would be taking their land had done. He was not well and had a mean cough that was not getting better. She knew he needed rest, not struggle. There was little in her basket, and she included her portion for him. She always brought a blanket to sit on, and she watched him cough with sweat rolling down his face. Near his end, he looked at her and talked to her different than any time prior.

"Maggie, I tell you straight. The farm be sick, and so am I. I heard your mom last night. She was coughing bad. This is influenza I have, and it be going after your mother. Tending us will no help. Rich ones with doctors are dying of it. Rich and poor alike. You will catch it if you are near. I may be none able to save the farm, nor us, but I can save you. Even without sickness, I would feel such. This is your chance. Your time in life to find a good man and marry. There be none prettier than you. I want you to say yea to Kevin. Be his wife. I know he wants to migrate. I think he will do well. Strengths and smarts, he has. With you at his side, you will save him, and he will save you. I know he will no marry another, no. He loves ya. Your mother and I give our blessing and know what be best for ya. Marry fine lad. Go to the Amerikee with him. It be your time. Daughter, it be your time."

She remembered the way he looked. The utter defeat in his eyes and his love for her. It was the only time she saw him cry, and he held her at arms length to not be near his cough. It was that day she realized that though nothing could help the crops, he worked them day and night to keep his wife and daughter from catching the illness. Two days later he was deathly ill, dying before seeing her wed. A hurry-up wagon that rode slow added his body to the others dead that day. Her mother had worked herself to hysteria and within a week she too rode the dreaded wagon to a mass grave.

Kevin was always with her when he wasn't working at the mill. He never once mentioned their future or talked of leaving. He knew she could not abandon her family. The night her mother was taken by the wagon, which was to prevent more from catching the illness, he arrived with his duffle bag packed and had one for her. He held her and said it was the wish of her parents. He had their permission, and their wish was they marry and leave before they too rode the wagon instead of the ship to the Amerikee. He had talked to the shipping line, and there was passage for his labor as he was a skilled carpenter from the mill on any freighter heading out. Then, stopping as they headed to the port and docks, held her hand and asked her if she'd be his wife.

Now, she was his widow. Not from too much work. Not from influenza, which is why he chose to live far from others to be safe. Not from anything other than the three holes in her body. That was the real sickness in the land of migrants and outcasts. Rape and murder by depraved men who knew no God and lost all sanity in a free land with no law, no rules. Kevin lay dead to satisfy the sickness that overtook men. She had been raped and ruined for the needs of a man no longer human. Living in a cave. He believed tying her down, chained with a collar, using her in ways she would never be able to speak of — all made her his wife. She no longer thought he was mad. She thought of him now as what men revert to when there are no restraints on them. That woman were just holes, and the male beasts were free to do with those holes as they wished only because they were large, strong and had no knowledge of God. Ultimately, they were fools. All men were fools. Instead of being loved, they were hated. She laid in bed for six months thinking of what her father or Kevin would do after years alone in the woods? Would they too end up stealing women or raping them? Her only conclusion was there was no way of knowing. She hoped that would not be so. She had only heard of miscreants doing such sick things. There are few mentions of a man isolated and without contact who was doing anything good, although that was possible as well.

During those months the thoughts went in a circle in her mind. There were no answers. Speculation was the only thing keeping her under the power of her rapist. His deeds had started her fearing even men she loved. She decided to accept each man was different, and there was no certainty. She had been consumed by fear. It wasn't helping asking questions when there were no answers. The world was full of sickness and there were many bad people. She knew the job of all was to stop them. It is why towns were established and lawmen hired in the move westward.

Preparing the plates of lunch stopped her reflections on human nature. Anne and Howie mattered now. They all ate lunch together and Howie looked a bit troubled after eating. Maggie asked if he had a concern. He looked at both, nodding.

"We are taking a break, and I thought it would be the best time to chisel words on the marker I made. It is fine oak. Good hardwood, and with care will stand the weather. I know it is a hard task to come up with final words, and I guess that's what has me so right now. Have you thought of what it should say?"

Patting his hands folded on the table, Maggie nodded and that put him at ease.

"Anne and I have talked on it. We know what to put there. We did a sketch that roughed it out some. Anne?'

Getting up, Anne took the plates to make room on the small table, went inside and came out with a sheet of butcher paper, laying it down in front of Howie, standing where she could point to it.

"Up on top, a nice cross. Under that, in the large letters, his name. Under that, smaller so, just Wife, a mark, and Father. Under that, larger sized, Left Us Too Soon, and finally under that in smaller size, this date, the day he died. It's a lot, do you think it will fit?"

Nodding, he said that it would, and he would mark it on the wood in chalk, and if he got it all correct and nice, he would chisel the letters then stain them to read well. Anne asked if he would need help. He said he could use some as it took a lot of careful measuring to make things center and straight.

Going to the wagon, he carried the board, and went back for a box with string, tacks, and chalk along with various sized chisels with a small hammer. Putting all on the potting table, he propped the board up with a heavy stone to keep it from sliding. Anne soon understood that he used the string to measure lines from the bottom up. To find the center, he just made a piece of string the width of the board, folded in in half, and marked the middle. Using an age-old method, soon the board had chalk lines where lines of words would be. Using a long roll of narrow paper, he wrote out the words the best size for each line, folded each line, marking the center. He copied the letters by holding the paper in place with Anne's help, writing them on the board with wax pencil. It took time, but both Anne and Maggie were surprised at how precise everything was. Getting approval from both, kneeling on the ground he began chiseling, which Anne thought went much faster than laying on the words.

He was skilled at it, saying his dad had him at it since he was quite young, and he took pride in making it perfect. Looking it over, he carefully blew all wood chips off the board and out from the letters. Finally taking a soft brush to get all wood dust cleared, he looked it over again and nodded, asking Anne to have Maggie come see. Taking a small jar of stain, he unscrewed the cap and held a cotton cloth in one hand. He looked at them both.

"This is the part that makes it special. The board has so much shellac, the stain can't harm it by soaking in. The chiseled parts will drink it up…"

He poured stain on the rag and rubbed it into the letters. Doing so quite fast, the blackish stain made large patches covering the letters and board. He quickly took the other end of the soft cloth and wiped the board. Suddenly, only the letters were black, the board free from stain. He made sure to get stain fully in the chiseled areas, and soon it was done. He looked at it carefully and said it was just about done. They thought it was, saying it was wonderful. Nodding thanks, he put the stain in the box with the cloth, took out a can of shellac and a beautifully clean brush. He looked at them.

"Water hurts wood, and the chiseled letters are raw wood. So, I'm going to fill them with a lot of shellac to where they are about even with the board face. This will keep all from harm."

He artfully applied the shellac, waited a bit, then applied another coat. Soon the letters and cross looked as if metal and it was far beyond what they expected. Maggie saw not only his skill, but the finality it stated. The husband and father who left too soon.

Setting it aside and away from where he had worked, he asked Anne if she was ready to continue. She nodded, looking over to the grave. Maggie said she had much to do for a special dinner, meaning that would keep her from seeing her dead husband transferred to the casket. Looking at the grave, Anne suddenly understood they would have to lift her father out, put him in the casket, and lower it into the ground. There was much to do, and it would be a hard task to face as she would be holding her father one more time. The last time.

Coming to stand with her, Howie thought of what she must be feeling and thought of saying he would finish things, but knew it was an act of love she faced and respected that.

"It was a fine job you both did in the dark of night. I'm sure you're thinking of how we are going to do the next part as it's normally done with several men, and then only to lower the casket. There is a good way, and your mule will help us. I brought ropes for the task. I'll drop down and put that large board I brought under him. The ropes go under plank at head, feet, and waist. I'll be having you hold the ropes as I hand them up. Then, I'll tie them to the mule with the same tackle for pulling the cart. You have him slowly walk four or five feet ahead. I'll be below, keeping the board flat and help it up onto the ground. We'll do the same with the casket after he is in it. Without a horse or mule, it would be difficult, but you will see. It is a gentle method."

Nodding in understanding, they both went and readied the mule in his harness, then Howie got the long ropes and plank from his wagon and readied all. Just as he described, he gently put the plank under her father's body, then each rope, handing the ends to her. It was done quickly, and he climbed out and tied the ropes to the mule, went back in, saying to lead the mule slow as she could. It worked as planned, and he kept the plank level when reaching the top and onto the ground. Anne stood keeping the mule from walking. Howie joined her, secured the mule, and released the ropes. He asked her help with the casket saying it was not too heavy but easier to position with two people. Taking the gate off the back of the wagon, he had the casket wrapped in canvas, and the two slid it down, putting it next to her father.

Taking a short break, Anne studied the coffin once unwrapped. It was simple but finely crafted and stained a beautiful walnut and had six handles. Howie saw her studying the hardware, and said no, there were not six to carry him, but the handles would help when lowering the casket, allowing him to keep it steady and even. He lifted the lid, and she was surprised to see it had been lined with white linen. She told him it was too much; she hadn't expected it to be more than a pine box. He smiled, saying he did things proper, and his dad had done most of the detail work.

The moment had arrived to put her father in the casket. Howie first put the ropes under it with care and said there was no graceful way to put him in, and if she felt strong enough, she could lift using the ropes tied round his feet. He would take the upper ropes. They both got placed for the task, and he counted. At the "Three" they both lifted and quickly had the body in place, lowered gently into the coffin. The fit was good, and he moved the body in several spots to center it.

"Anne, next, it is nailing the lid. I know your mom wished not to see this all, but it would be the time to add anything inside you want with him. Mementos, or things he would like, then a final prayer. It is not a thing I should mention, so I'm leaving it to what you think best…"

Knowing her mother wanted no more sadness to think of and remember, she decided to go ask her if there were things she'd like with him, always. She wished to add a note she had written to him the night they first buried him, and his rosary. She went in the house, got her items, then told Maggie she was doing so. Maggie nodded at the tradition. She said she had an item to add, and if Anne could place it for her, she would be saying a prayer for him as they closed the casket but couldn't take seeing more. She went to her bed table and came back, looking at what she had to add, then handing it to Anne. It was a picture of her from before the time she first met Kevin. It was a rare portrait with her mother looking so happy and fair. She understood it's meaning. They would be together, and she would put it under the ropes over his heart. Giving her mother a tearful hug, she went back out to the casket, placing the items.

Having placed a seal of caulk around the area the lid would lay, they each took the lid and that was the last she saw her father. Soon, lid nailed shut, lowering him with care, and each filling the grave with dirt, Kevin, Husband and Father, was in the ground for good. Howie had mixed some mortar earlier. He dug a trench at the head of the grave in the packed dirt, poured the mortar in, and set the marker in place, bracing it, making sure it was straight and true. The grave was finished and could be decorated with stones or flowers in time.

Looking at Howie, Anne said that Maggie planned to visit it, alone, after dinner.

After packing up his tools, he cleaned the area while Anne put the mule in his stall with care and left a green apple as treat. Soon, it was dinner time and Maggie had made a splendid ham, yams, greens and cobbler for dessert. She asked Howie of his future. With a nod, said he decided to continue in the family business because he liked the work and his dad had taught him to take pride in his skills. He explained he knew that some may seek greener pastures, but for him there were none greener than those of his home. He thought over time the area would settle down and more families would see the beauty of the land which meant more businesses, stores, and houses. His family business would be needed and prosper as more settled nearby.

Looking at both with some caution, he asked of their plans. Knowing their lives had been changed so by Kevin's death, he made sure as to ask in a way that would not cause more sorrow. Maggie understood what he really was asking was of Anne, and if she would be staying or was there plans other in their future. She had thought about the very same matters and had an answer for him.

"We came here a one score years back and building this cabin Kevin and I agreed this was home. This is where we spend our lives and that has not changed. This be home, and where I'll stay. Now, Anne, she has her own life ahead. With a husband some day, facing the same choice of where to plant roots. They be welcome here. If not, I pray she be not far from here."

That addressed everyone's questions. With Howie planning on staying in town, Maggie spending her days in honor of her husband's dream, with

Anne free to marry and not be far away, courting could proceed. Anne looked at Howie and smiled. She told him he had work ahead. They all laughed, and Maggie told the boy that it best to use the daylight left to be heading home. One never knows what could be waiting on the road.

Take Warning

Going to the pig roast proved to be another turning point for Maggie and Anne. An annual event put on by a loose alliance of what God-fearing families there were surrounding Pinewood, it was a chance for all of them to affirm hopes that people were fundamentally good. The event was growing slowly in numbers each year, and the future promised more good people. The ne'r-do-wells and social outcasts would continue to move westward as decent people grew in numbers and looked to gain stability for all.

Speaking at the pig roast, the owners of business ventures and the ones who had the most land proclaimed it was time to incorporate Pinewood, pay reasonable taxes and with the money hire a lawman for the protection of all. Agreeing with them, cheers from most all went up and plans for a committee to draft a resolution were made. Maggie was not one cheering the idea. Knowing it was needed, she was not sure if a committee or a lawman could change the nature of the evil lurking in all men. Kevin brought her to the mountains to get away from towns that all began with the same intentions but soon had saloons and whorehouses. She kept quiet, knowing it was tide that would not ebb. Saddened, she thought it the final nail in the coffin for Kevin, ending his dream of isolation.

For Anne, it was the start of her romance with Howie. She accepted his invitation to walk with him during all the speeches to the creek where they could be alone. Knowing him to have been brought up in a good family, his work burying her father had shown him to be kind and caring. He was handsome and he told her he thought her beautiful as they sat listening to the creek. Looking at her with affection, his admiration and attraction to her was clear. Offering the same in return, she had been dreaming of him since his visit and had fondness for him. Seeing no need to hide it, she let him know his intentions and affection were welcome.

After the speeches, Kevin's dad invited Maggie to sit with him for some punch on a bench he himself had made years ago. She told him of her appreciation of all he and his boy had done, and it was far more than she had thought possible for one young man to handle. He smiled, saying it was a proud day for him. Howie was grown and had made the planning — a sign he was no longer a boy. He had grown to be a young man. Maggie nodded in agreement, then saw it as the right time to talk.

"Yes, he has come to be his own man, and he was not shy making his interest in Anne be known. He sought my permission to invite her here and was respectful of our feelings on the matter. There are few their age here, and it seems they favor each other."

He was laughing at that point. "He hasn't stopped talking about her since he returned. Her working with him on such an emotional matter impressed him. He said your faith in Anne impressed him also. You gave her respect for dealing with things most girls would be fearful to do."

Thinking he hadn't seen Anne kill her abductor and burn him to cinders, how could he know how strong she was? How that day had her grown up, teaching of her of evil none should ever face. Unlike those gathered, Anne needed no law man. No committees. She had no plans to ever share the story and turned to the future.

"It hasn't been the same with Anne. I see her staring out at nothing and ask what is on her mind, and she mentions Howie. Well, they are at that age. She thought he would end up with the pastor's girl, being close and all. She will only seek a young man from good breeding, so it be good you sent him up to us. Has he expressed his intentions to you?"

Nodding, he said Howie expressed them after Anne visited, with hopes to start courting her. "His hopes are she has fond feelings of him, as he thinks she would make a wonderful wife. He has high opinion of you and asked what best to do if they marry someday. He would worry if you were to be alone. My mother lived with us, and you met her once. She was happy here with us. I told him when it comes to such, that is opinion only you could give. He will respect whatever you wish, but he is thinking of you as well."

Thinking of all said, Anne had also given thought to such matters since his visit.

"First, I guess we see if they head down the road together. I'd be inclined to live such if Kevin had died naturally before me, as your kind father had. I have trouble seeing myself anywhere but the cabin he built for us. I have no plan to leave his hopes and dreams behind. I could visit on weekends or long stays, but for now, I need to keep my home. There, with Kevin, eventually laying by his side as we did when we wed. I think that would be good for all. Anne could come stay if Howie is off to get supplies or such, and for now, that is what I know and will share with them if it goes so."

He put his hands over hers.

"I think it be a good decision. I know Kevin was taken from you, and you don't want to leave him. You will be welcome as your daughter builds a family with you part of it. I think all will understand. It's hard for me to think of my boy away from here with a house and family of his own."

Not surprisingly, Anne and Howie strolled back from their walk hand in hand, smiling at those greeting them with approval. They joined the talk going on, and Howie announced, as parents had given their blessings, he was courting Anne. She looked happy, and it had been expected. Maggie teased him a bit asking exactly what the courting would consist of? Howie looked with eyes wide, thought a bit and admitted he wasn't sure. That caused chuckling, and Maggie said it most likely would be calling on her often, gazing into her eyes, hunting for flowers in bloom, many a wagon ride, and even some fine attire. Anne nodded, saying she would expect no less, causing him even more embarrassment. His dad said he would figure it out soon enough and had a few hints to offer.

Noticing the time, Anne said they had no wish to ride home in the dark. Maggie nodded to that. After a long goodbye between the fledgling couple then to all there, they headed home.

Talking of things to come, Maggie asked if she had made any plans for the week ahead. Anne said they hadn't but would not be surprised if Howie showed up sometime soon, then asked why. Maggie said that it was high time to get some new cloth and other items to make some pretty dresses. Anne was all smiles at the idea. It meant a long journey to the large town, even staying overnight at the hotel there. Her mother said it would do them good to leave the shadows behind and look ahead, and such a journey would be one to remember.

Getting settled back at the cabin, they both worked on a list of what to buy and various things needed. As they finished, Maggie surprised Anne by adding an item when all else was done, saying only if they could find one used and not too dear. Anne sat stunned.

"A guitar! I didn't know you played one. When? Dad played his fiddle, why didn't you get one to play along together?"

Smiling, Maggie sighed. "Kevin loved playing so, and proud of his music. I never told him. I let him have his special gift. With the illness and us leaving with nary a penny, not something I thought of during those hard times. Now, I miss his music. I would never sell his fiddle, it's a fine reminder. But now, I want to sing the old jigs and tunes, and I have ideas for words I'd like to put to music. I learned to play from me dad when I was quite young, and I took it seriously. I want to fill hours ahead when you'll be gazing at the stars with your laddie. The music at pig roast made me think of it."

Two days later they made the journey. It was good weather and good for Maggie to be doing things again. They found all on their list, and the last purchase was from a used goods store that had a fine guitar getting dusty in a corner, willing to take almost any sum offered. The merchant had extra strings, saying if they bought it, he would make them part of the deal. With that done, they ate at the hotel and enjoyed the comfortable room they had for the night. Heading home, Anne drove, and Maggie tried the guitar. After tuning it and thinking of how long it had been since she played, she started with a simple finger pick and just a few chords. As they rode along, Anne looked at her with surprise, then tears running down her cheeks.

"That was dad's favorite." Maggie nodded, and there were tears in her eyes as well. Anne asked her to sing it. Closing her eyes, she sang with her wonderful Irish accent.

Some bright morning
When this life is o'er
I'll fly away
No more troubles
On that joyous day
I'll, fly away

Realizing that her mother was healing from the physical damage she endured, her emotional state was also getting better. Buying the guitar was a surprise, and Anne thought it a hopeful sign. It gave her a purpose and took her back to a time in her life when everything lay ahead and was not bound by some chain put round her neck. She was looking forward to hearing old songs and amazed she would be putting her own words to music. Riding home, Maggie practiced finding chords and notes she hadn't played in a long time. Finally, she laid the guitar down behind them, looking at her fingertips. They had dents from the strings and were red. She smiled and understood that steel strings would be hard when starting but in time her fingers would toughen up.

Maggie was rubbing her fingers with her thumbs and turned to face Anne a bit better.

"I've been thinking some, and like any mother and daughter, it is time we talked a bit about men. I know you are plenty smart, and good, but it's like our road. It can be a rough ride. Men are full of surprises and a young girl with her first beau best be ready for the ways of them. My mum had talk with me, glad I am she did. I want you to hear what I say. It doesn't mean that all will be needed, just good to be knowing. To understand men in ways other than how your father was."

Looking somewhat concerned, she nodded and told her mother she only gave good advice and would take all to heart. Saying the mule could use rest, they could use some treats. Being important, she'd pull over where it was shady up ahead and they would both do better there. Nodding, Maggie said it was a good idea. Finding a nice spot with shade and an area to sit, she pulled over and they used a blanket to sit on. The mule was eating at some bushes; they ate candies they bought for the ride home. Maggie took a deep breath and spoke in a gentle manner.

"We all go through changes as we grow, and our bodies, well, they be part of that. You've changed on the outside. A fine shape, your breasts, your monthly time, all turning you from girl to woman. You change inside too. You crave things like looking pretty and start wanting the attention of a young man. I'm sure you've gotten excited thinking about being held and kissed, and the lovin' that brings. We are each different, but with most young women it's a desire that leads to marriage, having babies, and having love making to please you. All good. For woman, it's about feeling wanted. Pretty. Loved. I see all of that happening in you."

Looking pleased, Anne nodded. "Those things are all as you say. It's not something I planned or thought about, it just happened. Yes, I want kind attention and to be loved. I'm a bit scared, but I think it's exciting to think about kissing, and what making love will be like. I figured it is how God made us, and what makes us want to make babies."

Rubbing Anne's arm, she had a sad smile. "Yes, it be God's will and nature, and with a good man be a wonderful thing. It's part of how you show your love for each other. The attraction is needed to make babies, but it is a pleasurable thing you crave. It be a fire that burns, that passion. How we show love and affection, as I said. Men, well, for them it is often different. They go through changes, and they grow strong and are made to be very physical. Loving, for many men, be a need they can't always control. Taking a woman and her doing what he wishes is part of being a man, for most. That power over women is part of feeling like a man. Some will want lovin' if you feel like it or not. They may want you to do things that please them but are not pleasing to you. With a good man, he will respect your body, and treat it with care. He won't force himself on you. A man who uses force shows no love. He's not one you want. I'm not trying to scare you, but it be truth."

Anne sat quietly and Maggie watched her reaction. She was thinking about what she had been told. Then, she looked up.

"I was thinking about what if a man is considerate when you first meet, but once married he starts making demands as he is the husband, isn't it the duty of his wife to honor him?'

Shaking her head, Maggie was very strong in her manner.

"That's hogwash, told to us by men. That is not so. Both are to honor and respect each other. The wife is not his property to do what he wants only. Forget that notion now. Never let any tell you such. Women want loving as much as a man. But she wants to be loved with affection, not like animals with no control. It is best to please each other, not the wife pleasing the man. I know many women are trapped in marriages like that, and that is a bad thing. If the man starts off sweet, then turns wild, you will not be happy. It's revealed quickly, so if it is shown before you marry, you call it off. Stop all right then. You think about it, and never do what you want not. Then there is one other trouble to look for…"

Knowing it was a lot to understand, Maggie knew it best to lay it out straight now as Anne was smart and would be best advised before starting courting. Thinking it best to use an example Anne could relate to, she went on.

"Daughter, oh, dear daughter. Oh, I was lucky to find good man, but he was in an isolated home with few women about. His world was small, and I was always aware men are victims to their own nature. I see you looking confused. Just as you've got a desire, natural like, to be a courting, we all have things inside that drive us to good, and sometimes to bad. Men, they have a roaming eye. They can have a faithful wife. A real beauty. A sweet family. One day, not even knowing why, they get the urge to stray. A woman they know or come across catches their eye, or she flirts with him, then it's all he thinks of. That urge can lead him to be unfaithful and ruin his marriage. In that, all men are fools. Many a good man has left his wife and family for some harlot. It be common thing."

Looking truly amazed, Anne said she couldn't imagine a good man doing that. Maggie understood she was sheltered from many things, so she wanted to be sure she understood.

"As I said, it's lust that takes over, and it blinds them. Think the hen house out back. We have seven hens, and old Bill, the cock. Does Bill limit himself to one hen? No, he rules the roost, and has all at his call. That's his nature, and there are men who see it same for them. Even with a fine wife, if they get the chance, they will be the same as old Bill. And what of faithful wife? The man rules the roost. She depends on him for so much, she would be in bad straights if she complained or left him. It not be all men, but me thinks most men be tempted time to time."

It was a sad thing to learn, and Maggie knew young women think it will never happen as love is true in the early days. She could tell Anne was figuring out what she was warning of. It was a problem she had no answer for. Anne had the look of that being her next question.

"How do you know who will, or who won't? And if they get that lust, what can we do? Just let it happen?"

Nodding, Maggie knew she had the idea right.

"Many a woman turns a blind eye, hoping it will pass. Men are not keen on being told what to do, and women think if they say stop, it will make the man want it more to show he makes the decisions. Other women see him leave for a chore and he never comes back. Women who make threats to leave are handed their bag. So, most endure, suffer in silence, even think it be their fault. When children come, they spend less time lovin' and more time tending young ones. Anne, babies change us. We get heavier and our bodies grow to feed the wee things. We don't think about it, but the man does. Then a love-crazed young woman looks their way. She be in fine form and no children wearing her down. She has strong hold over a married man who has to share attention with the babes from his wife."

"Mom, you had a baby. You are slim and beautiful. Dad was always looking at you with admiration and I could tell he saw you only as a beauty."

Maggie smiled. "Yes, he was always wanting to be in my arms and be lovin' me. It is true I am in fine form, still. I have my looks. That takes work. I made sure I kept myself fit and dressed pretty. I wanted him just as he wanted me. You are right on that. If his wife be a prize, he may be less likely to lust for women not as beautiful. It may still happen. It's like that old Bill. They need to prove they be cock of the yard sometimes. I pray you never have to face that. But know of it. If you see a man's eyes wander, you need to show him what he has a risk. Your heart. Your body. Your love."

Knowing they would have to get back home soon; Anne had the one question that had to be asked.

"I'm worried asking, but now I won't be settled until I find out. Did dad ever stray? Or were you worried he may? I guess it is always worry, but do you know if he ever did?"

Looking at her with a sorrowful expression, Maggie looked mournful.

"For so long, I was none sure. Now, I know the answer be no. The day he be killed, my first worry when he was so late was that he was stepping out and would say he got delayed tracking a poacher. Now I live every day knowing I had no cause to think that. He never gave reason to. Women have that fear inside them. It overtakes us. Fear and nothing else took hold of me many a day. It not be a thing I will ever get over. Anne, understand what really happened that night. Never change this truth in your thoughts of me. If I was not suspicious and thought he could stray, I know all would have been different. I was put low thinking how I doubted him. Knowing, well, knowing I thought such, Kevin wished me no grief. Rather than stay out looking that night when poachers do their stealing, he stopped early and took the fastest way home. Because I doubted him. I am sure it was his worry to rush home that caused him to not be alert to the monster waiting. I asked him straight before leaving, I said, 'Where are you really going? Is some missy out there a waiting?' Those were my last words to him. 'Is some missy out there a waiting?' And I remember the sadness on his face, and his last word to me. 'No'. He was so tired of my fears, and every time having to say no and no and no. I knew it was me killed him. Me, so selfish, making him worry only my fears, not worrying about beasts, or that ax…"

Some Loving Story

Knowing Anne to be quite a beauty and pleasant to be with, Howie smiled as she needed a husband. Living in a remote cabin with few young men to compete with anywhere near, she was not likely to do better than him.

He admired his father for many reasons, but most of all was in awe of the man having so many women to lay with near and far. Just about every delivery, trip to towns for supplies, or going to visit friends included a bed or two along the way. He was a dashing man and women couldn't say no to him. Many were widows, but also married ones who let him know that was no concern. Their husbands worked and should the man come home too soon, his dad had a reason to be there fixing this or that. He knew his dad was fixing them between their legs every chance he could.

Working with his dad since he became a teen, he often travelled with him. His dad told him when reaching teen years, a man can have what women he wants, and when older and married, no need for his wife to know his doings. Howie was told all was to stay between father and son. His dad said he was going to give him learning no schooling could ever provide. He knew his dad trusted him on the matter and he was excited at the idea. Found masturbating by his dad, rather than telling him he was doing wrong or taking him to the pastor, he said he could tell his boy was ready for some lady love and would show him that a picture from some catalog isn't as good as the real thing.

Smiling at such thoughts, the two formed a bond good for both. His dad was proud of his conquests and told him that he would be just as proud of him once he learned how to be a man no women could deny.

"Howie, one day I hope to say of you what I think of myself. You know those banjo boys over in the next holler? Yep, you know the ones. They have a song they sing that goes, 'He's got a chain, five miles long. On every link, a heart does dangle, of another maid, he's loved and wronged.' Son, they wrote that about me and it's their favorite. So, one day I hope you have a chain even longer!"

Paying close attention to his dad as he travelled with him, he had his first lesson when his dad said he should watch and learn. He'd wait in the wagon for his dad to go into some house to love a widow or wife, wait a bit then go peer through the windows. Watching without making a sound he saw his dad do things he didn't know possible and women squealing with delight. Most times he would masturbate while watching. When they started to get dressed, he'd run back to the wagon. His dad would ask if he saw this or that, and Howie complimented him and asked questions about the various positions and what women like the best. Howie was sure being watched made it more exciting for his dad.

After enough time watching, when he turned fifteen, they headed to a house with a woman he saw his dad with many times. Having a strange grin on his face, his dad was looking over at him and he wasn't sure what the grin was for. As they pulled up to the well-kept house, he was thinking of the woman. She was quite young, had a fine body and he thought her very pretty. His dad waited a bit, then looked at him after he jumped off the wagon.

"Betsy is quite a handful. Son, I don't think one man is enough. She told me next time to bring you along as she sure could use an extra man on the job. No more watching, this is your day."

Stunned, he thought his dad was teasing him. He told him to not do so, it was not right.

"Howie, get yourself down here. She caught a glimpse of you running back to the wagon last time and asked if you were watching. I told her I had you learning about loving the ladies, and she said she'd be so excited loving both a dad and a son at the same time. When she learned she would be your first, she was ready right then, but we had to get home. Now, you have seen me enough to know what to do. She's a fine one, none better for your first go."

Smiling to himself, he thought back that Betsy was fine indeed. That day was as special for her as it was for him. He tried to count how many times he had visited her over the years after, most on his own. She taught him everything he knew, and always welcomed him with the same affection of that first day. He was just glad it wasn't him or his father her husband found her with. The husband was not arrested after shooting Betsy and the cheater man. In those parts no man was locked up for shooting a cheating wife and her lover, or a man stealing his horse.

Warned that caution and discretion were part of being a successful lover man, his dad shared his wisdom of who to go after, when, and how to ride on by a lady's home if he saw a wagon or a horse outside. He had a special method that was helpful. He told his ladies to tie the drapes in their window into a knot if they were sure a boyfriend or husband was off elsewhere, and things be safe. There were a few close calls and he soon realized that having his son in the wagon outside would be a good precaution. Seeing the boy would involve hellos and there would be talking before the man would enter, giving his dad a chance to get dressed and have a reason for being there. Its was as basic as what man would bring his son along to cheat on his wife? His dad was a lover man who was also very clever.

Much of his dad's success with ladies was charm. He was certainly a handsome devil but had a polite manner and was always respectful until he got in the bed when he did what the woman liked best, even if not always well-mannered. Listening to the way his dad spoke to women influenced him. He got good at being polite, innocent in nature, and acting considerate even though the only reason was to get their bloomers off. Soon he had links on his own chain. One day he asked his dad why he married when there were so many fine and willing women about. His dad nodded his head saying it was a good question. He explained why it was truly the most important question to have answered.

"Being truthful, loving so many when you are married just makes loving your wife more exciting. It's something that she doesn't know about. It be coming home, making love to your wife after you've had a few ladies that day. It makes you feel like a real man. Before your mom, I had me plenty of those pretty things, but I asked myself a question I'll always remember. I thought *what kind of woman would I want to marry?* One who be fooling around with every cock in the coop? If she'd love me before we married, she'd love others after. You can't marry a woman who would cheat on you, boy. You need a real wife. Lover, wife. Those be two different things. She takes care of the house. Has your children. Takes care of you when you get old. And if you get the right one, she's the one every other pecker out there wants, but only you can have. That means everything. You don't only need a wife; you need a wife that would never cheat. Then, you have it all. If no ladies have the curtains tied, she's there waiting for you. You always have that. And truth be I love your mom with all my heart. She is my love, not some missy on the side."

Knowing that advice to be wise and enamored with his dad's wisdom in all things, he had been looking for a good girl he would have for a wife. He was certain Anne was exactly the one for him. Pretty as a peach, her mother very beautiful meaning she would follow and stay pretty through the years as well, and isolated from other men. It was rare to find an innocent girl in their part of the world and there were few he hadn't loved at some time or another including having many a mother and daughter in bed together just as Betsy had him and his dad at the same time. Anne would never do such a thing. Most important was if she found out he was cheating, she was not the kind to pick up some gun and blast him for wicked ways. No. She would turn her head and let him have his way with some daughter or wife and count herself lucky to have a good husband.

Star On a Summer's Morning

Moving quicker than any expected, the courting of Anne by Howie led to news from both at a Christmas church dinner they were in love and planned to marry in the Spring.

Knowing the plan, Howie and his dad would be building a house not far from their own, and Maggie would be sewing a wedding dress. She never had one as her marriage was the quick work of a magistrate just before she and Kevin boarded the ship to start their life across the sea. Although all were happy, it wasn't much of a surprise. Short of the moon falling from the sky their union was expected and made sense. He was looking for a wife, Anne a husband. They had seen each other since they were toddlers, and they had always liked each other. For Maggie, it meant Anne would have decent home in a safe area surrounded by decent people. She had no plans beyond visits and being there if needed. Her only wish is that Kevin was still alive to be with her once Anne had moved away. It would be lonely.

One concern, quickly addressed, was with Anne married she worried about money. Kevin, then Anne, we're skilled at trapping but she was not. Thinking of other ways to make money, she realized that dressmaker was the only thing she could be. She figured Anne's wedding gown would be seen by many so it would be an opportune time to show her skill and let people know she was willing to offer such fine work for others. Telling Anne, the news reached Howie and his dad. They said to worry not as they would be sure she had all she needed, even offering to build a nice shop for her to showcase dresses for sale and Anne could help run it for her. She thought it a kind offer and would give them both purpose as time went on. She thought

Anne was more excited than she was, and that was the best part sprouting from her seed of an idea.

Each day she drew ideas for dresses, and with cloth she had spare, started making some as samples of stitching, collars and embroidery. Anne looked forward to the time after lunch each day and waited on the porch for Maggie to play her guitar and sing her songs she learned when a girl in Ireland. Maggie had to recall her skills at first, but soon was playing any tune she wished with ease. Her voice was strong and full of emotion. Most days Anne would have tears as many of the songs were beautiful but often sad.

"Mom, you sing songs dad never played. Well, he mostly played fiddle jigs with no words, but each of yours has a story. They are haunting melodies, and most have some heartache or tragedy befall a maid, as they were called. Were men in Ireland so heartless to inspire such songs?"

Laughing, Maggie understood. "Yes, these ditties have many a young maid in distress or done wrong, haven't they? Well, I do none think they would write a song about the girl going the day and barely getting the washing done, now would they? At some time, all face some sorrow, such as losing your dear dad. Those moments are put to song. Some of these ballads be hundreds of years old. And they be ones I favor. They are prettiest. You don't hear me singing no happy ones. Those are drinking songs and Irish men love the drink, more then their women, I think. That may be why there are so many maids with such troubles!'

Laughing, Anne understood. "Yes, I guess that is the reason. I would guess that such songs are written in every land. It's just how things seem to go. So, I give you a challenge. What is the saddest, most heartbreaking song you know?'

Answering by starting a beautiful finger pick, she told Anne this one had her crying before she knew what it meant, but her favorite. Then Maggie started singing.

I never will marry. I'll be no man's wife
I intend to stay single for the rest of my life
One day as I rambled down by the seashore,
The wind it did whistle, and the waters did roar

I heard a poor maiden make a pitiful cry
She sounded so lonesome at the waters nearby
I never will marry. I'll be no man's wife
I intend to stay single for the rest of my life

The shells in the ocean will be my deathbed
And the fish in the water swim over my head
My love's gone and left me, he's the one I adore
I never will see him, no never, no more

She plunged her fair body in the water so deep
She closed her pretty blue eyes in the water so deep
I never will marry. I'll be no man's wife
I intend to stay single for the rest of my life

Looking at Anne, who was crying, Maggie put the guitar down and held
her hands out and took Anne's.

"When I was just a wee one, that song made me cry and I knew not why.
Now, with Kevin, he is gone. Maybe not for the reason in the song, but
away from me. The night we put him in the ground, as we were digging
this song was in my mind. I knew straight I'd never marry again. Just
him for me. And it filled my mind that I'll see him no more. I thought
of the poor girl sinking in the water. Now I understand this song. Losing
your love, no matter why, you lose yourself. I was sinking in my own way,
drowning in my tears. I was like the girl. If I couldn't have Kevin, what was
left? Do you know why I didn't go down to the same fate? Go to the banks
of the Ohio and throw myself in?"

Sobbing, Anne managed a tearful shaking of her head.

"I have you. You are Kevin's gift to me. See, that is why we marry. When I look at you, I see my man, and I see you."

Turning Anne's sadness to a smile with her message, Anne started wiping away her tears. She understood that her mother loved her dad so deeply, and despite all that happened, she had hope for the future where once she was drowning in sorrow.

Looking at her daughter, just as with singing her the song, it was a time to be sure she was making the right decision by marrying Howie.

"Daughter, you saved my life. I still wonder how you had such strength. Now, it is your life. I want to ask some things of you, and they be hard to think about. It be time to ask if you are certain of Howie and the life ahead. We live where there are few good people. Your choices were few. If we lived in a large city, you would have met dozens of men and had choices. Here, really, only one. Now that you have been courting him, it be time to ask if you are marrying him because he is the only one? Or, is he truly the man of your heart? If you were in a big city and had many proposals, would Howie be your choice? Is he all you think of? Is he your dream? You marry for life, so if not, that is a long time to be unhappy."

Reacting with understanding, Anne looked a bit frightened.

"Laying in bed at night, I have the same thoughts. I want to be sure, as you are right to point out. At first, I was unsure. It was not where a handsome lad came to town, and I was swept away in fury of passion. I have read of such things, and I am sure that is one way. I have known Howie all my life. I've always liked him from afar. The quandary in me is it still only liking, or is it love? I know that my body is wanting love and babies and that can fool me, so times I think that may be. Then I think of you and dad. In the middle of sickness and death, you would have been destitute or gotten sick, but he was there. Was that love's passion, or something where if times were different, you may not have married? I do feel liking has turned to love true. I see him look at me and it excites me. I care about what he says and does. I'm impressed how he is concerned for you. A fire that grew from small spark, starting to blaze. Maybe those that start with the blaze see it die out over time. I love him and I see in his eyes he loves me. I would not have said yes to him if not."

Such a Terrible Crime

Passing quickly, winter gave way to spring.

Maggie was amazed how well the dress-making shop was built, and far more elegant than she had expected in every way. Jimmy, Howie's father, said it would be the start of a new day for Pinewood. He planned to build other shops alongside. She asked of what variety, and he said first barbershop, chemist, offices for a doctor and lawyer, then a café. He said that the town needed many more, but those would start attracting occupants and new families. As the coach line stopped in Pinewood, he thought people moving westward would think twice before heading further as Pinewood would no longer be a ramshackle trapper town. It would have finery and why her store was important. Jimmy had strong notions of the future.

"Maggie, if you get the woman, which your shop certainly will, that is all that be needed." Little did she know the dark, deeper meaning of his plan to attract fine ladies for his — and Howie's — pleasures.

While Jimmy was finishing painting crown molding and donning the dressing room with silk fitting room curtains in the dress shop, his son was finishing up the house he and Anne would settle in. Howie had help from father and friends to raise the walls and roof but wanted to do most else himself. No log cabin, it had siding, a shingle roof, casement windows and hardwood floors. He needed help plastering the walls after he put up lathe and bartered with a craftsman from the large town in exchange for his labor later that summer. As part of the plan for making the town attractive to new families, it was near the road where all could see. A large shed and barn would come after the wedding. The house would be ready in time.

Stopping by often, Anne was overwhelmed. It was a grand house, so different from the cabins most lived in. Both she and Howie spent many evenings with Maggie picking out various things he couldn't build himself from the Montgomery Wards catalog. The Wells Fargo wagon would be busy delivering a stove, sofa and chairs. They were most excited to order a mattress for their room, and one for her mother's bed when she visited. Anne was feeling grown up as such things were what adults did. It was costing a tidy sum, but Howie explained he had saved all his earnings for just such a day.

Building in the new Pinewood was bringing people to town more than expected as news spread through mountain towns. Maggie worked decorating the dress shop. Although she lived outside the little town for more than twenty years, most people had never seen her. She rarely went to Pinewood, knowing only a small group of decent families from church. Kevin, sometimes Anne, made trips to sell furs and buy supplies while she stayed home. She was never fond of the wild nature the place had fostered. Working in the shop she saw new faces. Some walking by when the coach stopped, others coming in their wagons who were curious about her store.

As the elegant sign with lettering reading "Ladies Finery" was hung outside, she started having ladies stop in to learn what would be offered, complementing her as such an establishment was surely needed.

Maggie learned the hard way that love indeed betrays all secrets. Two weeks before the wedding, an attractive young woman in decent clothing stopped in to see when the store would be opening. She looked to be stylish, and Maggie could tell she was excited to have such a store closer to her home. The woman gazed at the fine carpentry and details and told Maggie her husband was quite gifted making the store something a real lady would be most comfortable visiting. Maggie saw no need to explain she was widowed, saying just she admired the work too, but it was all crafted by Jimmy, if she knew the man. The woman's face lit up. She glanced around then gave Maggie a knowing look and then a more knowing nod. She let forth a little giggle.

"You must be quite special in bed for Jimmy to do all this for you. I do give him all I have, but he hasn't built me a shop!" The woman pretended to be miffed and beside herself. She then blushed, saying, "You must share your secrets. No wonder he doesn't visit as often. If it wasn't for Howie stopping by now and then, I'd be loveless. You know how it is with no man to take care of all that as only a good one can."

Almost fainting, Maggie managed to keep her surprise hidden and led the woman on a bit to learn the whole story. She smiled, one of the hardest moments since her rape, and engaged in reply.

"Yes, I have been keeping Jimmy quite busy. He visits every day which be why he insisted on the silk drapes for privacy. But you, so young and pretty, I think it will pass and he will be back your way soon. Unless he has other chores to tend to." Maggie had to watch her manner as she about said "whores" but glad she had said "chores" to keep confidence.

The woman gave a serious expression. "That's always the problem, isn't it? Too many stops. Too many chores. I don't know how he manages it. I now understand why he sends Howie over so often instead. I must confess I'm actually quite impressed with the boy. He's as good as his dad in my bed. I'm sure you know what I mean. He's so charming. Acts so sweet and innocent. But the things he does! Why, those are hardly innocent, are they?"

Nodding, Maggie agreed. "No, the boy is far from innocent in his ways with me."

Saying she had to leave, the young woman asked when the store would be opening. Maggie told her an announcement would be coming soon, and she wrote down the woman's address, thanking her for stopping in and assured her all her needs would be taken care of soon, she was sure. Smiling, the woman had a dreamy expression.

"I do hope so. I love my husband, but I have such an appetite for love, and he's gone so much of the time."

Standing in the middle of the shop, feelings of dismay, anger and apprehension all swirled inside of her, and she felt sick. Anne was spending the day gathering skins from traps. Maggie had the cart and mule. She gathered all her personal possessions and put them in the cart, including her materials, tools and samples. She would never go back in the shop again.

Understanding the meaning of the revelation, a sudden wave of apprehension shot through her. Howie was a scoundrel, and she would need to ask Anne if he had already taken her virginity. She never asked and if Anne had done so, that was her decision and a private one although she would be understanding of such a need.

Sharing the news was a terrible duty that would devastate Anne and asking if she had bedded Howie even more upsetting if it be so. Filling the cart, all her thoughts were tumbling round and round. She would know no peace until she had a talk with Anne. She dreaded the long ride home then waiting for Anne to come back from trapping. It would be a hard day and the waiting would be the hardest part. She started up the mountain, the mule going painfully slow. She decided she would work on her song writing as best way to distract herself. It would be good to let out feelings that way.

Arriving back at the cabin Kevin had built, it was comforting and safe. No grand new house could match it as it was made with naught but love. Kevin had been a true lover and made them a real home. Back in Ireland, they had little chance at courting with such troubles around them. She realized that the real courting was when Kevin found ways to cut timber, build the home, and went about finding the stove and other goods to give them comfort. He went out in the world, not to defile maids, but to show his love for her. Building more than a house, he built their life ahead. Howie was out bedding others and was untrue to Anne before they courted, and that courting had been such a terrible crime. She knew deception would not end when married. He had been raised since young boy to believe a man could steal hearts of tender ladies. She would make sure Anne locked her heart away from that thief.

Making lunch, although it still hurt her heart, before eating she went to Kevin's grave and told him she was glad he was not witnessing the things that happened since parting. She told him the sad news and how Howie was bad as the monster who raped her. The decrepit creature had hurt her body, but Howie had hurt Anne's heart. That would ruin her faith in men. Bodies could heal. Hearts not easily so. Faith and love were fragile and now would be fleeting and gone. Like a star in the summer morning, they appear and then they're gone, never to be held true again. Anne's faith in men would to be hard to heal, if ever.

Telling Kevin her thoughts and how she felt made her feel less alone delivering the sad news. She went into the house, brought her lunch to eat on the porch and had put on her belt. It had the sheath carrying her silver dagger. She would wear it always from that moment on.

Eating, she looked out at the forest. It was the stunning bright green of Spring, and beautiful. The thick pines dark and lush, now dusted with new needles bright green, like dew. In time, the new pine needles would darken and become the dark hue of the forest seen from afar. Knowing hearts were the same, hers grew darker that day. So would Anne's.

Deep in the beauty of the hills, many animals were mating. Others, such as nature is, were attacking weaker creatures and snarling as they ate their prey. Few animals had a mate for life. Even the tiny cuckoo bird with no real mate would steal eggs from another's nest and send them crashing to the ground or claim it as his own. She had heard of men discovering their wives had been loving another, and people said them cuckold — and fools. Now living among the small birds, she understood where such a name had its roots. The world heard the bird's sweet warble, such a pretty sound it made while robbing a nest.

Finishing her lunch, she took her ink and quill and began writing down words to an old song as she thought of the truth looking one way but was sadly not as it seemed. Life was often deception, cold and cruel.

O the cuckoo is a pretty bird, she sings as she flies
She brings you glad tidings, she tells you, no lies
She sucks sweet flowers, to keep her voice clear
And never cries "cuckoo!" till the spring of each year

O meeting is pleasure, but parting is a grief
An inconstant lover, is worse than a thief
A thief, he will rob you, of all that you have
But an inconstant lover, will send you to the grave

The grave will receive you, and turn you to dust
An inconstant lover, no maiden can trust
They'll court you, and kiss you, poor maids deceive
There's not one, in twenty, that one may believe

Come all you fair maidens, wherever you be
Don't hang your poor hearts, on the sycamore tree
The leaf it will wither, and the roots will decay
And if you're forsaken, you will perish, away

Reading the song, it was her telling of the one she remembered hearing when she was very young. She had no idea what it meant then, but now sad she did. Listening to the chorus of the little birds round her, she thought of what their songs really meant. She remembered Anne saying it seems most songs told of poor maids with broken hearts. She shuddered. Anne would be such a song. She decided she would write and sing of her sorrow, but not until all had played out. Hearing Anne's sadness directly would be the truth in her song.

Folding the Cuckoo song, she put it in a box Kevin had decorated with gold paint for her keepsakes. Her songs were many, with only a few happy in lyric. There would be another sad one before long. She thought of how they told the constant sorrow of women in this life and could only wonder why God had made man and woman so. Men, knowing well how tender a woman was, had no trouble breaking their hearts. They did not care. All women could do is pine and sigh, letting troubles pass them by.

Having spent the afternoon with thoughts and songs, Maggie had left her goods in the cart. She wasn't sure if all should be burnt or kept. They were sad reminders of broken promises but also a way to make money and not rely on men. While she was thinking what best to do, she heard Anne calling hello from down the road. She had both hands filled with skins and would be happy of the harvest. Standing on the porch, she waved at Anne gently. She would not speak harshly or in anger as she told her news. She would be gentle and sympathetic which may lessen the pain.

Walking up to the cart to put the skins in it, she stopped and had a puzzled look seeing all from the shop. She turned and looked at Maggie and her expression became one of alarm.

"Mother. What has happened? And you have your knife on your side? Please, this is all upsetting. Are you alright?"

Sitting on a chair, Maggie nodded a yes to let her know she was okay, telling her to put the skins away and after cleaning up, she had much to tell her. Anne was showing fright, knowing no good news would be shared and made quick stowing the skins and washing herself. Keeping her overalls on, she went to the chair next to Maggie and just sat, waiting. While Anne had been washing herself, Maggie went in the house and brought out some cloths as she knew there would be tears to dry. She had them on her lap, which helped cover the dagger as it had concerned Anne. She knew little else but to gently tell her news and keep all her opinion out of the telling.

"Mother, you worry me so. Your goods in the cart, knife by your side. Please, this is frightening me!"

Maggie was having a hard time starting to break such news but saw it would be worse if she delayed.

"Anne, what I am going to tell be breaking my heart and will hurt to hear. I'm just workin' my courage up to speak the words. Yes, all my goods are out of the shop and here. I shan't be going there again. For good reason, I assure you. Today, I was getting all ready for the opening, and ladies have been curious and have stopped in to find out when the opening would be. Mostly ones on the coach during the mail stop. Today, one came in, and I learned things from her that surprised me. No, much worse. Shocked and upset me so."

Having a confused look on her face, Anne stopped her and asked who the woman was. Maggie nodded in understanding.

"She was not anyone I had ever met. I don't know many hereabouts. She was well dressed, made up nicely, younger than me, and married. She said she lived a few valleys away. We talked about the store and noticing the fine crafting of the place said I was lucky to have a husband so talented. She assumed that. It was nothing I mentioned. I didn't mention Kevin or his passing but told her that Jimmy was doing the fine work. She gave a look, as if putting two and two together. Then she had a sly smile and said I must be a good one in bed for him to be doing such for me. Then, thinking it through a bit more, with that same expression, she said it explained why Jimmy hadn't been stopping by for loving as often as she'd like…"

Stopping as Anne had gasped and was staring in disbelief, she understood her reaction and was the way she felt when first told. She held her hand up letting her know it was far from done.

"That was such a surprise, I almost fainted. But I needed to know the story and acted as if I understood so she felt free to speak. I told her, without a lie, that Jimmy was a very busy person. She laughed a bit and said he sure was with as many women as he made stops to visit, and she said I must teach her what I do to keep him away from so many others. At first, I thought she was joking, or angry at him for jealous reasons. As she said more, I was certain she was, with me, sharing her secret with another of his lovers."

Having to gather up the right words to tell the hardest parts, she paused. Understanding, Anne asked her how she could be sure. Sitting still, she just looked at Anne. It had to be told.

"As I said, she was revealing something that only one doing such would know. What convinced me was what she confided next. Anne, this is going to hurt. Dear daughter, it must be said, and there is no gentle way to tell it. The woman told me she was frustrated Jimmy was busy loving elsewhere, and she was so glad that Howie was making up for it with his visits."

Waiting for it to sink in, Maggie didn't want to elaborate more than needed. Anne was wide eyed. She opened her mouth, then closed it. She just stared at Maggie, then spoke quietly and with no emotion.

"Howie and his father are making love to many different women. Both of them. Making love. Screwing them. They're both screwing the same women…"

She was in shock, just speaking to herself. Letting it form as a sentence. That it was just a fact, and the emotional impact was yet to be felt. Maggie had tears rolling down as she watched Anne react in a state of disbelief, then trying to get it right in her mind what they were doing. Anne tilted her head slightly, then continued.

"And while he was doing all those women, he was so polite and proper. Only kissing me and would not want more until married. So respectful when he asked me to marry him. When he wasn't with me, he was out doing that. His respectful father as well. Just as if off to fix a barn door for them…"

Waiting, Maggie just sat, tears rolling down her face. She knew Anne was putting the picture together and understanding how she had been deceived. How they both had been deceived. She opened her mouth, and Maggie waited. Then Anne asked, "And you said the woman was young and pretty? Pretty as you? Or as me?"

Taking a deep breath, Maggie said she was pretty, but no, not pretty as they were. Then Anne said something that hurt to hear.

"Silly me. I thought I was the only one he hoped ever make love to."

Maggie contained herself, not wishing to make it worse. The tide was turning. Tears were rolling down Anne's face. The news had caught up with her feelings. The tears turned to sobs, and then wails of anguish.

"Anne, the boy is a fool. Both of them. Fools…"

Anne sat up straight. She took a cloth and began wiping her face. She said no, she was a fool to believe him." Maggie put a stop to that.

"No Anne. No. You were deceived. Trusting and loving someone is not being a fool. Men are. They tell you some loving story, then go away to love some other. For what? To have you sit and cry? Wicked lies. Oh, beautiful stories and terrible lies. I've been thinking on this waiting for you. Anne, it was good that woman stopped in. If not, you would have gotten married. What if you didn't find out until you had babies? Best you know now."

Anne nodded. She heard the same birds her mother had earlier. She thought how free they were. She looked at Maggie and had a faraway look in her expression.

"I wish I was a little sparrow… And I had wings, and I could fly."

Maggie asked her why.

"I'd fly away from all this sorrow."

Maggie started to cry again. Anne reached and held her hand.

"Mom, but I am not a little sparrow. I have no wings; I sure can't fly. I guess I'll stay right here with my sorrow. You are right. Best to know now. I'll have to let my troubles by. I want to ask you. Why do you have your knife?"

Maggie looked at it, then at Anne. "I don't know how to load the rifle very well."

They both laughed, and it was needed.

"Oh, mother. It's so easy. Pulling the trigger is the hard part. I think there are things that you will be wanting to be using it for, and that is another trouble we are both about to face."

Maggie raised her eyebrows. She asked what that could be. Anne shook her head.

"Howie said he was most likely going to visit tonight. I wasn't sure, but with you clearing out the shop, I would guess he will be wanting to know why. I suppose Jimmy will want to know as well. Hard as it will be, I guess we get it over with. Do you know the name of the lady you found all this from?'

Maggie got up, went to the cart, and found the card. She brought it back to the porch, handing it to Anne.

"This may be good to know. Mrs. Cummings. Did she give her first name?'

Maggie had meant to write it down but had been too upset before she packed the cart. "Lisa. Lisa Cummings. She didn't mention her husband's name. I think we'll just put his name down as Cuckold Cummings…"

Looking confused, Anne had not heard the name before. Maggie said it was one she remembered from long ago.

She asked Anne how she wanted to handle things. Maggie thought it best Anne stay inside to rest.

"Anne, I can tell the bastard liar you can't be his bride, and he's not welcome here, his dad as well."

Anne had calmed down from the initial shock and was growing angry.

"I'm hurt bad, momma. I don't know how I'll court another. I'll only have this one chance to face the one who did me wrong. It's not a hurt I can put in that gold box and tie it up with your silver twine from the sewing supplies. It would just keep falling out. I'll be back in a minute."

Waiting, she was glad Anne would tell the fool he had hurt her. She knew it would not change his ways. Deep down she knew when it came to such men, it would be like telling the sun to rise in the west. You can ask, but it will never be. Men like that have no care. Anne getting her anger and hurt said, that was right to do. It would help her.

Writing down bits of their conversation on a scrap of paper, she knew this would be a song to write. Another one warning young women about the dangers of courting.

She looked up, and there was Anne. She was in her finest dress, looking radiant and holding the old rifle at her side. Maggie could smell fresh powder. The gun was loaded. She got up and stood looking at her.

"You can't shoot him, girl. Or do you plan on just scaring him?"

Looking confused, Anne asked, "I thought you can't be charged with murder for shooting a cheater, or someone stealing your horse. Or is that just for men?"

Nodding, Maggie hated to tell her. "That's what Kevin told me. Not the cheater part but stealing the horse part. I asked if a woman shot a horse thief, would she be treated the same? He said he didn't believe so. He read in a paper about a woman, living alone. Tough old gal. Shot a man running off with her horse. She killed him. They hung her. It's a man's world and the rules protect them."

Anne stood vigilant. "Well, I had thought of telling him of my broken heart. I want to. But he'd just try some lovin' story or claim it was a lie. I don't think I could handle more lies. The rifle is just to let him know I mean what I say, and I'll fire at him if he tries to hurt me more. I just want to send him back down and tell him he has no bride. I'll say he is too busy with his Cummings and Goings to have time for a wife… and to say 'Hi' to Lisa for me."

A Little Sparrow

Maggie was visited often by Anne and her family. She had met a decent man a long time ago, had four sweet children, all now grown, and she guessed Anne was warning them about the nature of men as they were all daughters. She had turned seventy and was happy she stayed living in the cabin she and Kevin had made love in so many times before he died. She talked to him each day; knowing she would be joining him not too far down the road a bit. She was ready.

Most days, she worked on her songs, getting all of them written legibly. Each one held a memory, and her gold box was filled with songs sweet and sad. Looking up, she saw a man was walking up the road. She had the old rifle ready if he was peddling or none too polite. He was a husky man for such a climb, but smart enough to wear a hat to keep the sun from his head. She worried he was peddling since he had a large square case with him. She'd find out for sure. She thought everyone, even men, deserved that much.

Saying hello from a calling distance, he asked if she was Maggie, the guitarist and songwriter. Maggie figured if he walked that road to hear her songs, he was welcome and waved him up.

"Maggie, my name is John. I've heard that you are a regular encyclopedia of songs from way back, Ireland too, and a song writer yourself. Is that so?"

Maggie laughed, and pointed to her guitar. "I don't use that to keep the crows away. Yes, I know many a song. Write some too. Just to pass the time. So, what's in that box? Looks heavy."

He nodded and laughed, saying it got heavier each step up the road. Maggie laughed at that too.

"There are so many wonderful songs being sung in these mountains. I'm working to gather them up and share them. Preserve them. They are the story of our land and important as anything in a history book. I've been writing them down, but now I have this field recorder. Have you heard phonograph records?"

"Yes, John, my darling daughter has one now. It's magic to me. You plannin' on playing records in that box?"

John smiled and opened it. "Better. It records those. I can record you singing songs and they play like the records your daughter has. I'm out to capture songs so they are never forgotten. I'm hoping you'll sing your songs and let me capture you singing and playing your guitar. Would you sing some for me?"

Feeling honored he came so far to hear her songs, she said she would like that. She asked if any of the backwoods boys ever ran him off. He chuckled, saying it happens but once he tells them he wants to hear them play, they can't say no. He set up the equipment and they talked about her life and how she learned the songs and play the guitar. He took notes. She played him a few old favorites. She played *I'll Fly Away*, saying it was a song her late husband loved. He was impressed with her song knowledge and performance.

After recording several older songs, he asked if she could play her own songs. She said she had written many and didn't know where to start. He suggested starting with one she felt everyone should hear.

She gave him a look he would always remember. It was sad, but grateful. She had tears as she told him she knew the one. Then, she said she didn't know if everyone should hear it, but she hoped all women would.

She told him it was a song for her daughter. She said her daughter once said she wished she was a little sparrow, then sang her song into the box.

Wild Mountain Thyme

O the summer time has come
And the trees are sweetly blooming
And wild mountain thyme
Grows around the purple heather
Will you go, lassie, go?

And we'll all go together
To pull wild mountain thyme
All around the purple heather
Will you go, lassie, go?

I will build my love a bower
By yon clear crystal fountain
And on it I will pile
All the flowers of the mountain
Will you go, lassie, go?

And we'll all go together,
To pull wild mountain thyme
All around the purple heather
Will you go, lassie, go?

If my true love will not come
Then I'll surely find another
To pull wild mountain thyme
All around the purple heather
Will you go, lassie, go?

Fearless She Be

"Daf, they be. No sense. Dim as night witoot moon."

Standing with a ripe blueberry she carried quite a way for sup, Button looked at him with wonder. For centuries he knew all folk be daft, and no faerie need waste good eating time saying big ones be no too bright. Surely, it be true, but there be none more need said.

Understanding Bow only frustrated with young lad he be watching; she was just as bewildered by the lad — and her misfortune hearing more of him. Looking at the blueberry, she was entranced by how plump the thing was, wishing to be eating the beautiful find.

"Talkin' no gettin' me fed, now tis it? Nor do I see you eatin' any, with all ya pointless talk. I have ya know I fought off giant rabbit who be wantin' berry too. Fierce I was, Bow. I stuck him with sharp stick! Then flew up and punched his nose. Still, he stood, ooh, a big one, an' posin' mighty harm to me wee body. Hovering o'er his giant ear, I shout fox be comin' and he be off. All that I do, jus' for this sup. I be hearin' no appreciation comin' my way from ya."

Being hungry too, Bow looked at the dew on the blueberry and how excited Button was about her find. He delighted in her tale of battling giant rabbit. She was prone to expand tales of her foraging might.

"Button, be ya sure twas giant thing? I saw wee bunny, scamperin' away. No much bigger than sparrow new in nest. Be ya sure tha' was no the one ya challenged so fierce?"

Laughing, both knew it was a wee new bunny on its first outing she shooed off. Saying no more, he loved her tales of battle with every manner of woodland creature. Button was fearless, and had it been giant hare she would still have won the berry.

It was the purple time of year, the one they loved most. Blueberries grew so ripe they fell to the ground. The thyme was rich, all manner of plants sprouting purple. Lavender was about, helping air smell purple. Most purple of all, butterfly bushes; a sight to cherish.

"Button, do ya know what big ones be doin' wit' berries fine as this?" Thinking them rather limited in all things purple, she had an answer that she be sure of.

"What else but baked in pie? All sugared an' roasted 'till berry be gone. They bake all good tings in pie. Woodland creatures, wee fish, mushrooms, tangy apples. If rocks they could eat, they be bakin' rocks in pie."

Giggling at the notion of a rock pie, Button suddenly stopped and stared at Bow with a look of worry.

"Bow, uh jus' had fearful thought. Folk have sleepy time rhyme sung to wee ones, 'bout bakin' blackbirds in pie. Oh, the poor little tings. Oh, they pluck them from nest, put in pastry. Feathers an' all. Beaks pokin' out crust. Oh, Bow… What if they e'er should find us? They be bakin' faerie pie! Oh, ya wee feet sticken' out crust! Me wisps of wings wit' sugar on em. We mus' no be seen or surely we be dessert."

Bow had a look of terror. He agreed, fearing such fate.

"Ya be right. There be no ting, livin' or up from ground, they don' bake up without buttery crust on it.

Fateful Day

Carrying a basket filled with blueberries, Aiden knew it would be more than plenty for the pie her mom had planned. Her mother was home preparing pie dough rolled out many times over over, each time butter spread thin on the dough, folded, then rolled again. Her mom was known throughout the county for making a crust so flaky and light, without filling it would fly away. Thinking how hard her mom worked on the crust, she knew she'd be happy to see the basket full of berries she gathered. They were so delicious many came from counties quite far to pick them.

All through the year Aiden had good fortune finding excellent fruits for pies. Preserving was fine for most fruits, but not berries. They made delicious jams, but the time for pies was only when picked. Walking slowly to enjoy the smells of the earth, all around her nature was in bloom. She smiled knowing she was in full bloom like the heather she loved dearly.

Passing the McHenry farm, she waved at the young twins, lad and lass, gathering yellow flowers. She smiled as the wee lad had one in his hair. Each held blooms in their tiny hands, and she expected they were for the dinner table that night. Squealing with delight as they saw her, they ran to the gate where she was watching. Without a word, each found the best flower they had and gave it to her. Seeing her smile as she smelled the two flowers, they ran off to pick more.

Thinking back to when she was a wee lass, she picked the same flowers, always having one in her hair. Suddenly saddened, she thought of her poor brother. He never had a chance to pick flowers with her. Just a babe in his crib, he died one afternoon. He hadn't been ill and was a happy little baby. Her face showed her sadness. One day he went to sleep but never woke up. Just died. He would never taste the berries or jam, or court a bonnie young maid. He was but two, she only five when the Lord took him. The doctor told her mom and dad sometimes babies just die. No reason he could explain. Knowing no words of comfort, her parents feared having another child, leaving Aiden without sister or brother.

Living on a farm was wonderful, but often lonely. Surrounded by farm animals, rolling hills, heather and the beauty of nature, it was where she envisioned growing old. Feeling gifted with such a wonderful life, her only worry if she found a lad who truly shared her love of the land and the same dream of farm life. Though their county had a few good-sized villages, there weren't many lads her age living nearby. Many grew up on farms, left to join the army, or sought fortune in large cities far away. Most she knew expressed such plans. Her choices were few and being of courting age she considered it was possible she may never find an ideal young man.

Reaching home, her mother had pie dough resting, smiling at the sight of the basket and number of berries she brought. Loving to cook and bake, her mother had won many ribbons at the Summer Festival each year. The baker in the village offered to sell her pies for a good price, but she turned him down flat.

"My pies no be for sellin' ya know. They be for eatin' by friends and family. Gifts. It's the love in them that makes them good. Not coin!"

Growing their own grains, having cows for milk and butter, pigs for lard, and fruits growing all around, the only expense was the time and work her mother put into her baking. While growing up, her mother taught her baking and cooking was celebration of the bounty surrounding them. Most all they ate was from their farm and fields. Going to villages and visiting shops, butchers, and bakers, her mother would shake her head while looking at jars and packages. Always feeling sad people had to eat things from shelves when the land provided all needed, she understood those not having farms had little choice. It was her way to say they were lucky to have such fortune.

Visiting neighboring farms and attending mass at St. Cadoc's was the extent of Aiden's contact with the world. Most all families she knew lived in the county for several generations — all good friends and neighbors. Knowing any young lass need have a lad to marry was often discussed by those around her, including the pastor.

Securing the blessing of Aiden's parents, the boy Aiden wondered about his having true love of country life, Kane announced at the Harvest Festival he intended Aiden for his wife — if she'd have him. The proclamation was met with cheers and many rounds of ale. Aiden looked beautifully happy. She was, in the opinion of all, very pretty and a fine lass. Her long brown hair and ruby lips combined with beautiful eyes and sweet smile were much like her mother's. Her mom was a beautiful woman, and both were envied for their good looks and fine forms. Announcing the engagement made her even prettier as she glowed with joy.

After harvest came payment for crops sold to market and was a time to enjoy some pleasures including putting money aside for a wedding. Others were putting a bit aside for gifts and the pastor was reviewing his calendar and almanac to find a day with fine weather for the ceremony. Planning became good reason to meet and gossip for the mothers. Fathers thought fondly of their wedding nights and how Kane would need a night at the pub to get a wee bit of advice from those in the knowing — along with many a pint.

One morning, after the following year's harvest, Kane's father came to call on Aiden and her parents. Driving his carriage, he rode slow up to their house and was unusually quiet when greeting the family. They all had smiles as they welcomed him in for tea, but the man looked worried and pale. It didn't take long for Aiden and her parents to see he was deeply troubled. Smiles turned to looks of concern. Asking what worried him so, the man looked at Aiden with even more sadness.

"I have news that will upset ya, as it has upset my wife and me. We were happy Kane was to marry ya. We hoped for it, such. Yesterday, I went to fetch the harvest earnings to bank it all, and noticed good sum gone. I called Kane to help me find missing coins, but he did no answer. I went lookin' and no findin' boy, found letter instead…"

He took out a folded paper, put on his glasses, held it up, then red it out loud.

Dear Mum and Dad,

I know you expected much from me, and beautiful Aiden be waiting. I know with this note I will hurt all. Leaving note be best. I could no see your faces as I be telling I have thought hard, knowing leaving be what I must do. Staying I would cause worse hurt, I be sure. I know I have land, family, and sweet Aiden, but I would no be happy. It has taken much to be honest with myself. I be knowing I no be meant be farmer, or husband. Long I have thought of the ocean and new country. Both keep calling to me. I must answer call. Dad and mum, forgive me this. I have taken a bit of the purse for journey. I will repay it one day. I be leaving to join migration to America. I will write when I be settled. Please tell Aiden I be sorry and know I will miss her. She be what be keeping me here. I love her. My only comfort is knowing she will find good man who wants her more than I want adventure. She deserves good man, — not rover like me. I love you both and I love Aiden. Please forgive me. Let this no be goodbye, only fare well.

Kane

Shocking all there, the news in the letter was a complete surprise.

Looking at Aiden, Kane's father asked her if she had been told of his son's discontent or plans. She looked stunned at such suggestion.

"Mr. Tobin! No. Not one thing. I wouldn' be plannin' me wedding to Kane knowin' he'd be getting' on some freighter, now, would I?"

Crying and angry at the same time, realizing Kane had not written her a letter hurt the most. He led her on, never sharing his feelings. Feeling betrayed and foolish, she got up and went walking. Her parents understood she needed time to herself after the shocking news.

Without destination, Aiden walked through fields of heather, letting both hands brush the lush growth as she walked. The wind was blowing gently, creating waves in the heather, making her think the field her ocean to sail. Racing through her were thoughts of days behind, and days ahead. All her memories had been joyous but were now sad. Plans evaporated like dew on the flowers when the Sun grew high.

Gone.

She was a maid, and glad of it. Kane had wanted more than kisses. Sighing, she considered the lasses in America may be free with virtue and may be why Kane went sailing there. It not be a land known for honor, or virtue. If he wanted some strange girl on his lap, he would find such there. He had not found it from her, and glad she was. She had maiden pride, and her virtue.

The Sweetest Thing

Wings fluttering with haste, Bow almost tumbled off the branch setting down to join Button. She sat on a twisted branch on the ground outside their home hidden deep in the forest. She smiled at him, knowing such landing could only be he had shocking tales of a grand sort to tell.

"I be needin' nectar, Button. I'm dry as that branch. It's been long since me wings carried me so far or fast as this day!"

Still smiling, Button saw he was wee bit aflutter. Reaching for a small leaf she had made into a cup to put nectar in for herself, she handed it to Bow who nodded thanks. Still standing, wings flapping gently, he drank the sweet syrup till all was gone. Button watched then asked if he needed more.

"I feel bad takin' yours. I gather more for us later. But If there be more, then let us share it."

Nodding, she opened a little jar of nectar she had brought for the day. Pouring more for Bow, she bid him sit and gather strength. She took a sip from the jar, her eyes opening wide with delight as she loved nectar.

Looking at him with fondness, Button knew the wonderful stuff helped Bow feel better. He looked at her with pure affection. He opened his arms, and she leaned forward for his sweet hug, putting her arms around him. As squeezed each other, Bow began singing an ancient Daoine maithe song into her ear. It was her favorite aisling.

Her eyes to mine
My eyes to her
Made each one part of we

Like mist of night
Sweet she hold
All things thou make be me

I know sweet days
She be here an' true
Being all that I can see

She came my way
Oh she came my way
She my love she here with me

Button cried as she always did when he sang the old song. Although very little, her heart and love were larger than anything Bow knew. The look on her bonnie face sent him back to a place and time long ago. As only faeries can do, he was there again.

Being hunted by townsfolk, the big ones had fear of those such as he. Many thought wee ones be devils or evil sprites. They knew no better and were fearful of most things. There were faeries fond of mischief, but he was not one. Folk, being large and having hounds in pursuit, were quick and clever as they chased him. Taking to air, arrows whizzed near his wings. Fast as he was, in flight he was easy to see. One big one had a net on a long pole to capture him.

Heading down to fly near to the ground, he saw Button for the first time.

She was standing, hands on her hips, waiting ahead. In that instant his heart was hers. She was the smallest faerie he had ever seen. Her eyes were large and dark, looking lovingly into his. She was smiling at him as her near invisible wings gently raised her off the ground. She said not a word, only nodding at him then turning and gaining speed. Understanding she wanted him to follow, he knew that moment he would follow her anywhere. She never looked back. She knew he was there. Zipping through trees at great speed, she headed to a thicket so dense with trees and brier only ones wee as they could pass. Deep into the dense growth she flew into a hollow knot of a large oak.

The shouts and threats grew quiet, fading away as they flew where no folk could fit. Inside the hollow of the old tree, she stood waiting for him to realize he was safe, for he was with her. She had pine nuts on a leaf and looked them over, picking out the finest one, handing it to him. She found another good one for herself and sat down on soft nesting busy birds had dropped, nodding for him to join her. She wore a snug green fitting, making her the same color as the forest. Like all faeries she was ageless in appearance; a child who never grew old. Her dark brown hair looked like feathers where it met her sweet face.

When they entered the hollow knot, she had pushed a little plank over the opening. Looking, he saw no daylight or candles lit anywhere. Glowing gently, her wings were the light surrounding them. More than light, the glow was comforting. He was filled with a feeling he never had before. Sitting with her, looking at her gentle smile, he knew he must tell her what he felt.

"More than tellin' ya my thanks for savin' me, I need tell ya I be entranced. The moment I saw ya, all changed inside me. I have ne'er been bold, but now I must be so. I love ya. That be all I know. I love ya with all me heart. Yours is all I be."

Putting her pine nut down, she crawled close to him, knelt up, and put a hand on each of his cheeks, then kissed him.

Her wings glowed brighter then could be imagined. Moving forward, she wrapped her wings fully around them both. Looking more wondrous than anything he had ever seen in the light of her wings, she moved her head back, slightly, looked deeply into his eyes, telling him she felt the exact same way when seeing him. Putting her forehead to his to stare into his eyes, she gently told him,

"I be just a button, an' will hold us together snug forever. I love ya too."

Never having a love, at that moment he finally understood it the most precious gift of all.

As she looked at him, so tiny, just a whisper in his arms, her smile grew full as she knew he was her beau.

Opening his eyes, he saw Button looking at him with kindness and affection. She understood he travelled to that memory. She often went back there as well, and it gave her the same joy. Neither understood how or why faeries were bound and mated as they were. Both knew every moment past — the fearful folk, years of forest growth giving them safety, all things that day — all happened so they could find each other. Folk said faeries be magic. Love such as theirs was that very magic, so the folk were not so daft as they seemed.

Button held his hand, wondering what had him in state of such excitement.

Close to the Edge

Thinking his life over, Duncan stood on the point of the cliff highest above ocean without looking down.

If I look, I won't jump. I'm so afraid of what it will be like. I just need say my prayer, then step forward. That be all I need do. Just say my prayer.

Trembling, the sound of the ocean filling his ears drowned out his thoughts. He could smell the salt of the water. Wind blew strong riding up the cliff, but he stood strong.

Starting to step back, he stopped himself.

Doing it again. Stepping away. Then another, another, then turning to run. Coward. My whole life, afraid of everything.

Taking one step forward he surprised himself.

I did it. No more running away. Now, be strong. Stay with the plan. It is only a prayer. Oh, no, no. The final prayer. My last one. Ever. I'm going to say my last prayer. That is the plan. I pray for strength to save me and give me courage. To take another step. Just like the one right now.

Seagulls rode the wind watching the lone man standing. He hadn't any food for them. They called, but he paid them no mind.

The prayer. I can't remember it… Maybe it be better I just tell God why I need to do this. Talk to him. He doesn't need a prayer. He will understand the truth.

Looking up, he could see white clouds soft in the light blue sky. Taking his right hand, he quickly made the sign of the cross, held his hands together then closed his eyes.

"Laddie? Ya be mighty close to that edge. Tis a grand view, an' ya seen it, so come, walk with me."

Hearing Aiden, he almost jumped off the cliff from the surprise of her voice.

The lass from the road! You were ever on my mind! Now, at my end, you haunt me more. What cruel fate to have the one I've longed for meet me, now?

He didn't understand why, but he turned to face her. He had asked God for mercy, telling Him what brought him to his decision. Was this the answer to his prayer?

As he turned round, seeing Aiden shook him so that he dropped to his knees, then sat on the ground crying, full of shame. Aiden thought only she surprised him and he realized he could have fallen, but he was crying tears of pain. She approached him in a gentle manner, then sat beside him. Letting him cry, she sensed he needed to let out some hurt. Just as she was hurt from new of Kane's leaving but an hour earlier. Thoughts of her ex-finance faded, seeing the lad had even more hurt than her. He was heaving and wailing.

Not sure if she should, she reached out and her hand lightly on his shoulder. He didn't notice it at first, so she gave his shoulder a gentle rub. Still crying, he turned and looked at her hand, then turned away. Reacting to his wailing, she intuitively put her arms around his chest, pulling him to her. Resting his head on her shoulder he sobbed, and with that she whispered he was not alone.

With her comfort, his sobbing quieted to a whimper. Aiden waited. He seemed better and she would but wait until he could talk. She realized the lad was in a bad way, and she was glad she had wandered from the heather to see the waters. She shuddered, realizing his standing so close to the edge was to jump off and kill himself. She realized she came upon him to save him. It was God's will.

"Lad, ya worried me. I did no mean frighten ya. You be mighty close to that edge."

Taking a deep breath, he managed to pull out his handkerchief and wipe his face best he could. Somehow, her calling to him and the intensity of his crying had released the grip of death holding him. He sat, shaking. He realized if not for her he'd be on the rocks and waves below. Wiping his face again, he felt able to talk. This time, he would be brave and not cower from his pain.

"Yes, I was close to the edge. Not just cliff… my life. I was saying my final prayer. I was telling God I was at His mercy, then I heard your voice…"

He looked at her, his eyes wet but sincere.

"I think he answered."

Looking at him she was stunned by his honesty. What he said was hard to say, and hard to hear. She knew not how to reply and could only listen, trying to understand. She thought it best to get him away from the cliff. He could have a change of mind and attempt to jump. Standing up, she held out her hand. He looked up at her, not sure what to do. She was doing what he had dreamed of. Inviting him to join her. The decision of what to do when she looked at him and told her thoughts.

"I know ya have His answer. If ya accept God's will, He certainly sent me to ya. Come, I was takin' walk in heather. Will ya come? Go with me? I can use friend right now too."

Crossing himself, he stood up, lightheaded but feeling strong. He reached out and she took his hand, squeezed it, and nodded.

"I be Aiden. I live in yon farm, and ya be?"

He almost forgot his name, but out it came.

"Duncan."

He was holding the hand of the one he admired and dreamed of since seeing her from his father's carriage. One time. She was his age, but unlike him so happy running in the fields alongside the road. She had been in his dreams since.

Still in a state of wonder, he thought maybe he had jumped. Maybe he was Heaven. It didn't matter. He was walking away from sadness. He had been strong enough to reach the cliff and confront his sorrow. He had been strong enough to tell Aiden his darkest story. He realized the same strength was in him to tell Aiden he longed to meet. He had been given a chance to live and not hide from life any longer. He knew Aiden may deny his interest, but again, she may smile with approval. All he could do was walk with her and take that chance.

Saving Grace and Pie

Worried about Aiden, her parents talked of ways to comfort her. Her father, pragmatic in nature, said the best way to forget a hurtful lad was to meet a kind one. His wife agreed but explained the poor lass had just been jilted and would need time to understand it was best all happened now, before any wedding. She looked at her husband, and was upset and hurt.

"I can no believe that lad. A scoundrel, for sure. Goin' about, cavalier like, breakin' hearts then off like coward to find his pleasure. I be glad he's gone, Farrel. Tis for the best."

Looking at her husband, he was staring at the pie she made earlier. She understood that in a bad time, best to find something good. She brought two plates to the table, put the kettle on, then sliced the pie. Waiting for the water to boil, he looked at Bre, then took her hand.

"All for best, I be sure. I think it be long enough now to tell ya I had plan to run off before we wed. But Bre, I can only tell ya I liked ya pies too much."

Getting up to get the whistling kettle, she was laughing.

"I think it be more than my pies you stayed for…"

Farrel looked her up and down, nodded, and offered a smile.

"I think that may be so. You are bonnie lass. Better than ev'r. Pies, yea, they be bonus, but Bre, not even yon pie fills man hungry for love."

She smiled, nodding.

"And ya think bonnie lass has no such appetite?"

They both burst out laughing. Farrel managed to say he was glad she did as she put blueberry pie on his plate. He waited for her to take her slice, and they each took the first bite at the same time.

"I've be waiting for this all year. My God, woman, ya be amazing. Well, as I said, ya be better than ev'r. Pie's no bad either."

She gave him a wink and a nod. The laughing and pie helped with the sadness of the day. Farrel suggested cutting a piece for Aiden to have it ready, saying after her long walk, she'd be peckish and it would be a comfort. While Bre went to get a plate, the kitchen door opened, and Aiden smiled at the slice of pie waiting for her. Giving her mother a hug, she next gave her father a kiss on his cheek. As she sat down, they both were looking at her with concern. She knew they would be worried.

"The walk did me good. I left confused an' hurt, but somethin' happened. Somethin' that could only happen cause of that. A miracle, I think."

Her parents looked confused and waited as she took a bite of pie. She nodded at her mom and took another bite.

"I think all was meant to be. Kane did more than hurt all those loved him, he saved a poor lad's life.. "

Taking another bite of pie, she looked at her parents, knowing they were wondering what she meant.

"I know. I see ya two looking all confused. Ya will understand as I tell of my walk. First, I only wanted to feel heather brush by me and smell flowers. Without thinkin' why, I turned to go up cliff. I was no even thinkin' of the water but that be where I headed. When I reached top, I saw frightful thing. Duncan Folsom. Do ya remember all the talk of that lad? All said he be a shy one. Today, there he be. Grown up, like me. Standing on cliff edge, ready to jump! Sayin' his last prayer. No sure of intent, I went to him, an' saw one sadder than me. Not sure what to do, I gave his shoulder a tap."

Looking horrified, her parents sat, mouths open, waiting. Her father asked, "What happened when ya tapped poor lad?"

"It still be hard to understand… But, there I be. Putting me hand on his shoulder, sayin' be careful, ya too close to edge. That shook him, and he was plannin' to go over. Next I know, he be wailin' like a babe, sitting on ground. I helped calm him a wee bit, then he fessed up and told me he was about to end all. Was tap on shoulder pulled him back. After the cryin' stopped, I told him walk with me. He needed a friend. Lad took me hand, and to heathers we walked. I took him far from cliff. Had I no found him, that lad be dead."

Folk Tales

"Bein' swept away by ya song, I no ask what had ya so worked up, an' I have tale to tell too. Bow, be ya ready to talk, or do ya jus' want cuddle all night?"

Feeling comfort from his visit to the day they met, he was calm enough to tell things right.

"Folk be more than daf. We have much to fix. Kane had me in tizzy. I be lookin' in on lad and could no believe me eyes. Twas jus' time for Sun to rise, and there be Kane, scribbling' away some, in kitchen, lit with but wee candle. He had look most strange on him. Sinister grin it be. Next to lad was large sack, filled with all tings his. I knew somethin' be amiss, an' it were. He gets up, then, Button, lad goes to earnings hidden away. Withoot shame, takes most, smiling, takes pa's coins. Bad that be, then he goes to scribbles, folds paper, writes pa's name, then I hear him whisper, mean like, an say, 'Goodbye pops. Goodbye mum. So long, Aiden.' Grabs sack. Off he goes. Me little heart be beatin' so, I just sit on tree branch, watchin' him go. Gone, Button. With no worry or care. Gone."

Shaking her head, she held his hands knowing he was upset for those hurt by the lad. She waited for him to look at her, asking of her adventure.

"All be makin' sense, now. I be followin' hummingbirds as they know where nectar be best, then made way to see what lass be doin', takin' my time.

Before I reach house, she be out a walkin' to heather, looking hurt, ever so. I knew somethin' be bad. Now I know note from Kane had her such."

Bow didn't look surprised. It was a part of the puzzle that fit well. Button was seeing it too.

"Flew high, I did, lookin' if lad be about or if she be headed to him. Oh, Bow, far up as moon, I'm sure I be, an' I could see cliffs and water. Oh, there be sight terrible to see. A different laddie, ready to jump in sea. The sad thing be shakin' and fearful. Like bolt of lightning I be! Fast I flew to lass, giving her more than wee poosh. With mighty power, I whisper, 'Go ta ocean,' and heeding plea, off ta cliffs she goes. Seein' same what I see, she be none sure wha' ta do. Oh, Bow, with even mightier skill, I whisper, 'Go! Put hand on lad, he be needin' ya. She goes, puts hand on lad's shoulder. Touched so, he drops down, cryin' like baby. Yea, rescued by me cunning plan. Reveal all, he does. The lad be timid and be lovin' Aiden from afar. Fraid of bein' hurt, he be, nothin' more…"

Bow sat with mouth open, saying tell more. Proud of her might, she waited to make sure he understood all she had done.

"There she be, girl he dreams of, savin' him from doom. Tell, I could, she opened her heart hearin' tale of woe. That Kane, he true be gone? Good riddance ta him. She met one loves her true. Yea, tha' Duncan, lad of doom and despair! All for no havin' her love. Bow, he be yours ta watch now. I know ya will be mighty an' swift as I be this day!"

Doom and Despair

Living alone, Duncan hadn't changed anything in the grand house he inherited from his father. Although his father had left him the house, the largest farm in the county, and a large sum of money, he left the running of the farm to an able manager. Duncan felt all he really had been left was loneliness. Being an only child, his mother dying when he was an infant, with no relations his had been a lonely life.

Thinking often how his father could have found a new wife, made friends, and been part of village matters, he chose to live in isolation. Duncan only learned of the reason when his father grew gravely ill, knowing he was dying. Having to take care of farm matters, Duncan found himself searching through his father's files and papers. He found an ordinary-looking box that revealed why his father was reclusive, and why he kept Duncan away from the world — especially women. Duncan, in his teens, wanted to court maids but was never allowed to. His father had a strong manner and put him through endless grief for even a mention of courting. He had no wish to disobey his father, and even more so as he grew ill. His father had always been kind to him, but fearful of the world around them. Reading the papers in the box, Duncan began piecing the reasons together.

The box looked like several others used for keeping records. Each was labeled with the year of records held. Noticing there were two boxes for the same year, he knew the year was an important one. It was from the year his mother died. Opening the first box, it held an assortment of crop and financial records. Opening the second box, it was a collection of letters, newspaper clippings, police reports, and a journal his father had kept at the time. His father had always refused to tell any details of his mother's death, making him feel he was invading the sick man's privacy. Regardless, he felt he had a right to know all possible of his mother.

Making sure his father was settled with medications needed for the night, Duncan set about reading all items from the box. When finished, he understood why his father had been isolated and protective of him through the years. He was also angry he led a life controlled by his father's hurt. That was no way to raise a son.

Telling all, the box was a tale of woe.

Looking at pictures and items of his mother, Anin, he saw she was very beautiful and from a wealthy city family. Reading letters, it was certain his dad loved her truly and had been devoted to her. From the letters, ones written from his father to his mother, Duncan learned he was often away on business matters. It was easy to read between the lines of the exchanges. His mother had grown bored of country life. Burdened with an infant she never really wanted, her letters showed little love in her words. Her letters told how she felt stifled and was suffocating. She longed for excitement and passion, and in her words she reached the point of degrading his father. She was bold in saying he was neither exciting nor passionate and she needed to find such, or die.

Her words were as arrows in Duncan's heart. Written when he was newly born, there was no joy in her having him. She made it clear in her letters he was not her child, but rather an anchor pulling her down. He was not wanted. Though hard to read such sentiment, he could only continue reading.

Moving to the journal, his father had written of his feelings — and of torrid events. His writings shocked Duncan.

He wrote of how his wife stopped all affection for him or her child. She had started to correspond with men from before she met him, with him learning she had no virtue when they married. Once knowing such, she began taunting him of the other men. She told they were better lovers, knew how to please her right, and he was the worst lover she had been with. He could see tear stains on the pages, knowing how hard it was for him to chronicle such painful moments.

Reaching the end, he read how his father regretted hiring a crew of vagabond workers for the harvest. They worked hard, but he learned that offering work to those claiming to be hungry and despised by most all had been folly. They were bold deceivers and he soon learned they could not be trusted. Many valuable items were missing, but he feared confronting them. They carried knives and drank each night. He was anxious for harvest end — and for them to leave.

One, the leader of the crew, left early. The man, called Gypsy Davy, was tall and handsome, dark in color, clearly having eyes for his wife. Each time he was away on business, he fretted his wife was engaging the man. One night he rode home, finding the house empty. Upon going to the crew, asking about his lady, with disdain the only answer he got was she had gone with Davy, and taken his child. She had forsaken her husband and taken her baby to humiliate him. The last entry was filled with despair. He wrote he must rescue his son and find them both. He had no hope his wife would return, but his son was not for the gypsy to steal. That was the last entry in the journal.

Duncan moved on to reading a collection of newspaper clippings. Everything he read was devastating. Reading two major front-page stories from the city newspaper, using the dates to keep them in order, he read the first story. The large front-page headline was so strong that reading it felt like a punch to his stomach, making him wretch. He gathered himself and let it sink in.

Scorned Husband Suspected of Killing Wife

Each word was brutal in its candor. Having read what the reporter could not have known, the letters and journal, each word was a story by itself. Admittedly, his father was a scorned husband, yet there was no mention of Gypsy Davy in the headline. He struggled to keep reading.

Late last night, wealthy farmer Keith Folsom was taken into custody, suspected of shooting his wife, Anin Folsom, at the Brier Inn outside Sanshire. According to inn keeper, the man occupying the room with Mrs. Folsom was Davy Django, from parts unknown, an interim farm laborer. Django stated he was helping the wife and her baby escape her husband. Django stated Folsom had been mistreating her and threatened to kill her. Learning his wife and child had gone with the laborer, Folsom pursued them to the inn, entered the room to confront his wife. When asked by the investigating constable if he shot his wife, Folsom stated he had not killed her, and was at the inn only to take his wife and child home, stating she was under the influence of Django, knowing her to be from wealth. He stated he had no weapon, and the gun fired was Django's. Telling him to leave, Django brought forward a gun, not releasing his wife. Folsom stated he grabbed for his wife, with fear of being shot. A struggle commenced, and his wife entered the struggle to help Django. The gun went off, mistakenly striking the woman. The first constable on the scene stated he encountered Django fleeing the inn, telling the constable a man had shot a woman there. Folsom was found holding his wife, calling for a doctor. Both men are being questioned and held. Mrs. Folsom was pronounced dead at the scene by a local physician._

Staring at the account, it was more than he could imagine. He believed his father an honest man, and he was telling the truth about his mother defending the gypsy. It was her final insult to his father.

Holding the second news article, it answered his remaining questions.

Inn Shooting Suspect Released

Keith Folsom, held on suspicion of murdering his wife, Anin Folsom, was released and no charges filed. After reading of the shooting incident, a witness came forward stating that Davy Django robbed her at gunpoint earlier that evening. Her statement was confirmed. The witness was reporting the robbery to a village constable at the time of the shooting. The witness was asked to identify the robbery weapon from an assortment of firearms, and to identify the man who robbed her from a lineup of six men, one being Django. She identified the pistol, stating it had a unique appearance. She then identified her robber as

Davy Django in the lineup. The testimony of the witness confirmed the weapon found at the murder scene was owned and used by Django, and Mr. Folsom had brought no weapon, supporting his statement he was there to bring his wife and child home, defending himself when threatened by Django. Faced with the testimony of the witness identifying him as the owner of the gun, Django changed his statement claiming Mrs. Folsom had grabbed his weapon to shoot her husband. He struggled to stop her, the weapon fired accidentally in the struggle, and she shot herself.

There was no other article telling what happened to Django and he had no interest in finding out more. His only wish was that his father had told him of the events long ago. He assumed that Django had been released, causing his father to be fearful of leaving his property. Guarding him from women was also a fear based on his experience. Knowing his mother was not like other women, he had been kept from meeting a good woman which would have shown his father not every woman was like his wife. So much sadness, all for naught.

Seeing no benefit of confronting his sick father with such thoughts, he understood his father was still deeply hurt and he had no need to revisit his pain.

His father died before Duncan turned eighteen. Although young, he had land, wealth and title, but had never courted a maid and was unsure of what to do or say if he did. Sitting alone in the large house, he realized reading his father's papers was still weighing heavy on his mind. Starting to worry the same fate could befall him, thoughts of courting turned to fear of being hurt as his father had. Before ever trying, he was frozen. He had inherited the fear his father harbored. His mother had used him, he was socially awkward, not skilled at conversation, controlled by his father, lonely, and above all, fearful of the same fate. Without realizing it, he feared being written a letter someday from a wife revealing she had no virtue, thinking him a fool and a disappointment as lover. It was more than he could handle, and he had no one to turn to.

Lost and alone, Duncan found no joy in living. He saw no point in going on. There was no one who cared if he lived or died. No one would be worse off or hurt if he was dead. Existing without love or happiness had taken its toll. He knew it was a sin to commit suicide but thought it worse to live the sin of his parents. Looking around his home, he decided that the next life, for him, had to be far better than the one he lived. It would only take one step off the cliff overlooking the sea to end the pain he suffered in his home, alone.

Welcome Home

Looking at her parents, Aiden asked if they thought what Duncan tried to do was wrong.

Farrel and Bre looked at each other, then Bre shook her head and Farrel nodded in agreement. It was an important question, and Farrel decided to offer an answer.

"Only God can judge one, Aiden. Only He knows what be in lad's heart, or what despair drove him to such. Aye, church says it be sin, an' that helped save many from hasty decision. I think church fails to explain Jesus came to forgive our sins. He said we can seek forgiveness if we be sorry. Had the lad jumped, he may be treated as a sinner. Truth is, after your comfortin' he did'n run and jump to sea. He did no commit sin. Now, if sorry, confessin' his attempt, that will have him forgiven. Right or wrong? It be hurt and despair from ya telling. A poor hurt lad, no family or friends. He was lost, that be all. No right, no wrong."

Nodding she understood, she smiled, looking relieved. She put both hands in front of her on the table and tilted her head.

"I be fortunate to have thoughtful parents. I be much relieved, for a reason. Mum, please keep dad from the rest of pie. We be needin' it later."

Bre looked at her, not understanding her meaning and telling her so. Aiden smiled.

"Knowin' you both compassionate sorts, we need it for after sup. I could no let Duncan head back to his house without a friend in the world. I invited him for a lovin' meal here tonight, and piece of that delicious pie."

Farrel looked at Bre. "Now, which one of us gave lass such goodness? I be wantin' full credit, but admit I learned it all from you."

Laughing, Aiden was proud of her parents. They were kind to all, and she had learned from Duncan's story not all parents had such open hearts and minds. Knowing they would agree, she had already offered the invitation and she saw worry leave his face. He told her he knew little of social manners and the sup would be a first for him. If they could excuse any shyness he had, he was most glad of the invitation. Aiden understood, saying her parents were kind people and there was no need for worry.

"You will be as if one of the family. That is how guest be treated in our home. Don't dress special or fret your shyness. It will be fine chance to know all is not bleak. Duncan, do ya like pie?"

Helping her mother with cleaning vegetables for supper, she told Bre she asked Duncan if he liked pie, and when he said yes, she asked what be his favorite. Bre smiled at her.

"No need tell. It be blueberry. Aiden, that was a nice way to calm his fear. Askin' him that, a normal question and considerate it be. I bet that simple question meant much to the lad. So, did he tell more of himself?"

Scrubbing carrots, Aiden nodded. "We talked about pies, and yes, that seemed to get him feelin' important. And, yea, it be blueberry. I was none sure if asking too much would scare him away, so I asked how far he was from here. Do ya know mansion on way to Sanshire? The one ya always stare at when we pass it?"

Nodding, Bre said she knew the one, then asked if he lived near it or beyond. Aiden stopped working the vegetables, sat at the table, gesturing for her mother to join her. With a puzzled look, Bre sat next to her.

"Mum, he don't live near place. He lives there. It be his house."

Bre's eyes widened. She looked surprised, then grew serious.

"Oh, child. Now the lad's sad state makes sense. Yea, I always stare when we pass by, no for admiring, out of sadness for it. Such a grand place, but filled with tragedy and heartbreak. I was wonderin' why we knew naught of lad. Did he tell ya more?"

Surprised by her mother's reaction, she said Duncan told his father died not long ago, he had no other family, and his father a recluse wanting no part of the world outside their gates. She had not questioned him about any of it in his state, and he was certainly sad and alone. Her mother nodded, then thought it best to tell Aiden what she knew of the father.

"Duncan has right to be sad, for there be terrible history for burden. I ne'er knew the family, but most all know of them. Tha' may be why father kept lad shut away. People can make judgments 'bout things they know not. About time ya were born, papers told of the father being held by constables, accused of killin' his wife. Well, no easy way to say it. His wife had scoundrel lover. They had run off with Duncan, and his dad went to find 'em and bring 'em home. There was struggle, and gun fired. The shot killed his mum."

Aiden was sitting, stunned. She couldn't imagine such a fate. Gathering herself, she asked her mother to tell the rest. Bre was lost in tears but went on.

"All I know was what was said in papers. The wife's lover was a wanderin' worker, gypsy it said. He learned the wife had family money, romanced her, and no problem stealing her away. The wife went willingly, it was said. Then gypsy claiming it be wife grabbed gun to shoot her husband. Tryin to stop her, the two fought over gun, it went off and she was struck down, dead. The scoundrel fled, then was caught. Husband stayed by his wife, callin' for help. The lad's father never told who had pointed gun at him. After that horror, he locked himself and the boy away. People talked 'bout it for long while, most thought the wife be intendin' on killing husband. Nome know but him, an' wife be dead."

They both sat quiet, thinking of how horrible the event had been.

"Mum, the woman must have hated him to run off like that. An' to shoot him, or be with a lover who would if no? Was Duncan's father a wicked sort, I mean, one wife could hate so?"

Bre shook her head. She understood that being hurt would be a reason, but the woman went far past being unhappy with her husband. She looked sad as she shared her opinion.

"There was much talk of that at time. The man and wife are the only ones know. None knowing him thought him mean. Runnin' off with villain? That seems seeking thrill or to disgrace the man. It's no what women do if caring of their child. Whatever the reason, dying so was a bitter price to pay. It seems the real victim be Duncan. Father shamed, fearful of women after, keepin' lad from world. Him driven to jump off cliff? No good comes from bad. Duncan has chance to see world as good now. He may never recover, so we must pray he does."

Getting up, Bre continued preparing food, Aiden stayed at the table thinking how little Duncan knew of her life, and how little she knew of his. The account had shaken her. She was sheltered from such terrible news and couldn't understand why people would harm each other in such ways. On this day, her fiancé had abandoned her, and it hurt. She wasn't chasing after him to harm him. But people did such things. She wondered if she would ever understand, then thinking, she hoped not.

Mighty Poosh

Watching Aiden and Duncan sitting in the heather, Button looked at Bow, smiling. She had decided to see what the two would do on their own, and she was pleased with Aiden inviting the poor lad to sup at her home. Bow was ready to help Duncan, and knew much help was needed.

"Button, lass be sweet ta lad. Do ya see more ahead than kindness ta lost soul? He be taken by her this very day, but what 'bout her?"

Telling Bow to follow her, she landed in the heather near the two, hiding in the thick of it, motioning Bow to stand with her.

"Ooh, she no know yet, yea, she has heart for the sad thing. This day, she worries for him, soon, she be seein' handsome he be, and tha' he jus' be turtle with head in shell. Her pretty face already reason to be lookin' her way. Then she see him fine lad, her young heart will go pitter-patter."

Bow was peeking over her wee shoulder.

"I know tha' feeling every time I be near ya. And is tha' quick little thumpin' I be hearin' be yours doin' same?"

She turned her head to smile at him. "Of course it be doin' same. Silly Bow, ya just be wantin' me to tell ya. A question be no question when ya know answer. Look at lad. He be wantin' ta kiss her! If I give mighty poosh, lass be in his arms."

Bow studied the two. He heard the lass asking lad if he liked pie.

"Button, if he say blueberry, lass will think him wise. Tha' will set ship a sail…"

Listening to his answer, Button squeezed his hand tight with delight.

"Ooh, he gets some tonight! Bow! Oh, I see look on ya! I be talkin' pie, an' you be flyin' too far ahead. Let's make plan. This night, after he eats glorious blueberries in pie, you give lad poosh, I give lass poosh. A wee kiss mystify them both. A wee peck as he be leaving, thankin' her for savin' his sad life. Wha' ya tink?"

Admiring her knowing how magic a kiss for such lad would be, he smiled and nodded.

"Then Bow, we have our cunning plan. Tha' lad will no sleep tonight. Up he will be, thinkin' of her sweet lips on his. She will sleep like babe, no thought of Kane, tha' fool. She will be dreamin' sweet things. Time ta make dreams come true. It starts like this…"

Button flew up a tiny bit, leaned over and gave Bow a wonderful kiss. Tilting her head, staring into his eyes and smiling, she flew straight up, waiting for him to follow.

Book Learning

Having read hundreds of books from the library in his family home, Duncan had a good idea of what made a good dinner guest. In books he read a good guest was polite, mannered, had interesting stories to share, listened with attention to stories others mentioned, and put down knife and fork after three bites to pay more attention to the company then satisfy hunger. Laughing and compliments fit in when needed. He thought he could do most, but would have no stories to share, and knew no people to speak of to make polite conversation.

Having been told by Aiden nothing more was expected of him than his company, he decided he could listen and learn during the dinner. She had said not to get dressed up, but he wanted to look decent. He had clothes that were not formal but would be presentable. One thing he read in many books was dinner guests often brought small gifts or additions to the table such as dessert or wine. He decided a decent bottle of claret would be a fine dinner gift and his father had a cellar full of bottles that would be a good choice. He had never tasted wine and knew nothing more than names such as claret, burgundy and that the drink was white or red. The library had several books on wines, and he read that a red wine was often best for dinner.

Going to the wine cellar, he was surprised how many bottles were there. All covered in dust, each label was different, most in French or Spanish. He read French wines were well regarded. Trying to figure out which bottle would be a good choice, he found one from France with a beautiful label, his only worry was it was quite old. Most all the bottles were very old then he remembered that was good as he read older wines were prized. The bottle looked nice, and he decided it would be a good gesture even if the choice was not the best.

He had spent much time reading about manners and wine, and suddenly it was time to leave. Dressing and grooming were easily done. Looking at himself in the mirror, he looked presentable and friendly. He was nervous and hoped it wouldn't show. He decided on a dark green sweater over a simple shirt with a collar, and everyday trousers. He was sure they were right for the occasion. Carrying the bottle of wine, he was on his way. It was a cool evening, so the sweater was a good choice.

Deciding to ride his horse, arriving in a velvet-lined carriage could give the wrong impression. The family had a farm, so they would have a barn or horses for plowing and he could stable his ride easily. His heart was beating fast in his chest as he rode up to their house. He admired the farm as it was in excellent repair, and there was a small stable with room for his horse. As he was dismounting, a handsome man with a warm smile came out of the house, saying hello, offering to help stable his ride.

"Duncan, I'm Farrel, Aiden's father. I'm happy you can join us. Come, let's give your fine animal a good place to rest, and if he'd like, an apple or carrot."

Not knowing how Farrel managed it, he felt welcome and comfortable from the simple greeting. Once in the stable, he took the wine from his satchel and Farrel looked at it, then him. He was smiling and nodding.

"This be unexpected treat. That be a far cry from ale from pub. Me wife won't touch brew, but she likes wine. This will please her, no doubt. Come, let's join the ladies."

Relieved he had brought wine, he was also glad he chose a sweater as Farrel was wearing one, quite nice, as well. Walking to the house, he complimented the farm, saying he was impressed. It was more than the requisite complement; it was an excellent farm on productive soil.

Entering the house, Aiden was walking towards them wearing an apron and with a warm smile of welcome. She held out a hand, and he found himself giving his hand to her. She held it tight, saying she was happy he was there, and now it was time to meet her mother, Bre. Leading him into the large country kitchen, Bre was putting a lid on a pot. She walked over to him with a gentle smile and gave him a hug. He had never been hugged by anyone before. It was a wonderful surprise, and he was overwhelmed. She said she didn't expect such a fine-looking lad.

Smiling with delight, Aiden was impressed with the kindness and good nature of her parents. Duncan had been in their home but a minute and was given more affection and care then anyone had throughout his life.

He was reacting the way she hoped — reveling in it like a thirsty man finding a clear stream to drink from. Bre looked at Farrel holding the bottle.

"Now, what tha' be? Did ya bring tha' for sup, Duncan?"

"Yes. I must admit I know naught about the stuff. I hope it be a decent type."

Reading the label, Bre looked up at Farrel with a surprise only he would understand, letting him know the wine was no ordinary bottle of plonk. She looked at Duncan after admiring the bottle.

"Ya brought us a fine one. A good choice, for sure. Me hub knows ale, and, he knows ale. Me, I know wine. It's a fine treat. Duncan. A fine gift. While I get tings finished, perhaps Aiden can show ya round farm. It has been good to us, and wonderful home."

Holding out her hand for Duncan to take, Bre told her there was plenty of time before the food would be ready. As they left through the kitchen door, Bre held the bottle of wine, admiring it, then looked at Farrel.

"Husband, why ya no buy me bottles of this juice?"

He squinted a bit, saying he often brought home some good claret from time to time.

"No. I mean like this bottle. May it be ya don' have a few hundred in your pocket if ya could find one of these?"

Walking up to her, leaning over to inspect the label, he looked up at her with a question.

"I'm no sure what ya be meaning."

"I know ya don't, as ya no know wines. This be no common thing. I used to hear me mum say she wished she could taste this wine jus' once in her life. It's one of the most prized wines from the most honored of wineries. I would guess this sell for several hundred if it can be found. The lad no seems ta know what a prize it be. I be afraid to open it!"

Farrel rubbed his chin, then looked at the bottle again.

"The lad's dad surely knew his drink, then, and a purse to spend on it. So, tha' one bottle be worth more than a year of crops for many a farmer, then?"

Bre nodded. He thought about it.

"Bre, I know it's tempting to hide it away as prize possession, but I tink we open an' share it like a bottle of anything from the pub. Lad needs feel he did good, and he said he knew naught 'bout it. We may embarrass him if we make fuss. If we jus' open it, pour some out and tell him it be fine choice, tha' will do him right. So, enjoyin' the nectar, then, is best you can do for him. Do ya agree?"

She put the bottle on the table, went and got glasses just for wine her mother left her, then put them round the table. She had answered his question.

"Ya always amaze me with your kind heart, an' I could no agree more. But husband, I'll be keepin' empty bottle. What a treasure. I must warn ya' this be no sweet juice. This is goin' ta make your mouth pucker. It's wha' they call a dry one, so don' be looking funny when ya taste it. Me, I'll be enjoyin' it, and I'll be makin' a toast. Now here, learn a bit about such stuff..."

She took the bottle and looked it over.

"Tis very old, and tha' be good thing. Ya keep it on its side, then before ya drink it, you turn it up as it is now, and all the little specs from the grapes

and vine sink to bottom. Tha' takes time, but it will be fine as it's doin tha'
right now. Now, expert would open it and wait a bit, letting it breathe, they
say of that. We will no go through such fuss tonight. And when ya drink, ya
first sniff fragrance, then take wee sip. No gulps like ale. Ya savor it. I know
it sounds strange, but tha' how it be done. Tonight, we drink it like any
plonk. If there be any left, later I'll show ya why they do things so. My mum
showed me, an' I thought it daft, but we can no pretend we be in some
French chateau, and wealthy ta boot. Ooh, there be potatoes ready…"

Walking outside, Aiden was surprised at how little Duncan knew of
farming. He now owned the best, biggest farm in the county and had never
plowed the soil or harvested crops. She was sure to not show her surprise.
He was honest admitting he was not familiar with his own farm.

"Me dad hired man who knows all to do runnin' of it. He hires workers
ta help. I'm sure me dad knew it all. He never had me out working and I
think tha' I should have been out there like hired man. The farm means
much, I know it makes food be needed by all. It's a wonderful way to give
goodness to the world and must be done with care. Meeting your parents.
All this. It be new day. My pa has gone on, an' choices be mine to make
now. I will learn it all and be real farmer. Aiden, I don' know if ya pa would
consider it, but do ya think he would teach me a bit if I came to help here.
It be a fine way ta learn. I don' wish to embarrass the good man runnin' my
farm in front of workers."

Looking at him, she was proud of him. It was a grand idea. She said the
way to find out was to ask him, and she'd bring it up as they ate dessert.

"I jus' say you were admirin' the tools, but had questions about use. He will
surely be happy to show ya, an' good time ta talk about your wish. I be sure
he will want to help. I tink food ready, so, be ya ready for good eats?"

Smiling with a nod, Aiden thought of how earlier in the day he was like a babe crying in her arms. With some kindness, he was enjoying himself and talking about the future. She was feeling close to him. She had shared an important moment in his life. That never happened with Kane. Duncan was open, sincere and very nice. He was brave enough to come meet her family, and she knew it meant a lot to him. She liked the way he talked to her. He looked into her eyes when he spoke. He listened to her. He was not afraid to hold her hand. She also knew he liked the way she looked by many admiring glances he didn't hide.

Inside the house, food was ready and her parents were happy to have his company. Knowing his life had been difficult, they didn't ask too many questions and conversation was centered on food, the harvest, and weather. With dessert, Farrel opened the wine and Duncan explained he didn't drink. His request was respected, and Farrel teased they will just have to tell him how good it is, then. The wine was not what Farrel, or Aiden had expected. It was bitter with a nutty flavor, leaving an aftertaste there was no way to describe. Bre sniffed it, rolled it gently in the glass, taking small sips, then nodding with respect for it. She said there was no better compliment to pie than wine. It made the pie sweeter and even more delicious. She tapped Duncan's hand, telling him it was fine wine, and a good choice.

Aiden sat smiling, mentioning Duncan had a few questions about farm gear. Farrel lit up.

"I think we can beg ladies excuse us for such important matters. Normally I be scrubbing pots and washing plates as Bre stands by telling me how."

Laughing with delight, Bre was feeling the wine. "If only that be so! Well, I guess I must finally wash a few dishes. First time for everything."

She told the men folk to be off, also saying she and Aiden could manage fine without clumsy hands. The two knew she was only teasing them. Once they were outside, Bre asked Aiden how the lad was doing.

"He be fine. Happy from what I can tell. Mum, he is so different from Kane. Well, none like other lads we know. I be tryin to figure him out. He be innocent, but strong, too. Shy, but does no shy way from things. When he says something, he means what he says."

Looking at Aiden, Bre stopped washing and nodded. She was thinking about what was said.

"I noticed all that too. He be learning of things he's been denied and welcomes the change. I liked him right off. A good lad. I can tell ya taken to him. An' he has eyes for ya. It be good to remember he has no met many people. If ya have interest in him, ya need to give room and move slow. He does no yet know ya were engaged, or slighted. All may bring hurts to mind of his mum. The lad was taught wrong to think women be out to hurt him."

Looking out the window to the barn, Aiden was nodding gently.

"I know, mum. He needs to learn much. I can no imagine living as he has. I get wha' you mean. If he goes home an' dreams of me, then learns I was bound to other, could seem I am like his mum. When dad has him back, best I walk with him. Yea, tell I was courted by false love and was hurt. That Kane hurt a trusting lass. You be right. He has been open 'bout his hurt. I will be open 'bout mine. It be right to do. I hope I say all that jus' right. Mum, you know, up on cliff, after the news of Kane, I was full of heartbreak and hurt. Then, I find Duncan, and yea, I saved him, I think. But I know this. Findin' him so, he saved me."

Cunning Plans

"Did ya hear lass? Me whisper sent her walkin' into arms of love true. Across heather and away from hurt. Wise, I be, Bow... Wise I be."

He was smiling at her. "Tha' never be in doubt. Yea, ya turned all aboot jus' fine. I think we do big poosh when dey be walkin' next."

Button nodded. "Yea. Perfect time for mighty poosh." She was staring with a serious expression into the kitchen where Aiden and Duncan shared supper. Bow asked what she was so intent on.

"Tha' pie. All them poor berries. Smothered they be. Plump things swimmin' in sugar an' goo. Baked. Trapped in crust. Happy jus' bein' berries, they be. Now, they be pie. A sad sight."

Looking at the pie with her, Bow turned to her, his expression showing he was taken by a question.

"Button. I be lookin' at pie with ya. I do no recall ev'r havin' pie. Have ya ev'r had pie?"

Putting her finger over mouth, she squinted, obviously thinking hard. Then she tilted her head, mouth opening as if to speak. Then, closed it tight. She started looking here and there. Then, put her chin on her knuckles. Her face lit up, then she frowned. Finally, with look of certainty, said, "No."

Bow was very serious regarding her answer. "Button, how ya know it be horrible. Wha' if it be delicious? Folk, they make some good smellin' eats. Ya be boldest one I know. Be ya bold enough ta try pie?"

Button's eye grew large and full of wonder. She could not resist a challenge.

"Ya know, I ne'er thought it. Them folks like berries off boosh — and like pie too. Yea, I be bold enough, plenty, ta go at pie. Bow? Promise me this, Bow. Oh, ya mus' promise. Bury me in our special place if it does me in."

Both were peeking through the kitchen window, opened wide to enjoy the cool evening. All had been washed and put away, but they could clearly see one lonely slice of pie in the baking tin sitting on the table.

"Button, tell ya wha' we do. Over on yon' boosh be nice leaves. Ya get one, quick as tha' little bunny ya fought off. Give me leaf, I fly in, scoop bit of pie, an' we go under boosh an' give it try. Ladies be headed out front door, so no folk about."

Button didn't wait. At his last word she flew fast as lightening, tugged a leaf, then was back. Giving the leaf to Bow, he took a deep breath and said, "Wings no fail me now!" Flying into the kitchen, he scooped filling and crust as he flew without stopping. She was up in the air as he came out and they both flew under the leaves of the bush. The leaf had plenty of pie on it. Button crouched down, stood up looking down, circled around the pie, looking at it, then sniffing it. Bow watched her, always impressed with her prowess and smarts. She found a good spot, looked at Bow, shrugged her shoulders, took her finger and poked it into the deep purple filling.

She stared at the purple goo on her finger, looking up at Bow, then back to the goo. Slowly, she put her finger in her mouth. Her eyes opened wider than he had ever seen them. Her finger stayed in her mouth, and he heard her hum. Suddenly, she took her finger out of her mouth, poked it back into the filling, then stood in front of Bow, saying, "Open."

He opened his mouth and she put purple filling in it. She stared at him, waiting. He opened his eyes wide with surprise just as she had. They stared at each other. He was finally able to speak.

"Button! It be like nectar — and berry! All one thing! Tangy and sweet and it sent shivers down me. An' Button, there be crust. Let's try…"

Button broke off two pieces and gave him one, keeping one for herself. She managed to get crust with no filling on it so they could taste it by itself. They each took a little bite. They smiled with wonder, then ate the rest.

"Bow, it be wonderful. Oh, but we only have fillin' then we only have crust. Folk eat them together. Tha' be pie. Be ya ready for pie?"

He nodded with anticipation. She broke off crust, then covered it with filling. She handed it to Bow, then made one for herself. They sat cuddled up to each other on the ground, eating their pie.

Second Course

Walking to the barn, Bre and Aiden both looked at each other and smiled. Farrel was showing Duncan how to separate wheat from chaff from a bin they had kept for their larder. Both were very serious on the matter, not noticing they had company.

"Duncan, Farrel, do ya intend to be ignorin' beauties such as we all night? Such fine cool weather an' good for walkin' so Farrel, invite lad back as ya know it be better learned by doin' such durin' day."

He looked at Duncan, putting his hand on his shoulder.

"That be true. Bre is teasing us, but she really is saying we want you to come back, and we'll join together. Work the land an' learn wonder of it. Tonight, as she says, it be time for takin' a stroll or gazing at stars above. Why not ask yon maid there if she'd like ta roam heather with ya?"

Duncan was a bit unsure of himself, yet worked up his courage after looking at each of them and getting a nod of encouragement.

"Aiden, it be a beautiful night. Would ya walk with me? I'd like ta walk the heather with smile ya put on my face, none of my sadness earlier."

Aiden nodded sweetly, doing a slight curtsy. She gave him a sincere smile.

"No maid can deny such fine invitation, said so kindly."

Duncan recalled reading how gentlemen held their arms out for ladies
to hold as they walked, and he offered his arm to her. She put her arm
through his, then looked at her parents.

"Dad, I be most sure mum would appreciate such fine attention. Duncan
and I will provide you some time together."

As they walked towards the mountainside lit by moonlight, Bre asked Farrel
what he had been teaching the lad. He smiled, saying little things, and
the lad was plenty smart, may not know farming yet, but knew a fine lass
when he met one. He held his arm out for Bre. She put hers in his, leaning
against him with affection.

Bre talked sweetly as they passed the large bush outside the kitchen
window. "Was it really jus' this mornin' we heard Kane be off? I tell ya, it be
like someone be lookin' out for that lass."

Duncan was excited and frightened at the same time. As if in a dream, he
was out in the world walking with a beautiful lass, managing to relax from
the kindness of his hosts. Aiden was kind and gentle with him. No book
could describe how beautiful she was in his eyes. He knew she was a beauty,
but knew, somehow, that would mean little if she wasn't so sweet and caring
of him and her parents. She had a charm that made her wonderful to be
near. As they walked, he started to worry it was all a dream. It may be he
had jumped off the cliff, and such was a dream flashing through his mind as
he fell. Realizing that was his father's voice, he told himself he would heed
that advice no longer. Life was for living, not hiding.

Aiden was enjoying her walk with Duncan. Being new to so much, she
decided that he was doing quite well and it would be best to tell him a bit
about her engagement, going slow with the story and how in a mysterious

way, his visit to the cliff had saved her too. Finding a bit of clearing, she told him she thought it a good place to sit a while.

Once settled, she asked him if he was still nervous. He told her with such warm welcome, that helped greatly. He paused, then decided to tell her he had a bit of apprehension. That it all seemed like a dream. He looked at her and though hard to say, knew she would understand.

"As we walked, I worried how it be a lass so kind and lovely could no be married. Could such be possible?"

She was glad he asked, saving her raising the subject. Looking at him, she kept a gentle manner.

"Duncan, today has been an amazing day. For both of us. In rural life, all around people know each other. I be amazed ya jus' asked that as I was goin' ta speak of such. No worry. None. I was courted by a lad I knew all my life and, yea, he proposed to me. I knew him, had kind feelings for him, and accepted. We had our wedding planned and the day was getting' near."

Pausing, she could tell Duncan was confused as she was out walking with him, but engaged. She decided to relieve his concern.

"Like I said, this has been an amazing day. This very mornin' before walking to the ocean and findin' ya there, his father came an' gave unexpected news… for all. The lad got up before dawn, leaving only a note, sayin' he was off to America and goodbye to all. He took most of his pa's money from harvest with him. It was no expected by any, includin' me. Needin' time ta let it all sink in, I took a walk in this very field, and no knowin' why, turned ta see ocean. I found ya there. So, I am no engaged."

Looking at her, Duncan looked sad and concerned.

"Aiden, I feel so bad for ya. And there I be… ready to end all. There you be with such hurtful news, an' ya were no standin' there ta jump. With all that, ya put hand out to me, no mention of ya own problems. I feel so selfish right now. It were you needin' hand."

Holding both of his hands in hers, Aiden was crying tears of happiness. Duncan understood what she was saying and was able to see beyond himself. She was smiling as the tears rolled down.

"Duncan, meetin' ya such, learnin' of your trials, they saved me from thinkin' about a lad who cared for none. When ya opened your heart to me, showed me ya appreciated me for bein' there, I understood tha' be what I want in lad. The lad who left could do no such thing. I think tha' all good happened this day. We were there for each other. Can ya see now wha' I mean?"

Staring into her eyes, he was in awe of her. She was right. His desperation brought them together, and he was at a loss for words so simply nodded then smiled. She helped him by sharing her feelings.

"It be quite a turn of events. I will tell ya, and I hope it be the same for ya… I like ya, and I hope to be spendin' time getting to know each other."

Duncan was thinking of how to say the same thing, but didn't quite know how to do it right, and told her so.

Hovering high enough above the two to not be seen, Button was telling Bow, "Gather all ya might, get ready for mighty poosh!"

Aiden looking happy, suggested heading back to the farm. She said with his coming by to learn farming, they'd be seeing a lot of each other. They both started to stand up when each unexpectedly tripped over something. Aiden fell into Duncan's arms, and they landed on the ground, Aiden's face above

Duncan's. Laughing, she told him even that happened for a reason, then gave him a soft kiss. His first.

Change of Seasons

With the harvest over and winter coming, Farrel had plenty of time to do more than teach Duncan his farming skills. He grew to like him and enjoyed being a friend. Bre got to know him well, thinking him an excellent lad for Aiden. She watched as the two young ones grew close, Duncan clearly in love with Aiden who made no secret she loved him.

Duncan learned how important having a family was, feeling he had found one. Over the winter, into spring, he rebuilt his sad world into a happy one. No longer hiding from anything, he learned how to run his own farm and looked forward to the year ahead. He became active in church activities, attended social gatherings, and became a friend to his neighbors. His instincts were good, and he was learning how to be part of the world around him.

Every time he looked at Aiden, he knew that she had opened the door of life for him. With just her goodness, she had saved him. He loved her and felt that by the end of Spring, he would have his life in order, his farm running smoothly, and at the festival to welcome Summer he planned to ask her to be his wife. As much as he had accomplished, he still had a fear that he could be rejected. He also knew it was just a fear from his life before meeting Aiden. He knew she would say yes. Farrel and Bre had asked him when he was going to wed the lass. He was facing his deepest fear of rejection. He knew there was no need for it, but it was there. He was still healing. Realizing to do things right, when he asked for her hand, he needed to be free from the control his father had made him suffer.

With Duncan free to be a part of celebrations and church, Aiden guided him through celebrating Christmas, New Years, and Easter. Each one was a new experience, and he was accepted by the community with none pressing him for talk of his family's past. Aiden had worried that many would be curious, and she suspected her parents may have shared the care the lad needed with others. She became more certain of their influence as there was no curiosity of where Kane was, and what of her wedding. She asked them often if they were behind such cautions. They acted naive, saying they had no idea what she meant. Loving them all the more for it, they swept away reminders and let shadows fall behind.

With crops and planting readied, his confidence strong, Duncan took advantage of going to the county seat with Farrel to buy supplies to find an engagement ring. He shared his plan with Bre and Farrel, asking for their daughter's hand in marriage. They sat in their parlor while Aiden was bringing food to a neighbor who was ailing, and Duncan confessed he loved Aiden true and wished to marry her if they approved. They looked at each other, then Farrel told him they'd need time to consider it. Duncan said he understood, and he watched as Bre whispered in Farrel's ear, then he in hers. Farrel looked at Duncan.

"We've had time 'nough. Ya have our blessing."

They all were near hysterics, and when they calmed down enough to speak, Bre told him they had been talking about it for months and were full prepared with their blessing. Farrel looked at him and was earnest in his message.

"Ya have a yea from us, but we no be who ya be marryin'. The real blessing is when lass says yea to ya. When do ya plan on askin' her?"

Duncan had thought about it many times and was prepared to answer.

"I was hopin' ta ask at Summer Festival. If a yea it be, I will climb up mountain and shout it for all to hear!"

Finding a Claddagh was traditional for an engagement ring, and he asked Bre if Kane had given Aiden one. She told him that was so, and he explained he thought doing the same would bring up that sad memory. Bre was impressed with his understanding of such, and she agreed that looking at ring should not be reminder of Kane. He shared he thought an emerald, simple on a band, would be the thing to remind them of their first day in the lush blooms of heather. Green and beautiful. She was near tears as he told her, and she told him that was wonderful. He said each time he looked at her hand, it would remind him as well. That sent her into tears, and she hugged him, telling him the ring would forever tell their love.

Watching Duncan buy the stunning ring, Farrel was equally impressed. He was also stunned at the price.

"Lad, tha' be incredible, but I think ya be needin' ta hire bobbies ta guard it. Somethin' tha' dear has a price, surely, but ya sentiment be priceless. I know lass will understand wha' it means. Bre has been tellin' me of it. Tha' be good, lad. Good, indeed.

Riding home, ring safe in his pocket, Duncan told Farrel his last decision was a tricky thing.

"I could use some advice. I've been thinkin' there be two good times to offer her ring. One be right before festival. Just the two of us, private. Then I announce to all at the event. The second would be in fron' of everyone, wit' band playin' so all can share the joy. It would be the bravest thing I've ev'r done. She has made me strong an' I'll thank her for it tha' way. I think it be puttin' her on the spot, an' I don' know if tha' be fair thing ta do, iff'n she be not ready ta say yea."

Thinking about it, Farrel said he'd ask Bre when they got back. He said knowing Aiden, she will be saying yea, and she loves when others do such

grand gestures. Duncan unloaded supplies while Farrel went in the house, then back in short time. He was smiling.

"Lad, Bre said tha' was a good, thoughtful question. Like me, she say it be a joyous thing, an' to be proud of it. Aiden will be happy for all to see. She be tha' way. She did say ya may want to hint day before tha' you have big surprise ya may announce at festival. If she inquiries a wee bit, jus' say ya have an important question ta ask and wan' God and all ya know to be witness. The lass will know wha' ya mean an' watch how she reacts."

The Question

Being sure Bre knew best, Duncan decided to wait until the festival was in progress, then ask for her hand in marriage. Not nervous, he was feeling anticipation. The thought of looking at her, putting the ring on her finger, and her saying she'd be his wife was such a wonderful thought he felt like running to her and not waiting. Anxious as he was, he knew the wait would be worth it.

The night before the festival, Duncan was walking with Aiden and he realized he didn't understand why the Summer Festival was such a major event, so he asked her about it.

"Duncan, it be smart question as it be ya first festival. It be start of growin' and hard work. All there live off land. It be celebration of sorts, and it be time to trade and get help if need be. We sing, bring best dishes, priest offers blessin' and all tell tales. Ya be part of all now, so join in and I'll be havin' ya meet many ya don' know yet. I be lookin' forward to the music. In no time we'll all be singin' ol' tunes, together. It mainly be chance to all join together. The married lasses go pick new blooms growin' in the heather. Tradition be to give young maids a sprig of thyme, an' lads chase them about. If maid gives hers to a laddie, tha' be a sign she be fond of him. It be a joy to watch. See, flowers be in bloom, so is love. A sweet way to be like beauty of the land."

Duncan said he was excited about going and asked if she liked running with the thyme. Smiling, she said still a maid, surely she'd be given wild mountain thyme, waiting for some laddie to catch her eye. Duncan smiled, saying he hoped she had one in mind. She swiveled side-to-side in a shy fashion, looking up at him, saying she might.

Thinking it was a fine tradition, he asked how it started. Aiden lit up and told him the story handed down from long before any could remember.

"Shut in all winter, maids dreamin' of beaus, lads dreamin' of maids, all shy young things, it twas said faeries helped things along by givin' thyme to a lass to pair her with right laddie. If a lad be given her thyme, he would get her heart. It be said faeries still at it, and many a maid found sprig of thyme when least expected, an' the next lad she meet be one she be marryin' soon."

Engrossed in the tale, he asked how it came to be the ladies went pulling flowers and thyme from the heather on the mountain. She looked at him and was amazed he hadn't figured it out.

"They be lookin' ta find *faeries!*"

He smiled in understanding. He thought it a wonderful way to start in life. Wee ones helping folks find love. He realized she was in the heather the day they met.

"Aiden, don' be thinkin' me daf, but I be thinkin' it were faeries gave ya push my way the day we met."

Aiden stared at him, and he saw enchantment in her. She was seeing all anew. She hugged him with all her might.

"Oh, ya sweet lad. Ya be right. I be wonderin' er'r since wha' made me leave heather and go to cliff. I jus' found myself headed there. It mus' be that. No else makes sense. It be grand thing. I went to pick wild mountain thyme, an' picked you."

They looked at each other, eyes misty, knowing it was magic.

Duncan said he was looking forward to the festival and knew it would be full of surprises, and he was planning one for her… if she be ready. He had a question he may wish to ask and did she mind being asked with friends and family there to hear her answer, just in case he didn't hear it right with all the singing and noise. Aiden smiled, understanding his meaning. Holding him tight, softly into his ear she said yes, she wanted everyone to hear.

He walked her back to her house, and both knew the Summer Festival would be the start of their season.

Watching them from a tree, Button was telling Bow, "Lad be foolish enough ta believe in faeries." He thought about it, and nodded. She looked at him most serious.

"There be no rest for us, Bow, long as folk thinkin' we be real. No floatin' down the creek on leaf, no nippin' a bit of pie an runnin' off wit it. No. No rest for us, tha' be sure. We be too good at wha' we do. Folk can pick thyme, but no clue who ta hand it to. We be stuck. Like wee ant in leaf full of nectar. Stuck."

"Button, tha' we be. Tomorrow we have hard work, an' plenty of pooshin' ta do. If all goes right, after, we go stare at moon. Go float down creek on leaf and cuddle. Ya' work be needin' time to bubble n' boil. We always go float after festival, so why ya be worryin' of tings?'

'Oh, Bow. I feel the air. Somethin' be comin' an' it be blowing in on the morrow. It be comin' a long time, an' from far away. Mighty we must be.

Fraid of naught. Tis sure ta be time ta try a faerie's magic. Will be 'nother tale to tell."

All Go Together

Running across the fields, children plucked flowers pretending to be faeries. Tables were lined with favorite foods, and on a special table were pies all competing for a shiny green ribbon. Using a flat wagon, musicians watched bouquets of wildflowers put round it making a beautiful stage. Livestock stood looking at all the busy people, waiting for judges and bidders from near and far. Young lads were dressed proper, and all maids in their finery. Stories and gossip made way through crowds, and smiles ruled the day.

Holding Duncan by the hand, Aiden led him here and there, introducing him to those he had not yet met. Wearing a dark blue jumper, a checkered shirt, long brown hair blowing in the gentle wind, Duncan thought her most beautiful in simple country clothes. He wore a white shirt and tweed pants with suspenders. With sleeves rolled up, his arms had sprouted muscles from hard work done with Farrel. Women and maids commented on his good looks and the smile he wore. He was the talk of the event, his first year attending, a mystery to all. He owned the largest and most prized farm of any there and finally was part of the community, unlike his sad father.

Seeing all looked right, food and pies on tables, livestock lowing, children running in the heather or entering contests, the band started playing a lively tune. A good-sized area was left for dancing when all had enough ale to loosen their feet, and all cheered the first sound of the fiddle.

Duncan and Aiden were walking to the band wagon when a sudden change came, silencing cheers and chatter. It started from where wagons and carts were left, then like a wave, rippled through the crowd. All went quiet except for the fiddle playing, and sensing the change in merriment, the fiddler put down his bow and stared in the same direction as all there. Aiden grabbed Duncan's arm, looking to see what changed things so. People near the wagons parted ways, making a clear path. Walking with a determine stride, Kane had returned.

Gasps and whispers followed him, all knowing he had forsaken his family and fiancé. Showing no shame, he strode to the band wagon, ignoring shocked expressions and looks of concern aimed his way.

Duncan leaned over and quietly asked Aiden who the man was. She looked up at him, clearly shook, with no worry who could hear, told him, "Kane."

Having never seen him, Duncan instantly knew why all had stopped and stared at the man. His muscles tensed, his pulse quickened, outraged Kane was back, clearly coming for Aiden.

Farrel and Bre rushed to join Aiden and Duncan, knowing trouble was walking her way. Her father leaned over and whispered to Aiden, "Steady, lass." Looking Duncan in the eye, he simply said, "Steady."

Surprising all, expected to go straight to Aiden, he jumped up on the wagon, the band jumping off as he did. His hair was long, and he had not shaved for many days. His shirt was too large, opened at the collar. He wore stout boots over his pants and looked wild and fierce. He stood with his hands on his hips, staring at the crowd, then directly at Aiden. Giving her a slight nod, he went back to looking at all gathered. Shaking his head, he looked unsteady, and he clearly had travelled the night through. He spoke loud and bold.

"Take your looks. Yea, it be the villain ya all heard tale of. Take a good look. A failed man. Off to see the world. Off to make his mark. Back a failure. A disgrace. Begging for copper ta get home. Home, if it still be. I don' feel welcome, but here I be, askin' for forgiveness. Knowin' I made mistake.

Knowin' I hurt many. Knowin' there be price to pay. Pay the price, I shall. So, take your look. A broken lad. When leavin' I said it no be goodbye. Just fare well. So, I say sorry ta all I hurt. I hope Aiden be understandin' I came back as she be my love. I pray she still be mine."

Jumping off the wagon, walking up to Aiden, he stood staring at her. Duncan and her parents knew it was her chance to speak her mind. It was her moment, and Duncan was there at her side.

Ignoring the others, Kane gave her a little shrug of his shoulders with a sickly smile.

"Wha' can I tell ya, Aiden? I did wrong. Ya still be my intended. I be back ta marry ya. Will ya come go with me?"

Watching Aiden, not a sound was heard from any. She stood calm and poised, then answered.

"Kane, I must be a thanlin' ya. Your leavin' showed me I was no important to ya. And by leavin' ya ended engagement. Did ya no think I would surely find another? One true love who gave me thyme instead note farewell? There be no ring on my finger, and no Kane in my heart. Kane, up yon hill be mighty ocean. Climb up cliff, an' go jump in ya precious ocean."

A thunder of cheers and shouts rose from all gathered. She took Duncan by the hand, turned, and left Kane standing. The band got up on the wagon and started playing, all but Kane joining in, joyously singing.

I'll go home to my parents, confess what I've done
And I'll ask them to pardon their prodigal son
And when they have kissed me as oft-times before
I never will play the wild rover no more

And it's no, nay, never
No, nay, never, no more
And I'll play the wild rover
No never, no more

Walking to the heather, Aiden had to shout in Duncan's ear to be heard over the chorus.

"I tol' ya they'd be singing songs!"

Approaching the brilliant colors of new flowers in the heather, the youngest girl, just a toddler, went up to Aiden and handed her a sprig of thyme. The little girl ran off, and Aiden looked at the thyme in her hand, then at Duncan. She reached up and kissed him, then held the thyme to her breast with both hands.

'Duncan, was I right? Can there be any better than the start of Summer?"

All Join Together

Bow and Button took a seat in a tree as even the youngest ones were called in from the hills. They were excited to see their mighty pooshin' and brave acts working their magic.

Kane left, but not for adventure in the ocean.

All stood round the wagon the band played on. Duncan had taken Aiden by the hand and said he wanted her by his side as he headed to the wagon. Climbing up, he held his hand out for Aiden, the band making room. Aiden stood smiling, and her parents were standing closest to the wagon stage. Waiting for all to gather, Duncan held up his hand, and there was quiet but for one farmer drinking from his pint shouting, "Get on, laddie. We be waitin' since New Year's!"

Duncan laughed with everyone else and said he had too. With more cheers, he raised his hand.

"I see this maid be given thyme, an' it seems she be lookin' my way."

More cheers, even louder. Duncan, smiling at Aiden, saw tears in her eyes, feeling her love shine on him.

"Aiden. I heard ya say there be no ring on ya' finger. I do no know if this will do, but if so, I want ta put it on ya bonnie finger, an' ask ya ta be me wife. Will ya marry me?'

Nodding her head with a huge smile on her face, she gave him her sprig of thyme to a roar of cheers, then, held out her hand. Duncan took the emerald ring and put it on her finger. She held her hand up for all to see, and was met with hurrahs, shouts, and saw most wives had tears of joy. She looked at the ring and stared in awe. It was even more beautiful than the flowers and heather she loved so much.

The band started playing *Wild Mountain Thyme*, and everyone sang it to them. Aiden spent the rest of the day showing most everyone the gleaming ring Duncan had given her. A ring that was a crystal fountain reflecting the beauty around her.

Something Very Special

"Button, day be done. Ya did powerful magic. Thyme everywhere I look. I be worried when Kane come back so bold. I saw ya ready to go sen' fool on his way."

Nestled in his arms in their tree home, she took one arm and made a punching motion in the air.

"Sure as I be a button, I be mighty and fierce ta hold tha two together. Go at fool swinging, mighty, I twas ready ta do. Lass beat me to it. They be buttoned up, all tha' matters."

Her arm went down, wrapped snuggly around him. She nuzzled up to his ear, humming an ancient love ballad. He was happy as nectar on leaf. She softly whispered in his ear.

"I have somethin' special for me beau…"

He looked lovingly into her large brown eyes, and whispered back.

'Pie?"

Three Ravens

There were three Ravens sat on a tree, downe a downe, downe.
They were as blacke as blacke could be, with a downe, downe.
Then one of them said to his mate, where shall we our breakefast
take? With a downe, derrie derry downe, downe.

Downe in yonder greene field, downe a downe, downe.
There lies a knight slain under his shield, with a downe, downe.
His hounds they lie downe at his feete, so well do they their
Master keepe. With a downe, derrie derry downe, downe.

His hawkes they flie so eagerly, downe a downe, downe.
There's no fowle that dare him come nie, with a downe, downe.
Downe there comes a fallow doe, as great with yong as she might
go. With a downe, derrie derry downe, downe.

She lifted up his bloody head, downe a downe, downe.
And kiss'd his wounds that were so red, with a downe, downe.
She got him up upon her backe, and carried him to earthen lake.
With a downe, derrie derry downe, downe.

She buried him before the prime, downe a downe, downe.
She was dead her selfe ere evensong time. with a downe, downe.
God sent every gentleman, such hawkes, such hounds, and such
a leman. With a downe, derrie derry downe, downe.

Eyes

Perched high on scorched tree, three ravens looked to road below. Intently watching knight ride slowly past tree same, he be no aware they watch such. Making sound none, each knowing knight be one to follow, three be shadows of night. Looking to each other, scraggliest bird opened beak to squawk, decided nay, taking flight from tree in pursuit. Following scraggly bird, two other flew with haste, passing lone rider. Perching on decayed stone wall beside desolate road, birds be concern none to crusader. Standing as statues, birds showed interest none as knight rode near.

Having but small space between wall and road, stone perch gave full sight of rider and steed. Beads, being only eyes black, intently studied man, birds saw mighty sword. Much for worry he be. Knight man, nay, no wanted, no needed, glad only when he be rotting flesh. Presently — meal most craved.

Doubt

Longing for home, August understood feeling more than need. Journey be sacred call to him for riding home from holy land be ever more troubling than religious battles fought. Pleasure smelling grasses and barley was long ago, none for him more. Knowing desert and rocks, salt of sea, taste of blood, could he e'er again be in land of days gone? Surely all be fantasy. All such, yea, only thoughts. It be told dying warriors blessed be of solace such, brief, only given moment of death. Doubting explanation other, he wondered which frightened heathen issued fatal blow? What rock be catapulted blindly into savage fray, downing him nay any warning? Perchance it only simple blade sliced away his head. No man could stand in carnage, such, then be aside, choosing ride home one day. That no be so. He knew this be last ride.

Remembering men, knowing names none, all on last ride to homes or heavens strange to him, dispatching them such be duty of knight.

Dispensing death be told duty to God. Red-robe priests declared slaughter such be truly God's will. Crusader ne'er more, knowing no killing be will of God, nay. None holy, only sinful, red-robes be corrupt, lost in vision true ne'er. Shouting call e'er be death to all heathens, red-robes proclaimed right and just it be all knights vanquish non-believers with ne'er intent of converting lost to God. Holy war be none more than claim over barren scruff of desert land. Death be only for disputed ground, giving nothing except pleasure to red-robe priests. He knew church have call none to murder. He be glad his time had come, sure be ride was no to home, ride be to eternity.

Abandoning all possessions, away he be with nay goods nor gear, having garments none but what wore day of leaving. Casting armor and chainmail away, he wore but long shirt and leggings, brown up to knees in dried blood. Wearing blood of men dead such gave him pause. Blood, holy gift from God, red stuff be life. Now? Only part of dead left on rags. He knew no right to carry sacred gift, blood none his. Such life, the only possession sacred, now be stain on his rags.

Riding north through lands many, he saw world ruled now by church having passion always for power, dominating all. Shaking head in dismay, seeing holy crusade killed more than men in battle, holy crusade destroyed decency, all that be left, in lands travelled. Wenches in villages lifted skirts, offered dirty bodies for penny. Old men stood lifting hands, begging coin. Children tagged beside, telling mothers be loving beauties craving man such he be. Naked, mother be waiting for knight in bed soft, craving knight fill her with God. Seeing knights new on way to war, most rallied at such invitation, most to such depths fell. Many knights, men of God, stood brazen in courtyards, maidens kneeling before them in plain sight. None kneeling at altar, nay, wenches and young lads, mouths opened, ate body of man, none that of Christ. Drink and fornication vile be only victory he knew of holy crusade.

Understanding devil only victor e'er from battle, it appeared all people succumbed to dark evil. Seeing nuns run naked from convents to flee rape

by drunken priests and knights, he saw same many nuns, of sequestered
orders, who ran naught. In rapture, they lay with invaders outside convents
offering prayer only to knights, mouths open to receive communion, prayer
being unspeakable acts may bless them. Considering holy land be but
bloody field of slaughter, he soon thought carnage better than nuns and
maidens, most but child still, surrendering to serpents hanging from groins
of once-noble knights and ne'er noble clergy. Red-robed ones most pleased
by children, teaching lad and lass service only to them, divine ne'er.

Knowing such visage could no be real, he rode onward. Hoping only cast to
purgatory he be fated, it be his time to suffer; punishment thus for taking
lives in battle, knowing true it be unholy. Twas during last battle, looking
for God present in sliced bodies, heads thrown to mounds taller than he,
limbs being eaten by birds, he be certain killing such only sick pleasure
of men, ne'er will of God. Thinking more, he be understanding death
commanded by any truly be will of Lucifer. He thought how he be blinded
such by call of duty to crusade. Painful be his truth. He surrendered to
vile demon. If he truly be but captive for time long in Perdition, there be
reason fair. Once knowing he fought crusade of Satan, for such, he fought
no more. Seeing such light, before demon's gate he entered, no. Most
upsetting, now he be sure light shined always, on all. It twas there, yea,
brighter than sun, day he first killed. Moment of first kill, it shined on him.
That knowing be burned in him, yea. Looking into terror face of peasant
fighting be his devotion to Allah, Christ spoke no message of crusade to
him nor any other. He be sure. Now, witness to debauchery and depravity,
he knew Christ be nay part of any. He be certain only evil desire of dark
one be done.

Thus forever lost, he had but prayer one. He be content on road to
Perdition, he held ride just and true. His prayer be only for Kiera, his
betrothed, it she be safe from demon. Each day, riding on, fear he had
that ne'er be gone from mind. Fear consuming him be day when reaching
home, he be finding his love on knees giving service to demon. If he no yet

be in hell, finding her such would be torment same as hell for him through all eternity.

Debauchery

Making way through Spain and bottom of France, he be witness to less sin and corruption. Evil be patient, no yet consuming northernmost lands. Making sense, he knew like disease, evil took time to spread. Soon, he be sure, madness would reach green rolling hills of home, same as call for knights to crusade grabbed hold all good men there. If he be on road to Perdition, perchance green pastures be small reward given having true sorrow for wrongs. He could only hope it true.

Thinking matters such on journey, he considered every land rife with perils, e'er, but no madness from crusade be cause. Kings and nobles cared ne'er of peasants and poor. Towns of beautiful lands be home to drink and whore. Highways hosted thieves and deputies collecting tolls for baron or lord. All such no new to him, when heartless ruler be mighty, people succumbed sin such being only way to eat or survive. Sheriffs, many paid handsome to look away, sought bounty from travellers, even knights, riding past. Counting himself fortunate having no such encounter, it be very thing made him certain he be dead. He thought of warriors from northernmost climes having death with honor their home, called *Valhalla*. It be place dead go when victors of battle. No sure any be victors in holy war, priests told all they be such. Priests were ne'er on fields of carnage. Knowing red-robed priests laid with whores, fornicating, drinking wine, laughing while good knights died, his sword would have served them better than peasants he slayed when truth be told.

Thoughts of how man, any, hiding in robe red, could lay in palace looking o'er field of battle, a whore sucking him, a whore licking his arse, laughing watching men decent be slaughtered. What sickness be delight watching heads fly, ax bury in chest, limbs hacked off? What demon made such creature burst white flow into mouth of whore watching life taken for no more than such? Such was what holy war be, and church, ne'er stopping, could be only run by demon red like robes.

Riding along coast, after day long in saddle, he took pause to bathe and tend many wounds. Finding village small, he spied local inn, quiet, looking clean. Near was smithy to tend horse as steed lost fittings and be no shod properly. Inn suited all needs. He wished only hot bath, bed, and fire warm. The coast be ever damp and cold.

Hobbling horse, going inside inn, sitting alone at table was keep, eating cheese. Having fire burning, place be most warm and comfortable. Seeing it suitable, he greeted keep, asking man if there be decent bed for knight. Nodding, keep smiled, bid him welcome, inviting him join and share fare. Sitting, he told man he wished decent room for but night, desiring hot bath if such be convenient.

"Of course, grand knight. Of course. And, fine meal? Oh, my my, yes, indeed. Please, tell me, oui, what you wish? I have some nice grouse. You like birds, yes?"

Nodding, August said they be much his liking. Roasted, sauce none. Vegetables, only new, kind no matter. Spring water if any he had.

Hearing request, keep brought large jug and handsome engraved goblet.

"Clear, from my own tiny stream. Only this I drink. But, no wine? I have many fine bottles. Please, enjoy fromage. Refresh thirst with fine cup. I will ready hot bath. And, perhaps small mirror and lather for shaving? Please, be there any more you may need?"

"Ya be most gracious proprietor, keep. Yea, I be tending many wound. I wish ta treat all with ointment, and, yea, clean dressing if ya have such.

Something ta cover them? If ya have spirits, clear, pure from grain, and strong, I would make use of them."

Lifting his shirt, August revealed many cuts, most surrounded by bright red skin showing them in need of care. The keep looked closely, nodding.

"Tis good you stopped, agree? Those be red, yes, give any man worry. The harm they do, many times it be later, oh, that can be very bad. But, worry not. No. I have all what is needed. First, bathe. Cleanse them, then, medicinals. But now, I go, start water boiling. What of your fine stallion? Do you wish me tend him for you?"

Explaining his steed need special care, he ask call smithy to inn. He would give such request. The keep nodded, putting his finger to the side of his nose, saying it would be hot water, smithy, then treatments. He turned and was off to his errands. August carried little more than coin in purse. His tattered shirt and leggings had nary mending or wash. He first thought ask for their care while he bathed, then shook his head thinking best to find wear in shop if any be near. The village was small and there be time before bath be hot. Getting up, August went outside, looking at shops near inn. One had assorted goods in window, including garments. A small plank above door had but crude carving of needle and thread. It appeared be tailor shop.

Wishing quick business getting clothes, he hoped there be some made and ready. Opening door, he saw assortment of garments, some appeared to be right in fit. Looking at sturdy shirt of dark green wool, he heard footsteps so turned to greet shop owner. Knowing women skilled with cloth, he be glad when greeted by older madame. She spoke proudly of goods, telling such fine wear none common in villages. In short time, settling on price for shirt and decent leather leggings, she pointed to hats and boots, offered all for fair price. Thanking her, he explained he needed none more, then headed to inn. He be glad to rid his tattered battle garb away, now having warmer attire with no life of others staining him.

Returning to table, he heard comforting sound of water pouring into tub. Walking to splashing sound, he learned keep had all ready. Next to tub he saw welcome variety of cloths and soaps, plus polished hand mirror. Getting polite nod of approval from August, the keep bowed, leaving him to his toilette. Steaming hot water be soothing to muscles but harsh on wounds. He knew it best they be clean. Using soap, strong of lye, he found it most stringent, hurting much as swords to his wounds. Looking in mirror, he be surprised how ragged his face looked. Noticing a decently sharp razor near soap, he deftly swiped it about his face, soon recognizing himself again.

Knowing his wounds ready for treatment, he called for keep once out of tub whilst drying himself. Appearing, the keep nodded, saying he knew not what happened to man in bath. Now, much to his delight, there be fine gentleman. August said he needed help dressing his wounds. The keep said to wait but a moment, holding his hand up, leaving. August stood waiting when a young woman appeared. He be no expecting any but keep, also realizing he be naked. Grabbing for large cloth to cover himself, she said no to such bother, his wounds be in all parts and there be no shame in tending them. She spoke truth, and had gentle voice most sincere. Reaching for antiseptic, she poured much, freely, on new cloth, then set forth patting wounds.

Looking up at beams, he felt strange seen and touched by strange woman. She be young and quite pleasing in manner and appearance. Gentle and careful in her treatment, she hummed strange melody as she tended him. Standing back, she bade him turn about, making sure all tending done. Nodding, she reached for ointment smelling of weeds, gently applying to wounds with light touch. Finishing, she used roll of white cloth to wrap his chest and upper thighs. Still humming her tune, she reached for his new shirt, holding it for him, then pulling it over his head. Standing back, she nodded approval, then knelt before him to help put on the leggings.

Her kneeling such reminded him seeing women kneeling before men to pleasure them, causing moment of worry she too so intended. Only holding leggings for him, he slipped them on, telling her he felt much improved with ointment. He be surprised he boldly stood naked before maid, then grew thankful she helped him do what he could no do. Thanking her, he said she be most gentle and appreciated care such. Asking if she be keep's daughter, she laughed.

"No, monsieur. I be wife! Other things, too. Cook. Maid. And, as you now know, nurse. Have you wife waiting? I be not sure she will like your many scars. I do. They are marks of real man."

Surprised at hearing she be keep's wife, he knew it common for older men to marry young maids. With most young men off to crusade, maids had choices few. He be glad keep a decent sort.

"Nay, no yet. But, fine maiden waits for me. My thoughts of maiden kept me strong. It be year times three since uh left, but letters did reach me. She waits. But, married? When I return. Then. If she still wants me;."

Looking him up and down, she revealed admiration in her eyes.

"Worry not of that. You have everything any damsel desires. More, me think. She waits. She will be most glad she did."

Looking passionately into his eyes, he be sure he knew her meaning. He was unsure how to reply. She gathered up his tattered battle clothes, saying they were best burnt, then left. He stood wondering if she would surprise him that night. She had made her admiration plain to him. He would secure his door to sleep with nay such worry.

Seeing none more of her, sup waited, keep providing ample service and sup, all food hearty country fare. With needed sleep, rising new man, after hearty breakfast keep told his horse be ready. Paying keep, he walked to smithy, thanking him and paying him well. It had been a strange night.

The young wife kindled passion for Kiera. There still be mighty distance to travel and more nights ahead. With many men off to war, maids were plenty. He accepted most be looking for man such as he. He knew other knights would avail themselves of such temptations. The ravages of battle would do as much destruction to maiden virtue as it did to men's flesh.

With wounds tended, reaching northern France, his home in the far north be calling him. He found himself riding faster. Not far from his country, it be only few days more o'er rolling hills then he be with his love. The depravity witnessed on journey all behind. The world around him looking sane and decent again. France be beautiful with green hills. Green as they may be, they were no the hills of home.

Unlike the so-thought holy land, when leaving home to battle three years past, his country enjoyed a rare time of peace. He hoped it still be so. Without armor and chainmail to cause fear, villagers smiled as he rode through towns large and small. Welcome at farms and inns, he enjoyed seeing decency was no forsaken. Perhaps crusade was meant to preserve such beauty of land and people. Thinking more, he knew without battles, lands he travelled through were much like his home. People sought but peace and family. Crusades be no about preserving serenity, only imposing religion on world. He could no more see sense or right in such intent. There be but one God. Different peoples served and worshipped God their own way. Only creator could know those faithful to Him holy.

Passing village abbeys and churches, he wanted no part of their rituals or gatherings. Having no wish to force his knowing on others, he had seen true harm imposing beliefs on many. If flocks be happy and faith offered meaning, it be their choice. He now had beliefs his own. He wondered of Kiera. She be most devout and expected marriage in village church. Would she understand he had changed? Could she marry one who wished to ne'er enter church again? Would he bend and bow in rituals to respect her faith?

Nay, ne'er.

He knew doing such would be lie, and best explain he saw too much killing to follow laws of man. He had faith in God. It be stronger than ever. How could Kiera find devotion such wrong? It be his duty to explain his beliefs to her. He would share what he learned, hoping she understand him.

Riding, thoughts of how to return to her a new man were on his mind. He was a better man. No longer fool.

Thinking of young bride from inn who treated wounds, he could still hear her say he had all any woman could want. She spoke of manhood; of might. He thought often of Kiera's beautiful body, knowing that be natural. He saw many naked women selling themselves in his travels, women in attire most seductive, all offering their bodies. Knowing people more than body, he hoped he be seen as soul by intended. If she saw spirit, she would know him, most good. He thought of what attracted him to Kiera. Was it her beauty, or heart? Her smile, her care, her kindness? The words she spoke in his ear when alone? The way she smelled? How gentle she be with him? Her long legs and pleasing body?

Knowing all qualities such drew him to her, he loved her as man must love wife. She be more than young maiden of beauty, though knowing he craved body same as heart. He could no deny lust for her. God gave craving such, it be true and could no be denied.

Stopping to drink from clear stream and eat apple, he noticed large black birds circling above camp. Concerned, they surely be watching him, craving carrion as ravens feast on death. Perhaps there be dead animal about. They be attracted e'er to dead flesh. He could no smell any such rot. Finishing apple, he looked up. They had flown away and he be glad they moved on.

No far from home, he found himself thinking of Kiera, her humming same strange tune wife at French inn hummed.

News of While Away

Stopping at a shop in a small village, he gathered ham, cheese and bread for his sup and bought cloth to put fresh dressing on his wounds. It was late in day. With no wish to travel come night, speaking to shop owner he begged news of the land. Near home, he wished to learn all what happened during time he be away. Explaining he be back from crusade, nearing home, the man had interest equal to his, wanting news of battles. August told truth of crusade progress, keeping opinions from bleak description. The owner stood, saddened battle still raged with many men lost. August shared his sadness, learning man had son in fray, young, gone year times two. Told lad's name, he said they met, remembering him a decent sort. With trepidation, shop owner asked if he knew son's welfare. August be able to tell lad be respected, looked well when last seen, giving man comfort, some. No wishing to offer more, August knew day each could bring death. He prayed to himself that would be no, glad to see relief on man's face.

Asking of his county, Cragmont, and his village, Red Bluff, smile on man changed to concern. Getting fruit and water, he bade August sit in back of shop, quiet, to speak for there be much to tell. August grew concerned hearing man, wondering what news could worry him so. He begged man tell all.

"With good men off to war, dregs all be left, and yea, they be unchecked. Aye, dregs be ruthless, and, yea, foolish bold. Nobles, well, ya know them sorts. Keep kin from crusade, they do. With none to challenge them, meaning in county matters, they started in quick. Right way, imposin' mighty tax on all things. Even tax water from wells and streams. They care not what poor folks suffer. Drink makes them savage, aye, an' I know fact when in state such, why, well, no good way to tell ya… plunder farms and villages they do, grabbing all fine maids for their pleasure. There be many a bastard born since ya left, that be true. The sheriff, well, he is helpin' make it all easy as he be paid with maidens and bribes, an' paid well by rich land owner. The villains work old men folk hard in fields, then refuse wages. Any oppose, even speak foul of them, that ends quick, it does. Off in chains they go. A bad time, yea, bad for all. It looks peaceful like, but wait. They ride at night. Plunder an' rape be no sin nor law broken there. There be no stopping them bastards."

Worrying such fate had fallen Kiera, he felt urge to ride to her then. Asking man if there be news of his village, he worried a reply. Shaking his head, the man said he had no heard any, but warned all news be hushed, people fearful of reporting such deeds. August sat thinking of his road ahead. He be glad he kept his broadsword and knife. Hearing such news, his battle may lay ahead, no behind.

Watchful Eye

Riding long past exhaustion, August needed rest. Stopping at gentle stream, he changed wound dressing, seeing wounds healing. Eating, he considered even if Kiera be unharmed, he would face the lot running foul of decency and engage them. The only good he carried home from crusade was skill in battle. He long fought endless numbers of opponents, often many, ten at once, and prevailed. There be few skilled as he in the art, and he be ready to use it as it be true righteous cause this time. County news had him outraged. He would face any doing such harm, be sure of deeds they owned before drawing sword, but knew battle lay ahead. Having witnessed depravity such in many lands traveling home, the story rang true.

Building fire for warmth in cold night, he had camp ready. With mind full of worry he forced himself rest his thoughts as he fell deep in sleep.

One raven spied his camp from tall tree. Perched on a high branch, the black shadow watched his every move. He saw August testing the hone of sword and knife, then holding them as a man would in battle. Noticing both weapons be at his side for sleep, raven waited till man be still and quiet, then flew to tell of knight to ravens waiting on news. Once told, two conspirators joined him in flight. The birds, two, had been silent in wait, being none far away on tall tree having concern much of knight man. He would be assailed soon, three agree, yea, but certain man no would yield.

Stopping but once to feast on dead lamb, all pulled sinew and pecked red muscle. Scraggly one watching Knight man close pulled hard lamb's eye, showing it be prize after plucking. Nodding at other two, bird took flight. Lone eye be message for sleeping knight. Man knight to wake see eye staring, him knowing surely he be watched. Landing good distance from sleeping knight, bold, raven walked with nay sound to put eye on ground across from man, eye being to eye of knight who slept. It be tasty morsel parted with, but bird fret no, there be ever more such kill. Walking far distance with nay sound, bird took flight to join others. Circling over them, they flew to join in flight, deciding to perch on imposing berth along road man knight would travel. Landing, scraggly bird cawed at two other keep vigilant. They cawed in agreement, sleeping in turns on crumbling stone wall.

Suffering a night of disturbing dreams, wet with sweat from horrors filling his head, feeling their oppression even once awake, August woke seeing small eyeball staring at him. His hand headed to knife which lay at his side, only by instinct. Eye be no attached to living thing. Knowing it evil omen, it be put there such while he slept. Getting up, he looked for tracks in grass and dirt, seeing none. Quiet surrounded him, a morning new, he felt only wind and sensed it blew no good his way. His horse had his head low, at rest. The fire kept him warm and was still glowing, though only embers remained. He added dry twigs, igniting in flame to heat water for washing and tea. Leaving evil eye where it lay, he tended the fire then gathered his camp. None was amiss, but all around be most wrong.

Sitting on dry log, looking at broadsword, it be ready for use. Taking sheath from saddle, worked its laces, strapping sheath down his back. It be only weapon mighty kept from crusade and it served well — bad fortune for all he fell with blade. Few were men large or strong of muscle to wield such sword. Swung with fury, power built slicing through air downed any in its path. Sword cut men in half at waist. Heads flew like pebbles small. Limbs grasped at clouds in flight. Sword had reach near tall as most men; none survived its fury. Too long for belt, he wore blade down his back. In battle, he reached behind head, pulled sword, blade appearing to all foe as from nowhere. Having time none to think from where it came, its arc was the last vision foe would see.

Having armor or helmet none, he accepted he be unprotected from arrows. He doubted any archers left in villages. Skilled ones be called to battle years ago. He wore long knife at his side, his own before call to war. With armor none, battle was risk, but each day on Earth be risk for any. He accepted such, knowing well fear, in him if any, be only true enemy. He knew not if battle lay ahead. There may be errant knights or sheriff and deputies, but thought nay to all. All such no be likely warriors true so little concern. Any evil he thought wait ahead belonged only to cowards and fools. Nobles ne'er fought battles. Knaves and farm lads be handed that purpose, their lives worthless to all rich. Men, honest and true, be away, far, in battle or graves. None sure what he would face, he could only but ready himself for all, even if all be worst.

Finishing tea, dousing fire, leaving evil eye where it lay, he mounted steed and rode alert ever for dangers ahead. He could reach village by late afternoon but decided nay, ride slow, arrive at dusk. Dark time would be friend, allowing survey of village with attention hard given. Nodding it be good plan, slowing steed, he proceeded with travel slow. Ahead road be empty, fields wild and none tended. Twas sorry sight, yea, yet surprise none. He saw no farmers, no wagons, no travelers. It was as riding in troubling dream, having feeling all be most unreal.

Woke by dawn, same as knight, three ravens waited perched on crumbling wall. They true be bold deceivers; certain man knight would ne'er pay heed to such birds as they. Knowing all men and creatures die, they would have no breakfast hence yet be content, waiting patient, thinking him feast soon enough. Hearing knight riding near at pace slow, he seemed in hurry none to see his love. That be high importance. Riding slow, man be cautious. Knight no be easily surprised. He be smart one, they agreed with looks certain to each other. Though that may be, man knight no be smart enough to know their plan most cunning.

Riding past, he paid them no mind though they be fixed on his every movement. Having large knife on belt, they studied weapon, then mighty sword on back. It be long, wore askew to hang off saddle. It be weapon of war; he be warrior. He be large, well strong enough to wield it. He wore but clothes simple, but with muscles could no be hid. Skin, parts seen, covered with scars many. He rode with calm, nay hold reins, let large horse follow road, he be at ready to draw mighty sword.

Watching knight ride to village, they waited. Once he be away, ravens three cawed to each other, then flew high above knight such to be past with notice none. They saw much. There be none more to see. He be no coward. He be armed. He be at ready. He surely no be accepting what awaited him once he reach home.

Arrival

Feeling much like many dreadful moments before facing onslaught of enemy charge in war, there be only quiet and calm as he rode to his village. Nowhere were sounds of cart wheels, idle chatter in market, sounds of washing or cooking over crackling hearth. No smells of food in air or smoke from chimneys. No villagers about, visiting or on errands. He faced naught familiar. Nay, no such expected sounds, smells or movements. Being oppressive, he knew it all bad omen.

Silence broken when he reached first hovel at edge of village. Noise be cawing of ravens flying with menace above. Their ranting, disturbingly loud, only sound he heard. Looking at birds circling above while he watched, they turned, heading to parts north taking loud caws with them. All be silent once more, only sounds be his breathing and hoofs of steed below, slowly walking. Just turning dark, he hoped glow of candles or lamps in hovel windows, but saw none. He knew all in village had vanished, or perhaps he was still sleeping and all be frightful dream. Looking around him, he be sure he be awake, but knew there be evil about to make village such.

Pulling reins grasped tight in hands, he decided dismount and walk carefully through village. He knew not what he would encounter but even fearing worst, such would allow him peer in windows and doorways. Feeling such strange atmosphere, his horse be vexed, resisting lead. He understood steed, as himself, be keen battle-wise, alert to danger.

Seeming from nowhere, there came sound of hoofs, many, rapid in succession.

He considered noise belong to at least five horses, riding fast, all heading to him. Making quick work of right response, he mounted steed, ready to draw sword. Speed of riders told they had clear intent. Their purpose only be to address him. Years of warring taught him sounds of battle and aggression. There be no doubt what heard be none any villagers returning home.

Experience and instinct served him well. He saw horses and riders, five, approach from far end of village, galloping with haste to him. Led by one, four others flanked just behind, formation be leader with four to do his bidding. Five men approaching with mission bold upon but one lone man meant they be cowardly types, yea, needing strength of numbers. It could be nightly patrol, but pace being rapid was none that of observation, it be intent. He considered if they ride to confront him, how knew they his presence? He had no seen or encountered any on ride, nay, saw none at any distance.

Studying five riders now near, they true be rabble — vile in appearance and manner. Lead rider be in ancient finery none appropriate for riding. Sadder, leader had fancy-lad sword, small, hanging from gold belt. Flanking him were miscreants. Wearing worn peasant garb, two were heavy and slobbish, brandying ax, having assorted farm tools positioned as weapons. They be dirty, having sad look of ones pulled from lockup or cage. Other two be but lads, none more then twenty, skinny, proud, showing sneers and toothless grins. All enjoying power riding five against one offered. All four henchmen bandied common smithy swords at ready. One, clearly feeble of mind, had a large hammer hung on his saddle. They wore peasant ill-fitting cloth caps, having look of untamed drunkards spoiling for trouble. Wearing armor none, it be certain they be cowards happy striking down any they fancied just to feel power. They be no trained warriors. They be emboldened, yea, empowered by sheriff or lord to do no good.

No slowing pace as they neared, such showed arrogance and lack of battle skill. There be no doubt in August they ne'er engaged in battle true, possessing weakness of feeling invincible. He only needed draw sword, charge, then quell all in mere moment; then bodies be riding on with their mounts, heads on ground wondering what happened. Feeling urge mighty to do that very thing, he held fast, knowing they be only sad pawns in larger game he must know of. He would dispatch them after hearing words if such be their wish. He had no fear of them regardless what would come.

Sitting with concern none in middle of road, he be only quiet, looking, waiting. Giving reaction none, remaining still, he knew alarm none would confuse them. He knew it best play it through and learn their real intent if they had any knowledge worth the knowing.

Pulling hard at reins as they stopped gallop close upon him, air filled with dust from road and their foul stench. Leader man in foolish finery looked to either side making sure sad men be at ready. He tilted his head up, giving August long study. His expression be contempt. Finally, with manner superior, he spoke.

"What business have thee such? Ya be on Duke's road and have no business here."

August remained calm and mannered, holding reins and giving no clue to intent. He nodded slightly, studying their weapons and manner. He looked directly at the leader.

"Me business be my own. I be knight of king and do his bidding."

The five men chuckled and glanced at each other. The leader wore sneer on his face. He was sarcastic in response.

"Oh, knight of king? And, ya say, nay business but ya own? Well, knight of king, we see no king or knights here by ya side, and as ya ride Duke's road, ya business be his, none ya own."

Showing no reaction, August simply stared at fool man.

"Say ya, Duke, such, nay give respect ta knight on ride home?"

Again, chuckles and sneers. This time longer and louder.

"On his land, respect be given him. It matters no ya be knight as ya travel his road. Such privilege demands toll, which we be here to collect. Pay, and ya have his courtesy to travel on. If nay, ya have already used his road and be in debt to Duke, so again, pay toll. If no, then we shall arrest ya and ya pay toll with ya goods and gear, plus labor his land as payment for refusing his kindness."

August understood such tactics rose while good men were away. He had yet to encounter any arrogance such on his journey, surprised to find such in his home.

"This land be my home. I be titled land owner here. I be beholding to no duke, and pray ya stand down for ya be in my way."

Laughing harder than before, the leader looked at his men, then back to August. He shook his head and chuckled.

"It may be ya had title or land before ya left. That be no more. Ya have no land for Duke holds all title now. Ya land forfeit as ya long absent and ya return to nay land or title. Now, commoner, pay toll this moment while given such chance."

Sitting silent, August knew there be no reasoning with man. Testing him would reveal no more. He accepted he need dispatch crew and surely many more after them.

Remaining silent, showing no heed to demand, he watched as leader raised hand as command to henchman. They moved forward to encircle August which was all he expected and hoped they do such. Once in place, hands reaching for weak swords, leader nodded, remained ahead in front of August, staring at him.

"As ya offer no toll, we shall take ya prisoner to pay ya debt. Ya were…"

In a motion too swift to counter, August pulled broadsword from sheath on his back. In same motion he swung sword in wide circle round him to first strike two at his right, then without stopping struck the two on his left with but one mighty stroke. The sword be massive and long, easily reaching their necks, sending all four heads flying. The leader gave look of panic and fear, turning pony horse around as he saw heads fly, taking off at full gallop. August anticipated action such. After striking fourth henchman, he flicked reins of his horse and kicked ribs. It be challenge none to catch man wearing finery.

Knowing man coward, he deserved less consideration than his four headless henchmen. They had quick, easy deaths. August needed gain more account of matters, hence decided just strike him off horse, then ask questions knowing fool think he be shown mercy for answers. That be fool, indeed. Death be certain, answers or naught. August could only see fit send him join his men.

Riding upon man, fool attempted turn into field outside edge of village. Using mighty sword, dripping crimson with henchmen life blood, he swung at man. He cut swath through side of fool, causing him fly off saddle to ground. Having rider none, horse rode off, man lay on crushed barley with both hands trying hold bleeding side together. Blood pouring fierce from wound, August knew there be little time for questions. He dismounted, steed standing in place, then calmly walked to bleeding man. Pushing tip of mighty sword to touch man's throat, he gained attention.

"My toll, paid, yea, by my blade. If ya don't wish head in ya lap this instant, pay yours. Who be such duke ya defend?"

Shaking, clearly man feared his fate, but feared pain of violence from sword more. Gurgling, blood pouring from mouth, he uttered one name.

"Crowe…"

August knew of sad man. It be all he needed know or ask. Man, fancy leader, managed to look up at him. With words pathetic, he begged mercy.

Mounting his steed, August left fancy man sitting in the barley, arrogant head in his lap.

Troubling Tales

Turning back to village, he worried ever so. Twas where his intended lived, but no lived now. After meeting toll collectors, he feared what fate came to his love, pondering where she be. Traveling to village, he had been told by shop owner women be raped and all plundered. With no men of might such as he to defend any, villains now free to have evil way with maids and children. Passing by four heads scattered on road, he knew horses be smart ones of the lot. They be gone, surely taking headless bodies back to paddocks. He rode to small hovel where his love lived since birth, now empty, showing nay signs of living there for time long. Looking for signs or secrets left behind as message, there be none. Her clothes be there, all food and goods rotted in decay. He found small gathering of his letters in basket, tied with fine ribbon. All be from his first year away. More than else, bundle gave him pause. Blood surging hot through him, he felt intense rush, one such as comes in battle. Such surge grants power to strike, yet there be no enemy to strike at. Taking deep breaths, he knew it best leave and continue search. All of village be same; empty. If any lived there still, they could only be but ghosts of those struck down by same cowards he slew.

Having grown tired, he decided best rest and consider matters. His senses keen, he worried no should any approach. He be alert to them. Leading horse to abandoned barn, found decent oats, fed and tended fine animal, then lay in hay near him to sleep. Welcoming rest, he would need strength and be sharp of wit for the morrow. In short time he was asleep, having dreams most disturbing but none remembered when he woke.

Hungry, he found hens be left, so ate eggs raw to give strength until finding heartier fare. It be sunny day and he knew he could only face more battle. The first crew was naught but peasant fools. Heading to villainous Crowe, fights would grow fierce. He knew of the man. Like all cowards, Crowe would surround himself with many to protect him and do his fighting. He wondered what happened to allow villain such as Crowe domain over land and county, yet knowing he would learn soon enough. His mission first be find Kiera. He considered all he may do. Perhaps quick action finding her, taking her, being away, just leaving vile Crowe to his deeds. Shaking his head, he quieted such thoughts. Others be missing. He wanted no risk of battle riding away with her. He need end Crowe reign of terror, knowing then only would Kiera be safe. He hoped ever so he be done with bloodshed leaving crusades, but that no be his fate. On this day he had mortal fury driven by righteous cause, unlike in crusade. He would battle true villain for his love — and many others loved by knights dead or away in battle.

Once ready, he left village, passing headless fool sitting in barley with all finery now brown from blood soaked to cloth. Riding with caution, he surveyed all land ahead. Down road he saw lone figure pushing cart. It be older man, one he remembered, knowing him land owner who worked fields entire life. He had weapons none, looking only as one on way to tend crops. He be anxious to speak with him.

Riding to man offering greeting kind, man put cart handles down, looked all around, then gave August kind, though quiet, hello.

"Praise Jesus. I be glad ta see ya. It be long since men left to war. Ya be first back. Praise Jesus, I do say. Welcome. I hope ya remember me. Ol' Geoff. Land not far from ya own."

Smiling at man, he nodded, getting off horse.

"Of course I know ya. A fine harvest ya brought in each year, a kind wife and sweet daughter I be fond of. How be all?"

Geoff looked round fields. His face turned from glowing excitement to dire parlor. He shook his head, slowly.

"August, all be changed. Ya will soon learn such. When good men, them like ya, left to crusade, king command dukes govern all, to keep villages in his debt. He gave Crowe full charge of folk and land. That villain took charge, and yea, he took all. Farms, shops, all women. His miscreants do his wishes. He pays them no coin. Nay. Pays with maidens — even wee lassies. My missus, oh pray, oh, snatched and I no see her since. August, oh, it be hard ta tell ya. Same happened to ya sweet Kiera. All sweet maids. Took."

Geoff cried telling sad tale. August felt strong rush of blood in all veins from anger. He worried that all be so, but hard to hear put true. Putting hand on man's shoulder, he shared grief such. Trembling, man wiped at his tears, looking at August.

"Ya be but one. Be there more coming? Is holy battle done?"

Shaking his head, August told the man none followed, and expected few when any returned. He saw desperation in the man.

"Then be wary. That Crowe, fear him. I do. I be working land no more mine now. I nay be coward, so know this, and fear such. I be doin' so for fear he certain eat me wife an' lass for sup if nay I labor this plot. No, hear this certain. Nay, no jus' words. He feast on flesh, August. All here fear that fate. And… well, he be no sane. He be under spell. From wizard. From hell that wizard be. Hell!"

Knowing Crowe to always be but greedy noble, such news be surprise. All heard of sorcerers and wizards, but of times long gone. Dark arts all be long vanquished by church. Thinking, it made sense. Church blind, waging war on holy land, so nay vigilant of dark arts or such dangers now. He knew only art of slaying men, but none of slaying evil demons if there be sorcerer. All knew only dark tales from childhood; stories of magic and deception. If it be so, he was facing foe to be wary of. He recalled such tales thought only myths, none told as truth. The one spoke of may be but evil, a sinister voice in Crowe's ear. He prayed he have no powers beyond influence over errant duke.

"Geoff, be ya sure he be real sorcerer? Where came he from? Wizards and such, surely just tales told ta children."

Shaking again, Geoff had fear mighty on face. "So thought all. Just deceiver working Crowe. Aye. That be what all thought. Then, many a strange thing, they began. Dead crops. People screaming, terror taking them when no person be about. Children speaking of things none could know. Illness falling any oppose Crowe. Then, folk being cooks at castle, one day two be set free to tell all Crowe feasting on any oppose him. Some, oh, my Jesus, August, this be horror beyond any. Jesus where ya be? Oh mercy, two set free cooked own loved ones! Then, serving them on platter, watching Crowe and demon eat them… Then, to make all fear such fate, released ta tell all. That did us in. Now, I tend field lest I be sup!"

Geoff was in mortal fear, shaking next, falling to ground. Foam spewed from his mouth, his body in spasms. Eyes bulging, he grabbed at August and was able to say but one word.

"Run!"

Just as sudden, his spasms stopped. He lay dead. He only be corpse on ground in front of August, his finger pointing down road to leave county. Looking round him, August saw nothing. No person be near. Looking up, the carrion birds, black like night, circled expecting their next feast. August lifted Geoff, then put him in cart. He saw spade Geoff had there, took it, then with dead man tied behind saddle went to man's home and buried him.

Chamber Maiden

Looking out only small window in her chamber, Kiera saw three ravens swoop from high, entering through special hole in castle wall. Early that day, she saw all three ravens leave, heart sinking now seeing creatures return. Knowing them back, she moved from window to sit at table. Unlike others held captive in castle, she had small chamber to herself, locked. She be prisoner like many others. She thought castle cold and depressing, longing for her small hovel in village and, most, to be free. Her chamber had little comfort. Mattress filled with straw, small table, chair, oil lamp, basin, and pot. All walls bare, made of stone, but glad she be there was one small opening allowing her view of world. She left chamber only to serve perverse cravings of captor, now her master, Crowe. She be his pet. His slave. Her lot only to be submissive, obeying all commands given by master.

When thinking his name, seeing him, touched by him, acting on his desires perverse, all made her wretch and gasp though she could ne'er show reaction such. He issued relentless control over her, using fear and torture, all carnal, told it be for her pleasure. Effective, such, her fear so great she could do naught else but whatever he bid her do. Crowe, if human, still, be evil by nature. Bad he be to start, yet master grew perverse beyond all decency since she be taken, made pet now year times two.

She learned his sick ways be unleashed by alliance with unholy Avila, devil practitioner calling himself wizard. It be true the evil being had powers, but none be magic. He practiced dark art, obeying debauchery of devil. Avila arrived with Immunditia, a she-demon. Covered with markings made from ink cut in skin, she be near black, covered full in all places with sick symbols, images of fornication, and on her back be inking of giant tree with leaves no. Beyond all any could devise, it twas penis tree. Members, hundreds, hanging where leaves should be. Shocking in mantle with flaming red hair, she wore clothing none, spending much time fornicating, giving sleek body to men from village seized to feed her hunger, bringing them to state of such bizarre fornication they dropped dead, drained of life force. When Crowe and Avila sat court, she often be bold kneeling before them, serving them with mouth being unholy pleasure while they talked.

Avila commanded Immunditia be her tutor, thus taught her perverse acts to please Crowe. Dreading each lesson, Kiera learned ne'er to deny or complain. Immunditia had no hesitation causing all manners of insidious harm if she be no obeyed. She enjoyed inflicting pain, needed no help from guards to do such torture. Her method be most effective. Wanting no objection, she put a wooden globe in Kiera's mouth, no allowing words or screams. It had leather strap put through, globe filling her mouth, impossible to spit out yet tied around head to be certain it stayed. Once ball in mouth be, Immunditia had leather cover for eyes. During first weeks of lessons, being none able to see what may be done next was most frightening thing of such torture.

Immunditia smiled as she slapped her using gloved hands or leather lash. Other times she melted hot wax from candle onto her breasts and back. She enjoyed most suspending Kiera in air, binding her hands and feet to pulley on ceiling, leaving her hang for countless hours. Worst torture was being hung upside down while Immunditia would lick and kiss her most private parts, growing excited doing so. Kiera be pet and prize for Crowe, thus all done without leaving slightest mark on her body. Done for so long, her body used to torture such, all prepared her for obscene acts Crowe had Immunditia ready her for.

Immunditia removed all clothing from room, leaving her naked but for leather collar with triple ring. Told ring be nay different than if she be barn animal, Immunditia say new wear waited her. Thinking it be some covering, nay, it be leather cuffs with rings for wrists and ankles. Standing in chamber, ever naked, only bindings for wear. An older woman came each day, arranging her hair up and off face and shoulders. She bathed her and shaved all hair from body, making her feel more naked than only with nay clothes. All meals be small portions, vegetables, making her thin with no fat. There be no mirror, she being glad she could no see what she looked like for her master. She knew he be master of nothing but depravity, but master was what she be told call him always if she valued her life.

Once Immunditia thought her properly trained for carnal torture, one night Immunditia came for her, saying master waited on her. She brought chain, having handle to hold, clamp on end other. Immunditia smiled, admiring it, saying it be beautiful leash. Kiera, slave, must wear it evermore when leaving room. Telling her to follow, she clamped leash to collar, leading her to Crowe's chamber. Kiera needed but one tug from chain to know follow near without fight. Pull of leash be harsh reminder she be no more than pet, same as any hound in favor, one led by leash wearing collar on neck.

Reaching Crowe's chamber, Immunditia stopped, stood before it and hung leash handle on hook outside. She blew at the door, then heavy thing opened from her breath and naught other. Immunditia's smiled at her, turned, then walked away. Crying with fear, Kiera saw Crowe emerge from shadows of dark room, hand taking handle from hook, tugging it hard. Pulling her inside, chambers dimly lit, she saw room lined with fur skins on floor, burdened with grotesque stuffed birds hanging above. Most dreadful was large bed with posts on each corner, chains and cuffs hanging from each. It be place of torture and perversion beyond all she feared. Crowe, wearing strange garb made of black feathers, looking much as the dead birds above her, wore mask with orange beak. The sight of him thus made her wretch though she hid all spasms as he lit black candles then walked around her many times. Looking at her, intensely, asking her to bend fully over, rubbing her every part, putting his fingers in her while making a squealing noise much same as pigs made running for slop. It be worse than any nightmare, beyond all fears.

Finishing painful inspection of her every part, he went to table and retrieved silver goblet. Handing it to her, telling her drink all, she could naught but obey though fearful he would drink same, letting strong spirits make him more vile. Drinking with caution, it be bitter tasting wine. He remained fully covered in bird feathers. Finishing her wine, he stood holding his chin, staring at her which was worse than his probing. After time long, taking wine cup from her, he put cup on table then ordered her disrobe him. Having trouble finding seams behind feathers, it seemed as if he wore nothing, feathers being part of him. Pulling at feathers and chains he wore, her master started changing before her, becoming different sizes and shapes. Colors all ever changing. She could no understand all happening as nothing was normal. The world became strange in all ways, all things different, yea, alive. Her master be floating, seemed to be liquid, then transparent, or made of stone. All about him swirling, all changing, she felt her own form doing same. She became sleek black cat, crawling round him as cats do such hunting birds. Pawing at master to free him of garments, she purred, being panther pet, seeing giant bird now be fire, but burned her paws no. His arms became but feathered wings, his voice loud caw from orange beak, his screech echoed and sounded as if musical instrument. His words plain yet making no sense. Grooming him by licking paws then rubbing him clean, the last she remembered was him flying round the room. Black as spade, cawing at her. He be raven.

Guard

Having buried Geoff, knowing Crowe influenced by master of dark arts, August accepted fate of his love be more than captive. Such dark practitioners used maids as tribute to Satan, intended for rituals of human sacrifice to dark lord. Gasping at realization such, he knew he be fool when warring in Jerusalem when such true insult to Christ lurked in his own village. The dark one sent all good men away for folly, claiming maids pure and chaste. Devious he be, having good men away killing each other thinking it righteous. The enormity of how demon cast evil overwhelmed him. Knowing such thoughts best saved for later, his attention needed center on thwart of evil duke and demon enchanter. He be no priest, knew little of such matters, but certain of one thought. Be they flesh and blood, his sword would care no if they be devoted to Satan. Sliced in two, tricks and spells, none be much use without living body. He would wage his own crusade against real evil. It would truly be holy war.

Back on steed, he worried no of surroundings. He had but one destination, one purpose to address all worries. Dispatched to hell, Crowe and demon would have power none over people and village. His mission be simple.

Ride to keep, cut down any try stop him, enter, slay oppressors. Twas then he understood years in crusade taught him killing skills, thus giving him confidence to do God's will. He be training for this battle since first blow he struck against those red-robes called heathens, and he be ready.

Having all matters straight in mind, riding forth, he saw first challenge waiting in middle of road not far ahead. A man, seeming same in size and shape as raging bull standing upright be waiting for him. Massive and brute, bold henchman ha large ax in each hand, ax be ones used only for beheadings. Bold with one in each hand, two death givers be crossed in front of him. He wore skin from bull's head over his own, animal dead eyes still in place as be large horns. Bull man had body bulging with muscles, dead bull hide giving him massive berth and fearful countenance. He had full beard, eyes in shade from headpiece covering much his face. Bull man stood brazen, defiant, certain of his might for he be guarding road to castle. August realized Crowe knew of his arrival, though he knew not how.

Facing adversaries in such guises times many, all be intent on intimidating any in battle. August knew hesitation only folly. Giving brute time to lift heavy axes would be disaster. Bull man reveled in guise, waiting on direct contact to win with might and muscle. Knowing such method, August had no plan of riding into arc of swinging ax. Choosing not to draw sword, he continued normal pace and approached bull man. Having one hand on reins for villain to see, his other, hidden, held trusted long knife by blade. Expert at throwing knife great distances with dead accuracy, he saw man wore no armor. Task be simple. He need only throw knife swift and true. If brute saw blade coming, no matter, he would have time no to raise axes and deflect hurtling blade.

But twenty paces between them, eyes staring at target, August watched bull man grasp tight each ax handle, locking on them. Without warning, August threw knife true, so fast it be impossible to see in flight. Knife landed fully center in bull man throat, so powerful it cut clean through to spine under skull, severing it. The brute collapsed and could no move. Axes at sides, blood spurting from throat, dark eyes in death stare, August made certain of matters. Taking one ax, raising it high, then striking down with full force letting it split bull face to two halves. It was gruesome, but nothing worse than he had seen done to knights. When those losing battle lay injured, victors went about taking pleasure finding ever sicker ways to finish life. Skinned, impaled, quartered, roasted, wrapped in entrails, scalded, crushed, beheaded with small, slow, dull knives. All were common fates waiting any foolish enough to be wounded, laying such begging for mercy. Mercy never be part of holy war. Warriors killed or were killed. No victor cared for wounded men. None was victory if finished with mercy leaving any living warrior to pray. He knew bull man no warrior. He just be large and, yea, had been executioner. A cowardly post. Killing with nay threat be killed. That be why bull man be useless as guard. A warrior true would anticipate knife and have armor. The fool far better off in Hades where all such cowards be once dead.

Looking back to where he buried Geoff, he nodded, saying righteous kill was in his stead. Getting back on horse, he feared no opposition ahead. He faced no true foe thus far. If any wait ahead, he hoped it be human. Mortal, like dead guard. Demons and wizards were not ones he knew from battle. Smiling as he thought it through, he reminded himself that if flesh, they would bleed.

Summons

Having seen three crows return, Kiera knew Crowe, Immunditia and Avila, back in human form, were angered. She sensed dark matters at hand. Just growing dark, she be always at master's service each dusk, head between his legs as court ended with all visitors seeing his pet and her servitude. This day, she be nay called and though glad to no be displayed so, it worried her. Their flight, caws screeched coming back, no having pet at court — all be sign trouble be about. A frightful hour past her normal calling, Immunditia appeared at door, but with leash no in hand. Looking at Kiera in serious manner she told her only but follow.

As they walked, two stout guards appeared, walking but two paces behind them. They kept pace into court where her master sat on tufted chair, Avila lurking off to side in shadows. Their gazes intent on her, making her worry, having no idea why. Avila told her her not to service her master. He bid her stand before Crowe, answer him true. Nodding, she felt cold and fearful. Crowe looked at her for long while, then spoke with quiet manner.

"Immunditia tells us your belly grows round. Uh assume ya have noticed such?"

Kiera had, and nodded.

"Immunditia tells us, also, that be my child there. My prodigy, for ya had no other in ya. We all pray you had no other in you, that be so?'

Again, she could only move her head in fear, this time moving it side-to-side to indicate no, there be no others.

"Even so, and uh do grant ya say truth, pretty pet, there be other who wants ya. No, nay as sweet pet as master does, but bride. Do ya know any such?"

If she had learned any as slave, it be his questions were nay questions. He asked only when he knew answers. She could only but say that which he already knew.

"Master, ya be kind ta me, and understanding of men, yea, I be sure. Yea, long ago I be long betrothed, that be true. Before here. That be only man who would want me. But, master, what of such? I know no of him. Ha left to Crusade, abandoning your pet, gone year times three."

Crowe looked at his two evil counsels, then back at her.

"Use ya head ta think, no just ta bob up and down on my lap this one time. I know ya be disappointed of no doing so this day, but pray, imagine man surviving all battles, returning ta home. If that be, would man venture forth to find ya? Ta claim maiden fair?"

His suggestion stirred fire inside her. She knew her love must be back, searching for her. There could be no reason other for questions such. She stood, wide-eyed, knowing not what best to say. He grew dark in tone, sitting, staring, vile, waiting.

"Your master asked ya plain. If back love be, would he be bold to claim pet?"

She caught his meaning. It was a trap. She be glad she waited a reply.

"Surely, ha would wish me, want foolish maid he left long ago."

He nodded, face forming sick grin.

"And if, perchance, he be so bold ta make it through doors behind ya, bade ya go with him, what would happen?"

She be prepared for such trick.

"Nothing. I no be his. I be yours."

Tilting his head down, he chuckled.

"Oh, what well-trained pet ya be! Immunditia groomed ya well. It be only what ya could say ta save ya own life… and his. I be no twit. I know it be what ya must tell me. But, I know well it no be what ya truly want if that were to pass. Avila, what say ya? Is yon pet servicing me with pretend words same she services me bodkin with that sweet mouth? Lies, none true?"

Arms folded, Avila shrugged.

"No sight be needed for this truth. Her heart hurts hearing such mention. But, as ya say, she be taught well by master of such art. Pet be knowing to no surrender to maiden passion. Filled with ya child, such attempt would damn her, and knight, and thy child in belly. So, tha' be true. Pet told ya true. Nay, she no would run to him…"

Crowe nodded, satisfied at his dominance, knowing himself ever strong. Avila held up hand, having more to say.

"Where dark lord offers his gracious power to help, he grants me knowing deeper truth. Pet be thinking it no question to ask, having sinister reason, sadly, more insulting to ya. Her real mind be thinking knight, learning ya spoiled her virtue, taken maid in the manner ya have, that righteous knight would nay want maid now. Nay, pet knows same truth knight will know. She be made filth by ya being inside her, allowing ya seed ta grow in her, such. True maid would take own life an' no be worthy of ya. Pet be certain she be unclean by you. Defiled. Filth. No worthy of knight, thus."

Crowe rose with fury, filled with rage. He went to to her, seething, snarling.

"Is that your mind? Tell master. Now!"

Feeling a calm inside… the first since enslaved, she nodded gently, head moving slowly up and down, staring into his eyes.

Turning to face Avila, he intended to ask the most hideous and painful torture to use before he killed pet, then stopped, having new thought. He looked at his evil counsel.

"Wizard. There be worse pains than those but only to flesh. I wish pet watch her true love suffer. Be splashed with his spit and blood. I want knight ta watch me fill her her every hole with my might, me juice flooding out bitch, knowing he will no have bitch, yea, and I do. Show true she craves me, no knight. Hear bitch obey me, do me wish. Crawl to me. Have him watch her mouth swallow my cock. Pull hard on leash, parade bitch in front of him. They will suffer. Each shall have true pain only fools in love feel. Then, oh, this be sweet stuff, pet will tell she bears my child, no his. Knight may be of might, but he be fool. Dark lord, Avila, fool never had bitch before ha left. Maiden virtue! How pathetic. It be me life in her. She remains my pet. This be my revenge. She has one master. No God. No knight. Crowe! Immunditia! Prepare bitch. For all ahead, have ya black knife at ready. If pet disobeys my wish, say no words, stick her! Stick her and hear her cry for my mercy. That be grand spasm it give ya, if so foolish she be. Better than any spasms with countless other bitches ya sent to hell."

Visage

Looking up, August saw three ravens circling above, same as day prior. Certain they be same birds, he knew them bold to follow thus. Soon they would feast as he be true giver of dead fools now but carrion. Doubting any to come bury fool men he downed, left as carrion, raven sup, appropriate reward for service unholy. Their choice be vile, thus be what send them down scavenger bird gullets.

Recalling fields of battle, hot desert sun roasting dead warriors, there be more kinds of scavenger birds imagined possible. Birds of prey, feasting on living creatures, be many in shape and size. Buzzards, hawks, eagles, owls, vultures and ones he knew not names of. All fond of woodland or desert creatures. Having talons to grab prey, all knew fly away with meal. Raven be foul bird most pleased feasting on dead flesh, letting nature or others do killing, raven waiting for rotting scraps left laying. Thinking how ravens sought no fight, he thought them most cowardly. Raven be no bird of prey. It feasts on death, ne'er seeking food from own victory in battle. He recalled sad duty between battles, writing families of men dead in battle under his command. He could ne'er tell loved ones lads bones be picked clean by ravens. He could but write young lad fought brave for God, true be with Him now.

Flying boldly, near, he wished for arrows to pluck ravens from sky. He knew them cagey, smart creatures, some imitating words. Looking back, road rife with corpses, if smart they were, there be rotting flesh behind him. That be plain to see yet they held fascination for him only. Deciding best to ignore birds, he rode on.

Leaving steed follow road ahead, he be suddenly weary though well rested. There be reason no for such exhaustion. Letting head drop to rest eyes for while short, he thought it right to first offer prayer for those he killed, then prayer of finding Kiera. Feeling steed stop, unexpectedly, something be amiss. His horse be alert, as he, all times to warnings or threats. Opening eyes, ahead be fallen tree near road, hidden none in tall grass. Sitting on log be woman, looking to him only, patient in waiting. She had weapon no, sat hands at sides, both resting on tree, and she be alone. There be no horse or cart about. With clear view of road ahead, surveying it well before his brief prayer, he had seen fallen log, but no woman there or anywhere near. It be as if she appeared from but air. He be no alarmed, but none sure how woman appeared without notice.

Looking, she was none he knew from village or county. Her countenance be none like any woman seen by him any place other. She be perfect to his mind. Tall, thin, fully woman yet still lass. Breasts small but perfect shape, skin, aye, most fair. She wore but slight garment, light as air, thin so it surely be gossamer wisp of nothing, lovely as it blew gently in wind, following lovely form, revealing plain all beauty under as she be naked to eyes. Marveling at vision of body none hidden by dress, gossamer be most clear as if water floating about her. Her hair, softest brown he e'er see, moving as only rays of light can do. Flowing long, locks too followed wind. Her face, beyond his knowing of beauty. Eyes loving, he be certain eyes change color with each blink as he stared into them. Her cheekbones high, her lips soft and smiling, she waited on him with gentle grace. She had nay bodice or maiden finery under gossamer. Her feet with no sandals nor lacing. Her head tilt slightly, causing elation in him as she be looking at him only, pure with affection and understanding. He ne'er saw any like her. He be mystified, entranced, thus finding himself taken, fully aroused as man, yet only of seeing her, such.

In awe, stunned by her every breath and move, he be transfixed; he could no look away. Knowing he but have gaze for her only, yet knew it take time forever to know beauty such. He be elated, yet at peace. At that moment, he understood her more than mortal. Thanking God for her, she nodded, most kind, then spoke his name with voice gentle, filled with love. Hearing call to him, saying his name, he be beyond ken as her lips moved no. Her voice, no voice, hers, be in his mind. Sweet voice be call. Realizing such, his eyes opened wider, knowing true blessing from God she be. She sat, content, smiling at him, nodding her head, patting place on log next to her.

"August. Come."

Her voice, sweet and clear in his mind, calling to him, had him floating above horse, such movement be wonderful felt. Off horse, then on feet, he walked calmly to log, feeling loved ever so, wanted as ne'er before in life. Reaching log, she patted it, smiling, gazing into his eyes. Seeing her close, he stopped to fathom truth. She be made of stuff magic, only light. She radiated like brightest star of night. Feeling glow, it gave comfort and joy. He could no stop looking in her eyes, yet managed to get on log, sitting next to her, close as touch. Once at her side, she lifted one hand, put hand

on his cheek, rubbing there. Ne'er had he felt such wonder and it be e'er more than mere touch. Filling him, aware she be in him, giving him all love she possessed. All fears left. She nodded, understanding how all felt. Taking her other hand, putting it on his cheek other, she leaned forward then kissed him, blue green gray purple rainbow eyes still looking in his. With kiss, he could no be sure what happened, but all about changed to light. He was, as she, the stuff of stars.

Keeping sweet mouth on his, she took both hands from his cheeks, then began rubbing her hands on his many wounds. Each scar she touched healed, all aches vanished. Her mouth be all he could feel. No pain. No wounds. Gone. Her open mouth was sweet, yea, wet with passion, filling him with grace. He be filled with more than nectar delicious from sweet mouth. He be filled with knowing only he could exist such, having sweet mouth on his for all time. Her kiss, her love, her being. Those be all that mattered hence.

None pulling lips from his, she gently put both his hands in hers, then moved hands about o'er her body. All thoughts left his mind. All he be was how she felt to touch. She be but cloud, yet be of form he could embrace. Guiding hands o'er her every place, it be spiritual journey. He be in flight, sailing o'er mountains and fields into lovely valleys. There be no beginning, no end, no destination. She be his only home, the only place he could e'er be.

That moment, reaching such enlightened state, she took his left hand, put hand on her chest, nodding yea, yet ne'er moving her head. She pressed his hand into her, hand going inside her, gently down beyond her soft breast. He entered, be inside her, then realized he be holding her heart, feeling it beat. With him holding her so, caressing her heart, she took her other hand, one rubbing his cheek, then let it move to his chest, reaching into him, then, holding his heart. Her eyes gently opened and closed, her words came, filling his head.

"Dearest August. This sweet dream give ya this heart, ya grace me with thine. Dream I be certain tis mystery, but worry, no. Ya be in me, I be in you. Safe we be. Wanted. Loved. Cherished. Blessed. This be what all dream of, but hark, this be nay dream for ya, August. Feel me. Oh, yea, feel me such ya do this moment. Know this true. Look at this dream ya hold. Know I be only flower. Ya be glorious garden. I blossom in ya. Ya be me heart, and dear one, I be heart of ya, yea, ever true."

Moving hand inside her, she guided his hand down to places most sacred. He caressed her from inside, understanding only immense beauty of each part touched. She gently moved her lips from his, pressing her cheek to his. She prayed him hug her. His hand slowly moved from inside her, hers from inside him. Sitting in full embrace, both again full in form, he hugged her tight, feeling her breathe. He felt the heart he had caressed beating ever so from his embrace. No knowing how long they held each other such, it mattered no. Holding her be all there be; all there would e'er be hence.

In time, she whispered her arms down his sides, then showed her face in front of his. Her beauty ne'er ceased. Beauty such overwhelmed him, again, again, new, ne'er seen before. At first touch he understood she be ne'er of mortal world, only but true Angel of Heaven. He understood only he died. She be there to take him from sad place mortals suffer. Thinking thus, she knew his mind, smiled ever so sweet in understanding, then kissed him soft, again, many times more. All be but simple touch of sweet lips to his. Affectionate, and certain in loving.

"Dear heart, nay. Ya have no left ya mortal coil, yet. Ya be now as ya have been. I have longed to embrace ya kind heart an' have done such this day, and oh, most yea, for ya to embrace mine. Me heart an' me love, yea, they wait for ya in yonder home. Home, oh, it waits and longs for our love, know ya that. I can hold ya this day as ya be in place most special. Aye, ya true be living, and aye, ya true be dead. Here, and beyond. Man, and spirit. Both. If ya be only but man, I could no be one this way. This Angel has touched and embraced ya this day to help ya be what ya truly be. My man, my spirit, my love. Ya have awe in ya eyes. Tha' it be. I showered divine understanding on ya. It be wonder, I well know. Oh! Joyous I be, most yea, for I feel tha' joy in thee. My love, tell me true, do ya wish be knowin' more?"

She smiled, knowing his feelings and mind. All said be sense, but he could no fathom how such came to be. What point be there more? Living, oh, such be only suffering and pain. What be holding him from her, and Heaven?

Kissing him again, this time long with intense passion most certain, she then leaned back, sighing breath such it blew through him, him to feel sadness of sigh. Looking over her shoulder to castle keep, then she be looking back into his eyes.

"This wonder, this joy, this love tha' be me, it awaits ya. My love be yours, oh, too much I can no wait, no, nay forever. Know ya this, kind heart. Ya be blessed of special gift, for ya be true, an' most yea, good. Father, oh, such, gave His light. Light shine on ya hoping ya finish tha' which ya stood true for. Ya be one to end such pain brought to this lonely place by hurt of sad, fallen child. He who causes all suffering. This land, here, around us, be under his dark cloud. Oh, he bring all only sadness. Glorious love of Father, oh, denied all here. Nay, no never, tha' can no be so. All here suffer. Know this. There be one suffers most, yet be one who deserves such suffering least. Kiera, one chosen, has sad burden to placate dark minion of fallen child here until ya come back. Angels, know this now and e'er more, we can only but watch, forbid to meddle, oh nay, ne'er change such fate. Father gave all divinity such as He has. Thy will, free. His Angels can never, nay, never, be in way of will. These be sad times, true, for dark, fallen child denies His love. Kiera, all souls here, they long only ta be free in will. Dark fallen child, oh, yea, darkest child denies them most precious gift from Father. Tha' be true woe. Then, this be for ya this day. Only decent one, true, free in will, may choose change such course. August! Tha' be why ya still be of body, thus free ta choose do such. And, yea, ya be spirit too, here, inside me. Oh, August, be knowing! Here, inside me, forever, an' soon! Ah, tha' joy be ahead. A full being, us, one heart, oh, yea, tha' be what waits us both. Oh, my light an' love, such joy has nay description. Joy be no words, joy, ya know, joy only be felt. Beyond what any hope be described in scribbles or songs. Still bound ta body for now, ya may choose. Know this well. If ya decide so, ya may ride both roads this very day."

August was understanding, but still not knowing how it came to be. She nodded.

"It had ta be so. Ya chose ta strike down those ya once thought demon only as demons with red robes tell ya those be demon, ne'er of ya free will. That be done, sad be, and shall be again. Doin' battle such allowed me ta embrace ya, here, as we have done. Close ya eyes. I reveal answer. Good. Now, open eyes. Ya be ready for knowing."

Opening eyes, he stood holding her hand, outside Jerusalem, on palace terrace overlooking battlefield. Looking at battle most familiar, then at her, she nodded, then turned to look at battle.

"Oh. Love mine, look. This be gift ya be given. Father, I thank Ya with all I be for this day. August, ya know day well. It be day ya road home. Ah, heart, look at ya! Ya might. Oh, most certain I say yea. Ya strength. Ya knowin' most certain red-garbed war ne'er be for Father or His will. Ya knew it be only for demon. Most certain, ya knew. There, look. Both legions led only by Father's wayward lost child, Lucifer. There but no seen for he be coward. Ya chose ta leave, yea, knowing war jus' sin of man. Hark, this be moment most beautiful… Oh, sweet heart, watch. There. Oh, glory! Ya be run through by ne'er-seen blade. It had aim true for it fell ya. Yea, we be there. Tis tha' very day. Heaven knows nay thing ya call time. Ya died. Only dust ya be then, but wait. Look! Oh, glory. Ya rise, walk away, none about thee movin' ta harm ya. August, ones such as ya be gifted. Die, an' come back bein' as if ne'er left. There be more ta do. Ya left tha' land of sin, going home as it called out ta ya. Ya be back ta do right. Look at what ya be. Glorious! Living, and dead. Both. Ya shall come to my sweet lips when all be done. It will no be long. Now, smile at ya love, an' gently close ya eyes."

Closing them, she then softly kissed them, then told open again. They be back on log. Understanding he died, he be still of body to fight sick servants of fallen child. Once done, he need only lay down to return his dust to earth. She nodded with sweet smile.

"There. Ya be knowing… understanding all, an' tha' be good, ya be most blessed. Dark minions, those follow errant child, those sad ones have mighty plans for ya. They know ya be back from battle an' fear ya. They plan ta place Kiera between knight and righteous choice. Seeking ta change ya will. Oh, I am going to bless ya with Father's love, giving peace to thy mantle, oh, it be joy ta spite such evil. It be right and just. Ya choice nay lay ahead, no, it be done. It be made day ya died then returned. All love I give shall keep ya free from their sad plans, most dark, most evil. I shall kiss ya, love, once more this day, and my kiss be only my love. When lips part, I be no seen for wee time, and ya shall but remember sweet mouth on ya as dream, but only for now. Oh, nod yea. I know e'er truc uh I be dream far beyond any! Tha' be so, and jus' what be. When ya lay down ya bold, mighty sword, soon, I shall be there. Then, we walk home together. I will be with ya. My hand holding yours, my dream, I must say, true it be, evermore."

Rising in air, her gossamer dissolved, her body all beauty could e'er be. Circling round and round, showing what true beauty waited, she smiled such understanding. Being all any could want, she was all any could imagine. She, flower of Heaven, light of the Way. Angel of Holy Ghost. Blessed of Father. Stopping, facing him, her arms open in welcome, she filled his mind with peace. She moved to him, then using only gentle breath, hushed his eyes, then they closed.

Sitting straight up in his saddle, August shook himself to be sure he be awake. It was foolish to rest his eyes and doze off in land of such evil.

Plans

"Ya saw him. Ya be new to this domain with much to learn. Being corrupt and without light does no compare to knowing. Ya be only possessed by master. Do no dare step past little ya know."

Avila was somber, certain corrupt Crowe making mistake. Blind arrogance kept duke from knowing things as they be. Avila stood holding tall staff while Immunditia waited back, watching events unfold. Both she and demon wizard nay wish displease dark one. Both knew knight cast peril upon pathetic duke, peril fool could no understand. Crowe looked at the two and sneered.

"Yuh dare tell me what I know? Ya forget ya be in my service. I sold my soul and lord gave me ya both ta do my bidding. Deal be made certain. Bargain of the dark one. In it be ya servitude. My dominion, here. My slut pet. All maidens fair and other. And, know ya this, master o'er ya two village Faire puppets. No decent bargain, I tell ya that! And knight? Yea. I saw him. Same ya saw on flight. Mad! Talking ta himself on dead tree. Hugging air! Such knight be insane. And be easy kill. My only reason ta wait on him is ta torture bitch into full submission. Bitch pet needs understand it be she I be repulsed by, yea, for bitch had touched mad knight."

Looking at Immunditia, Avila squinted and knew she agreed Crowe be fool. He turned to Crowe, changing tact.

"I was sent to advise ya, yea, teach his dark ways. As Immunditia taught the pet, I teach ya. Now, all saw knight, talking ta air. I understand. It be good reason think him mad. When ya made the bargain with our dark lord, ya had guards present. So, answer me this. Did they run, insane, seeing devil?"

Crowe stopped, thinking of the matter. Slowly, he recalled his guards just looked at him strangely. Avila had point worth noting.

"Nay. No. I never thought of it. Nay. None showed fear. In such presence I would expect men flee in terror. True. Nay. They but looked at me and had looks to each other. Yea. Oh, yea. I do understand. I could see master, yet they could no see dark lord. Oh. Yea again. Do ya mean knight be making such bargain? Oh, that be worry!"

Avila nodded with mock admiration.

"That be why I be here. Ta enlighten ya. Yea, knight spoke to one no of earth, but sadly, nay, no our master. His tongue wagged ta Father's most precious servant. Angel."

Crowe looked at him with shock and disbelief. He stared, thought of such news, then understood.

"Mistake tha' mus' be! Man be more than mere knight? Have powers we know none of? Heavenly powers? Nay. Ya must be wrong. If so, I worry no. Ya job be protect me. That be bargain!"

Avila turned to smile at Immunditia. She smiled back and nodded. Avila turned, looked stern at foolish duke.

"Crowe, we be no here ta protect. We be here only ta teach darkness. Teach ya ta take shapes as ya do when we be ravens. Ta advise. Teach. Ya battles be ya own, just as bargain made purest maiden be slave to ya perversions. Dark lord fulfilled all bargained for. Tha' knight, oh, yea, knight will come. He be on way. Ya have rabble with weapons. This fortress strong. Ya can shape to raven an' fly away if he gets near. Tell me it be no so. Never! Crowe, worried?"

Snarling, Crowe was livid. He was not going to lose his soul only to have some knight usurp him such.

"I be no afraid of any, both ya included. I demand meeting with dark lord. This be no bargain. I need speak of such. Call him ta my presence."

Avila and Immunditia laughed, near hysterics. Crowe jumped to strike them. Avila swung long staff, striking him down without touching him, sending him flying across room. Immunditia jumped same distance in leap, landing at side, black knife pressed against his throat. Avila walked to him, stood in threatening manner, towering above duke.

"Oh, another helping lesson for duke. Know this. Now, fool! Hear it true. Ya demand nothing from dark one. Deal be done. Struck. There be no more ta say. He may giggle, or, perchance, laugh at ya when ya join him in hell. Worry no. Hell be soon if tha' knight gets ya. Now, lesson next. Ne'er tell Immunditia nor ma what ta do, ever. Hear ma clear. Never! We watch property of master. Just as slut be ya property, ya be his. Ya be his bitch. His little, ah, what be ya name for slut? Oh, yea, you be his wee pet. Da ya need ring on ya cock for Immunditia ta put ya on leash?"

Both turned, leaving Crowe with truth of bargain.

In panic, he began obsessing on knight. He knew he must destroy him. Show all who he was. He be no bitch, no to any. Nay, none to Satan. Nay, never. He be Duke. All must cower before him. He be no bitch. No pet. He would stay course. Honor only his pledge; teach slut he be only master.

Birds

Shivering, overwhelmed with shame, Kiera prayed August be away, let sick duke do what evil he wished with her, keeping August from him. She be lost, damned, doomed. She chose sin to stay alive, offending God with acts of perversion. She knelt on hard stone floor of pet chamber, knowing only she sinner be. Accepting hard truth, she had choice, always. Honor God, or, honor Crowe. Or Immunditia. Knowing her choice being life mortal, God would no welcome her spirit, she true be naked slut on leash, demon ruling her, knowing she be craving him. Praying to him. Worshiping him. Yea, she be fool and lied in mind, pretending all desire be only words to stay alive, ne'er worship or prayer true, but said it was. And, o'er time, truth. All such be mortal sin. Worshiping false god. Words tha' be only for true God. In death, there be no Heaven waiting. Nay, never, no more. It be fire and darkness to come.

She be one succumbing to evil and fornication whilst other maids died. She be living. Her good man fought holy war to serve God, now fighting to save her. Should he battle path to Crowe, she could only say Crowe be her master, she craved duke, no knight. That she must say to save him. He must walk away, leaving her face shame and sorrow. She must deny. She be no worthy of saving or love. She be what she had become. Demon's bitch. His toy to flaunt. To believe he be such good master, she, maiden fairest, choose be slut, true only to him. No. August cold no save her. There be naught but slut on knees in front of all, in collar, her leash in Crowe's hand, his sad shriveled cock in her mouth. That no be maiden knight e'er could love. There be no maiden left to save.

Sobbing, she knew no how to reach August, to tell she be beyond saving. Crowe held her with dark power. Shuddering with such truth, she could only admit she truly be his slave. Flooded with guilt, she knew horrible truth. Secret only inside her. Many were times she thought him kind if he used her name or approving her acts to serve his lust. She sunk low, craving his attention. Her need for his eye or approval be sign true she wished please him. Such be what slaves do. Crave approval from master. Please. Center all being on his joy, no that of Father's love.

Ne'er expecting to be called on darkest day, she shook with terror hearing door unlocked. Looking up, knowing she look pathetic from sobbing, there stood Immunditia. Kiera huddled in fear as she entered.

"Get off floor, bitch. Be ya stupid as ya look in tha' collar? Ya don' have clue, do ya, wench? Do ya know what I be? Me think ya should by now."

Kiera made it onto chair, knowing to study question quick. Immunditia had league to stab her if resisted any. She realized her death could save her knight. She must enrage dark demon servant.

"Ya be demon bitch from hell."

Against the black ink covering her face, Immunditia's white smile was revealed for first time.

"Amazing. Ya have wee bit smarts after all. Tha' be so. Uh be evil bitch, and yea, uh do devil's bidding. Uh do love my work. I loved turning ya, fool virgin maid, to pathetic cock hole. That I did, yea, quite well. But, ya be just three holes, no much more. All bitches have 'em. This day, there be bigger prize to win. One I will savor destroying so, and ya, duke filled student, shall do my bidding. Do it true, and ya shall be free ta suck whatever cock you wish in yon sad village. Ya knight may no be there, but every other pecker will want ya, well, perhaps if ya live an' do wha' I say. That be fine gift."

Immunditia handed Kiera her black knife. She laughed as she held it out.

"It no be trick. I give this and ya can decide who best stick it in. Oh, yea, surely ya can slice own throat. That be one way ta be free. Then, know ya this. If so ya chose, ya remain pet, but then to the true master, Satan. True slave an' coward and let ya knight die, Crowe free ta continue evil. Tha' be tha' choice. Or, at right time, ya kill Crowe. Avila and me will then have no puppet here, village hence free from Crowe, one who done made ass of himself from fool deal with devil. Ya save them all with but one poke of tha' blade. Yea. All, with that small little sliver of metal in ya hand instead of pecker duke puts in it. It be easy thing. No harder than putting Crowe's cock in you. This be no different. He has had much delight poking ya. Now, ya poke him with like delight. He killed ya sad soul. Killed all ya maiden virtue. Ya have all right ta kill tha' disgusting pervert, sending sick soul to dark master. Know ya this. He goes there no matter what ya chose do. I think ya know true best use of my sharp gift."

Immunditia turned and headed to the door. Kiera called out to her.

"How will uh know right moment, when ta slice?"

Immunditia turned, stared at her, smiling.

"Ya ever cut up chicken?"

Wide-eyed, thinking, Kiera nodded head. Immunditia shrugged.

"Chicken. Raven. Both bird. Same thing. When raven lands before ya, chop off head. He may make tasty soup. Ya already know how he tastes as he be filling ya mouth each day, true, wench? If that be your liking…"

She turned and left. Kiera stared at knife. Immunditia spoke true. She had good use for it.

Caged

Watching guards carry body-shaped iron cage from his chambers, Crowe smiled, reviewing cunning plan. Feeling defiant against Avila and Immunditia, he would thwart knight and supposed Angel protector. There be many ways to kill such man. Tempting him with lost maid would serve best, show to dark lord he be man none trifled with.

Telling guards set cage down where he pointed, him standing, he grinned admiring its design. Made of iron bars, each bar spaced enough apart to allow hands or pecker go through, yet close enough to keep pet inside, standing. Shaped with same curves as pet, bars kept pet standing, tight, trapped. He delighted at plan putting pet in cage, trapped such, many sweet nights. He loved seeing terror on her face when inside. Made of two halves, each joined by hinge, when closed, secured by simple clasp and at most loving times, secured with lock. Looking closely at clasp, he nodded. If pet be in cage, to rescue love knight need pull clasp to open cage. It be simple. All need be done it put pet in cage, wheel cage to open field, leave her there, unattended. He and evil partners then take raven form, fly above, watching rescue. It be perfect plan. Knight would soon join Angel.

Calling for court chemist and smithy, he grew excited more. He greeted them, then swore them keep acts secret or face death. Fearful, they took oath. Both joined him round cage, awaiting tasks.

"Smithy, fine job ya did making thing. This day, uh need quick work made to clasp. Ya made it fine an' smooth for me ta open with nay effort. Yea, clasp be smooth as pet's bottom. Now, ya must make it hard to pull. Ta open, make it hard very hard pull I say. As ya do so, I need ya add wee barbs on back side of clasp. Tiny, sharp things. Hidden from all view. Ones right where fingers hold tight ta pull cage open. Barbs sharp, sturdy like knives, pointed like spikes, sure to poke through skin on fingers. Do such, now. Many barbs in tha' one place, hidden. Small, yea, again uh say, but enough to pierce fingers grasping it."

Confused as to reason, metal worker nodded, saying it be simple and quick job. Crowe called his guards and cage be wheeled to smithy's shop. Crowe turned to chemist. He smiled and bade him sit. None else there, Crowe gave his order.

"Ya saw cage, ya know clasp shall have barbs most sharp ta cut into blood of any opens it. I need potion, thick, ta stay on barbs. Enough ta stay potent in air outside. A potion most fatal. Yea. Death mixture. Stuff tha' will fast kill man once poked by barbs. With haste make such poison true. With only touch of the barb, drawing blood, potion be there. Tha' poke must kill one touching it so. No in day. No in hour. Nay. Minutes after prick from touch. Have ya such mixture?"

Sinister looks were exchanged between them. Understanding request, old chemist nodded, slowly.

"Aye. There be such stuff, and uh have all needed make it. Nature be abundant in ways ta stop folk. Fatal toxin from sweet looking plants and creatures. Me make mixture combining meanest ones. Together, stop any man dead just from wee touch. Faster ever so if in blood. There be no turning back from it. Once poked, in minutes few, he be dead."

Crowe was delighted. Instructing chemist go straight way and prepare bottle, all be in place. He would put pet in cage, put poison on all barbs added to clasp, have cage wheeled out, final act to set cage in middle of innocent pasture. Knight will come ta free her, open clasp, then go meet Angel. He must insist Avila and Immunditia fly above ta watch true evil work, asking why they offered no such plan. Cage be torture for pleasure, now torture for death. He thought how useful his little pleasure chest had become.

A Swan

Encountering the divine, though no remembering such, left August dazed. He thought he but fell asleep, dreamed, and in dream gained certainty of path ahead. Fearing nothing, he felt most certain he would seize Kiera from Crowe. Feeling calm within, it be same like calm he knew before leaving to fight battles. Such times, quiet before siege even if large and looming, fear none known to warriors true. Nay, they relaxed, saved strength and accepted they leave battle but one way. Alive, or dead. No worry, calm in certainty. Conquering warriors finished all foe with fatal blow. Then, for any wounded on field of battle, merciful death blow. All wounded useless to them, finished with a quick cut or hammer blow, their bodies piled in mounds, set ablaze, birds of prey feasting on any they could find first before fire.

Remembering the stench, he thought truth of war. Such victors breathed deep the foul smoke, it being but bodies and bone of men. All dead warriors had hopes, dreams, plans and most had loves and family. One moment they be all such things; a man living each day with gifts waiting. With slice of sword or arrow in head, became only blood on boots, smoke in chest of victors. Nothing more than boots to clean, a cough from body dust in chest. That all they be then, none more. They be downed by his hand. Being too much to dwell on, he recalled last battle. He was struck down. He had thought sure it be fatal wound. Laying in blood and sand, counting the moment his last, twas no so. Without struggle, he rose up from field of battle raging round him. Having no worry of danger, walked to find steed, then was away. Having no concern for duty or any coming after him, his crusade and warring be over. That day he heard a call. Kiera begging him home. His dreaming woke the memory of that day of battle, then he looked down at wounds. All be gone. Stopping his horse, he lifted shirt. Looking all about him, he was smooth of skin. There be no signs of battle on him. Knowing he tended wounds with care, there would be scars, surely. Letting his shirt fall, he shrugged, then stopped wondering where they be. He needed them not.

Being close to duke's castle keep, be be ready for all battle ahead. This be his cause, this be his day. All his roads led to this unholy place. He knew but one thing; that be he ready. He soon be at destination.

Shaking his head in disbelief, ahead he saw another lone figure. Unlike the bull that be man earlier, he saw figure small, yea, slight. No weapon, no stance. Closer, he saw it be wench. Young, dressed in fine silk, timid, and most fair. She stopped, thus he worried trap lay ahead. Looking at wench, being in open land, none other near, no walls nor trees to hide behind, he decided it be but wee lass waiting on him. There be no choice. He need approach her and discover what be waiting for him.

Coming upon her, he was no sure if knew wee maid, for she be quite young. Pretty, dressed in decent manner, she stood shaking as she be fearful of him. Towering over her, hand on his knife, she had reason to be. Seeing no threat, he released his blade, remaining in saddle, looking at her without expression.

Surprising him with a gentle curtsy, she bowed her head, then looked up at him with look of tiding.

"Kind sir, me bid ya welcome and appreciate ya stopping so ya may hear me this day. I know ya be grand knight, August of Red Bluff. I be but wee lass in same village when ya left ta crusade. I be Swan, and bring news of ya betrothed."

He then recalled her. Long ago he heard her speak and her voice be most sweet. She had changed from duckling to swan, indeed. He worried that same like all maids from village, she be maiden no more, defiled by Crowe or his legions. It saddened him.

"Yea, I recall ya when ya be young lass. Tell me true, have ya been defiled by Crowe or his savage brutes?"

Sadness showed on her young face. Her eyes told the tale.

"Kind sir, much has changed. My parents killed. Village plundered. Yea, uh can no deny I be only ten when taken by Duke in that manner. I served him such, only as point of his knife be at my throat. Yea, serve him my goods I have done, yea, as all maids of some beauty be forced ta do. Now, e'er sad for it, I have lost pride, yea, honor too. All I be now is alive. Others be no living more. But, hark, kind sir! That be reason of my being here to greet thee. I be only little thing, pretty, I hope in ya eyes, nay threat ta ya, charged with calming ya fears. E'er so happy ta have good news of ya love."

Looking around, there were no others coming, no traps laid. Only Swan, and she appeared happy in her manner and news. He could but only listen, hoping her words be true. He needed hear right her words. He remained stoic, yet nay wishing to be cruel.

"In matters of Crowe, I know not how any news could be good or glad ta speak of. Creature be vile, yea, servant of darkness. He defiles all honor, Swan. Know this. All have but three things be value in life. Things true and be all we have. Ya parents, ya honor, ya life. Life be all ya think ya be left with. Pray, I shall make sure ya can use what be left most well on road ahead. Where is my maiden fair? Hear me. Maiden fair she be still if no for him. Him. And Swan, giving virtue of ya own wish be only true way ta lose it. Taken from ya by force, nay. Know this. Maid with honor ya still be. Know that. Understand?"

Lowering her head, his words cut deep. He could see though captive she had her own mind on the matter. Having been robbed of virginity, her parents, and freedom, he wished to avenge such crimes. He would tell her such.

"I be here to save all, no just my intended. Take solace, fine maid. There be time soon when ya body, and most sacred, ya heart, both be free of dark duke. Ya are no to fear me. Know that true. I be only friend, here to save ya. Ya be sent to me, posing no threat as ya be wee lass. The duke, oh, be true coward as he no come face me with sword in hand. In his stead, hides sends ya silk. Duke be only like tha' between ya legs. I know an' understand such. Ha gave ya message for this knight. Tell message, for I will hear ya in word and manner. I beg, speak only true."

She nodded, then looked at him with a soft smile.

"Grand warrior, duke tell all in court ya pose mortal worry with ya might. The matter be debated at length, decision made most true in ya favor. Duke told all such order. That be no harm be done ya. Ta let ya pass free, finding Kiera waiting for thee. Then, all told, give ya leave and wide berth. Duke wishes no battle, declared ya mighty threat, telling all battle be folly. Ha bid me greet thee, say no terms be said, nay, none needed. He wish only ya take Kiera and be away. Duke bid me tell ya such shows him reasonable on this an' future matters. He bid me explain what ha begs ya ta know true. Using words I must say jus' as he said them, this be message from duke."

Swan stood a moment, wanting to say all as told exact and true.

"Duke proclaim he set forth only ta but protect all from invaders. Tha' be done. He be misunderstood. This be offer of peace, mighty knight be last matter at hand. Let all know his wish ta return all peace ta village, county, and pray, to all of this land."

Knowing the lass repeated what she was told, he knew it all be lie. Even such, rescuing Kiera was first order and task, hence he must set all lies aside until she be safe. After, he would no accept such deception.

"Ya have delivered tidings most clearly. Tell Duke this be my reply. I understand meaning, truly. I be hoping them sincere. That be message ta deliver. Now, with that matter attended, pray tell where Kiera may be, and if vile duke will be present."

Nodding politely, she smiled, glad he heard message. She had all details he wished.

"Knowing ya be wary e'er so of surprise, worried ya love may run in fear of deception, Duke thought matter through. He has simple contrivance to hold maid in safety. It be no locked. She be in wait, in it she be, no even knowing ya be on way. There be large field, free from places any may hide, and maid be in middle of field. Duke bids ya go to maid. Open holding, it be held shut only with simple clasp. Take maid, pray go with wishes of peace for ya both. Field is one ya must know, surely. Tha' large one, before castle. It be empty but for Kiera. Sweet maid be there, now, waiting."

Looking up at him with eyes filled with longing and passion, he knew what be in her mind, and certainly her heart. Having suffered so, hope stolen from her, a pathetic cock given in place, his heart cried for the lass. She be but bonnie, he knew she be all crusade holy should be waged for. It would be so. Looking about her, she started to weep.

"Oh, knight, I say this on my own, and but it be only my heart filling with hope. I want ya know what ya mean ta little Swan this day. I wish it be me on ya saddle, in ya arms tonight. Think of me tha' way if ya so wish. I be only a wee thing, I know. I be dreaming of ya hence. Oh, if ya e'er dreamt of me I would true be maiden, new, in such dream. I pray ya be wishin' me so, on ya return. My love be in wait, for ya only, any time ya fancy if such wee maid ya desire."

Near tears, Swan turned and ran down the road. On her own, none came to gather her. August watched her go over a crest and saw no others. He thought her every reason to slay the demon. In Crowe's chains, her heart was yet free, hope remained.

Thinking of message delivered by sweet Swan, it be true he intended any form of battle or devastation to reach Kiera. For Crowe, coward ever, it made sense losing but one maid when he had many more, sweet and blithe as wee Swan at his call. It be set Kiera free or be run through by his long sword. Thinking, yea, there may be archers in wait, he then shook his head thinking nay, with field so large, none trained in such arts, that would be folly. Beyond arrows shot at him, he knew no other danger he would face. The coward picked careful his spot. It was as described. If Kiera be there, he had but ride there, gather her, then take leave at full gallop, alert, ready for any blocking his way. After all thought, he understood there be no choice. Deception or true, to Kiera he would ride.

Courting

"Crowe, uh admit ya devised stout plan for knight. I confess I thought ya could no do so. This cage be death. No for one in it, trapped. It be death ta one grabbing hold outside it. Damnation, yea, forevermore. Quite good. I say true master shall be pleased. It be handy craft. Immunditia and me fly with ya there, most delighted ta watch fool open cage ta save defiled love. Yea, fine sight. Oh, yea, all hearin' ya pet squeal and moan when knight dies in front of bitch so. All hopes an' prayers shall lay there at her feet, dead on ground with nay battle fought. That will be delight. Immunditia, be ready. We three shall fly above. When knight falls, Crowe, honor be yours. Feast on his eyes. Rip his flesh. Let pet see what mortal stuff grand love warrior be made of."

Sitting at court, admiring cage in the center of the room, they drank toast to plan. Crowe be smug, feeling superior to wizard and she-demon companion. He delighted both knew folly of underestimating his resolve and cunning. This changed who be teacher, who be student. Crowe went on to tell of sending young sweet morsel to stop August on road, then absurd story she must tell. Again, they delighted in his scheme.

"Crowe. Well planned. Ya will down knight without sword raised. Most impressive. Ya will have endless perversions to delight in for night ahead with your pretty pet. This day pet learns true why ya be master. Only ya be protector now. She will know that be so. Brave knight will leave again. Ya are the one to protect pet from such weak man."

Smiling, basking in praise, Crowe held up his hand and looked at the cage.

"The sweet young morsel has left. She will soon deliver message. We must take wing without delay. Immunditia, get my pet, but to no send knight into dismay, let her no be naked as I like her. He be none smart ta understand clothes useless on pet. Dress pet in some finery. Aye. Black, yea. That be apt honor to master. Make pet stunning so knight can see what be mine. Oh, yea. See pet he will ne'er have. Can ya make pet such? Quickly?"

Immunditia smiled and was glad as dress would conceal black blade, hers given to Kiera. A black dress was perfect for such deception.

"Yea, uh have lovely black bodice and skirt. Bitch be enchanting after me dress her. A true surprise for ya, black duke. Yea, wait! I must haste. I be back shortly. I leave it for ya to tell ya pet what comes next."

As she turned, she saw the chemist with small jar she knew be the potion of doom and death, standing clear less old man trip and spill it on her. She had all right in her mind. Preparing Kiera, she would share secret plan, telling Crowe would be raven form, busy gloating. That be time to cut him. All depended on keeping Kiera true to plan.

In her chamber, Kiera had practiced wielding black knife. She wondered when she would have chance to use it. Immunditia entered, holding embroidered black corset and skirt. Explaining all things to come, she dressed her, then slid the blade down corset seam where ties concealed it best. All was ready.

"Ya know he takes raven shape. No let on ya have knowing of such. No word duke be raven who land before ya. Be confused and scared in manner. Do no raise ya arm in cage. That be upsetting to Crowe. Hear me this, only let hands hold bars. No, ne'er, try open cage. No matter what, hold tight bars in front of those small breasts. Do no touch parts elsewhere. Heed my words or plan fail."

Leading her to court, she gasped entering, seeing cage. She managed to look embarrassed being clothed, putting her arms round herself in pretend shame. Immunditia had suggested it on way, and it be fine touch. Duke looked at her, holding his hands out to her.

"No, worry no. Ya be beautiful though true beauty be covered with pointless cloth. Only for short while. I have special treat for my pet. A day in sun to make ya skin glow. I will join ya later for ya favorite acts of passion. And here, lovely cage where ya enjoy countless pleasures. Ya will ride in it ta visit lovely field. Bathe in sun, pet. Glow for my pleasure. Enjoy day. Sun will kiss ya skin forever more. Men, ya have orders. Pet, in ya go. There. Very comfortable. Lovely surrounded by bars of passion. Think of me true, yea, as bars holding you…"

Once in the cage, duke closed it, careful to let it shut with the lever hinge snapping in place. Old chemist had coated handle, it had barbs quite sharp under it, waiting only for knight's grasp.

Unleashed

Holding tight bars of cursed cage she hated since first she saw it, four farm lads managed to carry it upright and place it on walled cart. Three stood round it, keeping it upright, fourth drove it to large pasture well past the castle. Stopping in middle, the four carefully lowered it to level ground, making sure it be secure and true. Once so, they left cart they carried her on, then at fast pace ran back to castle. She be alone, in perverse black corset laced tight, it holding fast the long black blade hidden inside.

Having been prisoner for a year times two and more, it be first time she be outside castle, prison true. Overwhelmed feeling sun and wind, she be overwhelmed more at events putting her in middle of field. She wore covering, she knew August would come for her, elated she had knife to cut Crowe dead if he did appear in form raven near her. Knowing him in league with devil himself, she knew devil — and his evil servants — took many forms. Immunditia, though depraved in all manner, was certain of matter and it be clear she be glad to find way rid of vile duke.

Having been treated as naught but mindless animal, some insane notion of pet, Kiera understood she be long past redemption. Killing Crowe be sin, true, yet killing be only but one more in great number of sins blackening her soul. Doing such would keep duke from damning more maidens, that reason enough for such sinful act.

Looking down at her body, she be glad she be dressed to some degree. It be tawdry attire she knew only whores wear, and woe, she be pale and thin as whores be if no immensely fat. Twas better than naked with collar clamped by leash, she conceded such. August would understand she be controlled by sick minion of Satan, her countenance be his command, nay hers.

Cawing above diverted her attention from vengeful thoughts. She looked to sky. As Immunditia told, she saw raven. She looked at black thing, then two more appeared.

Three ravens.

Circling above, they be looking only at her. She shook in fear as they be demon creatures, oh, up to no good.

Watching them closely, all three ravens changed course, flying to edge of field, then sat high above field, watching all perched on branch of tree. Cawing at each other, she realized the three were indeed the dark three evil wardens of her prison. Crowe, evil wizard, and Immunditia. Three demon minions, three ravens, waiting feast of bodies dead, her knowing most precious feast of demon birds be dreams and virtue. Certain they waited on August same as she, her only hope was they stay as ravens giving leave August take her away. Then, one raven, one making noise loudest, flew from tree, leaving other two on tree to but watch. The thing flew right near cage, walking on ground, evil eyes looking up at her. She knew it be duke, but let him know naught she had been so told. Bird duke looked to road, to tree, then her. Bird stared at her, then gave a loud caw that shook her. It took flight, returned to tree in haste. The three ravens stayed there, hard to see, now silent.

There were three ravens sitting on a tree. All be as it should be.

Hearing sound of hooves galloping, she understood why they be in tree, no making noise. August approached.

Having good view of road, she saw dust first, then shape of man on horse, then made shape to be her love. He saw her the same time, making haste to her. As he grew near, she cried out his name, he cried out hers. Once fully on field, he stopped suddenly. It caused her fright, but saw him circle about, surveying all around field. He being certain it be no trap be wise. She understood. She was crying, calling his name, ecstatic to see him once more. Certain no folly waited him, he was at gallop again, this time stopping no. Just short of her cage, he pulled tight reins, jumping off steed.

"Kiera. Love! Glorious day! I thought it be trap, or lie. No matter. Ya be here, I have found ya, thank God most holy. My love, we shall be away."

She was filled with emotion. Tears. Sobbing. Calling his name. Thanking God.

Wasting no time, August studied cage, finding it but simple shell held tight only by simple clasp with nay lock. He looked at her, smiling, full of love in his eyes.

"It be simple thing. Now, let us leave and talk once gone from this hell. Be ready to join me on saddle…"

Grabbing the clasp, August winced from pain. Pulling the clasp, after opening cage, he held hand up to study it. It be red with blood. Looking at her, he said it be sharp thing, then naturally sucking blood from fingers and thumb to catch bleeding. He winced again. Fingers and blood had taste most bitter. Taking hand from mouth, he studied wound. He looked at her with dismay, then bent to look at the catch. Seeing it had been shaped into barbs on hidden side, he quickly pushed the clasp back in place, telling Kiera to leave cage, to be no near clasp. She had seen his reaction pulling it open, then blood. She thought it just be sharp edge. He looked at her with sadness as she stepped out. He stood, looking at her with tears and desperation. She cried out, asking what be the matter.

"All that matters is ya be free and I love ya true. Kiera… From this evil, be away! Just… just be away…"

Looking at him with fear and confusion, she grabbed him and begged him mount his steed, be away with her. He was shaking, fingers and thumb bleeding. He held all blood away, warning her against getting any on her, to no touch cage or his wound. Crying, she saw tears and terrified look on his face. He went weak, dropping to knees. She kept tugging at his shirt, saying they must be away.

Hearing a loud caw, she saw demon raven duke land near to watch from ground. Raw anger rushed through her. She knew duke caused all misery and peril August be in. Ignoring demon, kneeling down, she started kissing August, telling him stay awake, she would get him on horse. He slumped, then head fell in her lap. His eyes opened wide, looking into hers. His skin was changing color, his hand was swollen twice normal size, he was gasping for air. He managed to speak between gasps.

"The cage… poison on latch… a trap… my love, I will see ya again… I be yours… yours… Go, love. Run…'

His head fell, his body went into a convulsion, he gasped for air, then was still. The raven stood watching. It let forth a shrill caw of victory.

Kiera fell forward over her knight, protecting him, wailing in pain and grief. Crowe had used her again. This time for his true perversion, his only pleasure true, killing.

She held August tight, uttering loving words to him, telling him she was his. As she said so, the raven cawed louder than she thought possible. The evil bird started taking steps towards them. She knew ravens picked flesh from any dead. She be sure duke bird sought eye for prize. Rubbing her side as if she ached, she felt knife Immunditia hid there. She looked up quickly at tree Crowe flew from. The devil ravens remained there, watching. Knowing them to be Immunditia and wizard, they waited her dispatch of Crowe. She would no fail in her attack.

Brazen as if he were in human form, the raven stepped up to study her love's swollen hand covered in blood. Cawing again, she gently slid August from her lap, laying him on the ground, acting like any frightened maid, telling the raven to shoo, to be away. She said she had no intent on giving black bird any flesh from her love. Crowe be looking only at fallen knight, no her. Seeing his attention so, she pulled knife from her bodice, keeping it from sight. As duke raven started to lift beak to pluck at eye, she seized moment, thrusting knife low from her side, long point going through bird breast. Blood squirted, creature squawked in pain and shock, wings flapping to attempt flight but leaving no. The thing fully impaled by blade in her hand.

Squawking, flapping wings, it was desperate. A might rose in Kiera most unexpected. She lifted the knife quickly by handle, bird flaying on blade, raised it, then turning its tip downwards with haste, drove tip of blade down with might into ground, keeping duke raven captive. Squawking louder, she ignored it. She watched August riding to her. He had his mighty sword sheathed, hanging from saddle on steed but few feet away. She sprang to horse, grasped handle of sword, then with strength she knew ne'er before, pulled blade from sheath, raising it high in air, then struck blade down straight with perfect aim at raven laying impaled on its side, looking with hate at her.

The sword sliced through its neck, sending the black bird head flying.

She laid down sword, pulling her love's dead body, moving it away from bird. Movement near gained her attention. Duke, in bird body and head cast away, began shaking and shimmering. Thinking she may have touched poison causing strange visions, she knelt next to August, watching all happening to duke bird. In but minute, bird duke changed, before her eyes, back to true form. Before her lay putrid body, and severed head, of Crowe. Black knife be sunk to hilt in his side, his departed head lay facing up to sky. Standing up, she went to make sure he was dead, seeing his pathetic face had a look of surprise. Nodding with smile, surely image before her would be her only remembrance of creature. He be most dead, but, shuddering with certainty of events, so was August. She knelt down at his side once more, rubbing his tortured head, so kind, praying for him.

"August, dear love. I have avenged your death this day. It be truly most unfair. Yea, I will see ya again. That be joyous day. Oh, laddie. This, I know.

It be ya give me strength to brandish tha' sword. I promise ya, holy sword will be ya marker when ya be in ground. Oh love, and this I promise, and know true. I will lay by ya side. I be glad ya ne'er had ta learn uh have demon seed in me womb. I can no let it see world. Nay, never. Crowe ended here, this day. His fruit will no see sun. No, nay, never. No fallow doe be I e'er more, nay, never. Satan bastard has no home in me. I be no his temple. Worry no, I must leave ya for but short time. Jus' wee time, that be all needed. I will tend ta all. Lay at peace. Ya maid be back, soon."

Laying his head gently on ground, she got up, again using strength she knew never before, and dragged Crowe's headless body to iron cage. She lifted him up and propped him upright against the sick iron bars. She took head by hair, pulled down his tights, then put what little cock he had in mouth of his head, holding all in place with tights pulled up about his middle, him looking like very fallow doe. Closing cage nay touching clasp, she stood, looking at dead duke now nay master to any. Nodding, told him certain he now be his own pet and hence have pleasure to service himself, and most pleasing to his master, Satan, forevermore. That be true, she be sure.

She had other matters to attend.

Pulling at mighty sword, it felt somehow light to her. She lifted it easily, laid the flat side over her shoulder, then leisurely walked to tree other ravens perched in. She looked up to them, sword shining in sun, reflecting in their black eyes.

"I no wish ya two be peckin' at tha' good knight. If ya don' wish ta be next feel this blade, ya best be back ta hell an' far way from here!"

She watched them leave the branch, heading down. She pulled at sword, holding blade out to her side, ready to strike true, ready to finish captors. As they descended, they transformed from two ravens to their human form.

Standing before her, Immunditia and evil Avila held their hands up, calmly, indicating no threat. She was wary of tricks, telling them so, sword fully at ready.

Nodding understanding, Avila looked at her as if for the first time. He nodded again.

"Be wary of any offering anything ya no know be safe. Yea, ya should be fearing of one's such we be. We serve evil, that be so. Today, know this. Today, we pose no challenge. Our work here? Done. Tha' fool paid his due. Ya knight? Knight died for love. What finer death can there be?"

Kiera could do naught but nod in agreement. Her battle be with Crowe. They intended no more suffering in his place and would be gone. All suffering now gone with Crowe's head. They both be called back to hell. Best let them go.

Immunditia held up her finger, black knife flew from Crowe's chest, landing in her hand. She admired it, licked all blood from it, then held it at her side. She smiled her white smile, looking into Kiera's eyes.

"Yea. Ya did him proud. Ya did fine work with that bird. I will remember that. I have my blade back. Oh, that be my favorite corset. I can no tell ya how many ones I done had in me whilst wearing it only as none can no count so high a number. My lucky bodice, so I do no think ya be minding me having it back. Yea, I think ya be liking one ya wear now a wee bit more…"

She looked confused, then saw Immunditia was wearing the black corset and skirt. She looked down at herself, and she was amazed. She was in same maiden frock she wore day August left to crusade. It felt wonderful. She looked up to question Immunditia. Both demons had vanished. They said they would go, she be glad they left. She now had no worry of ravens pecking away at her knight. Turning back to August, she saw they had done more than give her sweet dress. The cage was gone. August be there, his stood with the stout cart hitched to him, and there be spade laying in it. She looked up to top of tree. No ravens. Their deed be done.

Fallow Doe

After walking to wagon, she laid giant sword in its bed. Going to August, she knelt at his side, telling him she be back; worry no.

"But one more ride. Tha' all it be. This one, aye, this one be with ya love an' it be my crusade to be with ya. Love, know uh be fallow doe this day. August, no bein' from ya, that can no be so. But, no for long. Nay, no, never. I know place most special and dear, down road, ya know it too. The grove ya first confessed ya loved me, and aye, where I told ya this maid love ya true. Let us go to tha' sacred spot. It will no be long. Ya be good company. Now, tis special day, so this be special frock lass have for ya. Confess ya noticed. I hope ya remember! It be very one I wore day ya left. Now, it be one I wear when ya came back to me…"

Dragging his body, she was careful lifting him into cart. She still be stronger than she thought possible, but many unusual things belonged to that day. Describing countryside and road to August as they rode, she started singing his favorite ditty. An old tune they heard at Faire before he left. In no time, they reached the shady grove she promised, telling him she be about, making wedding bed.

Taking spade, she sang old ditty over and over as she dug deep the earth below her.

The water tis wide
I can no cross o'er
Nor have I
Wings ta fly

Build me a boat
Can carry two
An' both shall row
My love an' I

The hole was wide and deep. She looked over to him, singing more of the ditty.

There be a ship
Tha' sails tha' sea
Loaded deep
As ship may be

Nay, not as deep
As the love I'm in
I know no how
Ta sink or swim

Going to cart, she took his sword, then standing at head of hole, drove it deep in ground, placed well in its middle. Looking fondly at mighty thing, it formed a beautiful cross with its hilt and handle upwards. She nodded at him. Climbing down into hole, she gently pulled at his shoulders, bringing him in, then laid him down on right side of the hole. She knelt next to her love, gave him sweet kiss, then took long knife off his belt. Kissing blade, making sign of cross over him with blade, holding it to her breast she laid down beside him. Saying a prayer for a kind soul to pass by some beautiful day, seeing they laid without blanket o'er them, to praise God, be kind, and cover them safe as it be their wedding bed.

She lay, ready for forever, then felt great comfort. Hearing barks, sniffing and panting, she looked up one last time. Laying at edge of bed she made were Jake and Max, her love's grand hounds he sadly left behind, as he had her, being off to crusade. They found him at last. Their stately heads hung low o'er edge above. Then, closing her eyes, she used her love's blade for to join him e'er more in the land that knows no parting. Max sat up, raised his head to moon just showing its jealous face above. He began howling to Heaven. Jake sat up, joining in wondrous harmony. Heralding as trumpets divine, telling God this be special day. Pray, make way.

Love Here And There

"My love. Oh! Look at maid. Her love for ya true. Yea, that it be. Be it all ya dream love true be e'er, or be such even more?"

Sitting on downed log where they first met, the sky held vision painted on soft cloud. Holding each other, they watched Kiera battle for his life, then tend his remains. Smiling at each other, they kissed, sharing same true admiration for her love. Looking at cloud again, each saw Kiera digging grave from on high. A green patch of earth amongst beautiful trees. Slowly, green gave way to dark circle, growing larger, becoming square. He squeezed her tight seeing his much loved hounds find him at last. He heard Max, then Jake, both calling to God. A beautiful howling.

"This be mystery. Yea. Look. There ya be, yea, there. But, oh, who be this by my side? Oh, ya be here too. Dead, but alive. Gone, but back. Long ago, but yet to be. Ya save lass. She save knight. Is it any but beautiful? Could ya true know this joy, here with me, without tha' knowing?"

She kissed him again and sighed softly in his ear. Just a sigh. She was the air he breathed, the thoughts in his mind, the whisper on his lips. Taking off her wisp of gossamer, she pulled his mantle from him. Glowing with passion and shining rays of love that took form, she stood before him, then turned round and round, sharing all her infinite beauty, letting her turning motion send rays of purest love fly endlessly to the wonders of creation.

"Oh, I be knowin' ya seen many images of Angels in many a land. Paintings an' statues. In holy places, some gracing streets. Is it no sad none can show beauty such as I be? Such wonder, here, in front of ya?"

He agreed. Nothing of man could describe the beauty before him. Her form was divine and why the word holy existed. It be far more than perfection or ideal. It was all things one dreamed of. He told her it could no be so in that sad life, nay, none could be alive if they saw perfection such. Who would live when such beauty be but end breath away?

Seeing her as body, he saw her as soul too, as both be her. Both created perfection. One without other made no sense. He could no understand how anything could be desired if form only. Spirit shaped form. Once understood, once death brought real life, there be no remembering life and limits. Walls. Beginnings. Ends. This. That. She knew his mind; she could feel his thoughts.

"August, that be important stuff. Without sadness, how would any know joy? Light would mean naught if we had no any dark. Kiera had Crowe. Tha' evil seed inside lass. She had dark in her, yea, and around her. Imagine if she no had ya? How would she know that darkness if lass ne'er had ya light? Ya light be wha' she loved. She made choice. Tha' deciding, it be place where eternity waits. Tha' deciding leads here. Oh, it be true deciding can lead one ta dark. Each one decides. Ya faced many choices. Ya deciding, oh, know this, love, ya deciding brought ya here. To this sweet Angel. Oh, an' sweet I be… My deciding brought me to ya. I know ya be just woke from dream. That be all life is. A wee dream. No much more. I welcome ya back, though I ne'er had worry of ya. Know this, ya have always been, ya will always be. I know ya be just waking from dream. My sleepy-time knight. Ya see all as new. It be why we dream. To know this waits. All this beauty and love be waking on new day. When ya be knight, before tha' grave, ya loved Kiera. Do ya want ya bonnie maid here, now? Together, as ya both be in tha grave?"

He was certain he did. He had no doubt. She smiled. Both sitting on log he woke from, she bid him stay. She raised in air, was slight above him, then

lowered her form to be on him. Sighing her passion louder in his mind, him feeling her breath inside him, she sat on him, pulling his head tight to her breasts. He realized how complete he be inside her as they became one. As she moved up and down, sighing so, he understood she was inside him too, the river he felt running up through him, filled with her sparkling stream. Knowing making love such was becoming one, he thought how bodies stop true union. Being only sad things, trapping spirit in shell, loving with bodies be attempt of two trying to become one when living. As she moved up and down, on and off, inside her deep as love can be, kissing, hugging, all were but gestures and invitations. All be openings, true, to join each other in spirit. In love. To see each other, in each other.

Looking into his eyes, she knew her loving would wake him wide, giving him all her heart and soul. They be only what he always had, love and joy he be graced with forever. He smiled and nodded. At last he knew her name. The same he had called her in life when knight. The name he realized once inside her. The name when thinking of her laying by his side that day.

Smiling at each other, he told her his eyes be awake, then laughed, telling her true, "Kiera, ya really do look same, ya know. I know ya well by ya sweet heart an' kind thoughts. One, an' many, yea, at same time. I be needin' more waking to know how ya do so! I do know this. Ya be my love, ever. Love, same then, same now, same forever, always, again.

Here I Go, Singing Downe Ditty Dew

Hiking down a seldom used dirt road, the young man decided to stop and check his messages and email. He finally had service and took advantage of the good reception. Looking down the dusty road, then up at the trees, he thought it a bit hot even for the last month of summer. Though hiking at a leisurely pace he hadn't realized what a long distance he'd travelled. He was distracted, hard at work on a new song taking shape in his head, working the melody and on occasional stops playing it on his antique tin whistle.

An amateur musician and songwriter, hiking was peaceful, giving him inspiration and time to think.

It was a sunny day and he was happy to finally be outdoors after being holed up, chained to his work too long. His boss finally took the advice of some consultants and insisted remote workers get some vacation time. Stuck in his one-room flat, a long hike would get him exercise and some Sun. He had hoped to hike a historic trail in Israel he read about that sounded fascinating, but, as always, there was some war going on so he finally decided on Norway where his family migrated from. He was a history buff and he hiked roads used in famous marches and battles, having a great time learning about places his family told stories about. But, it was hotter than expected, so time for a rest. He was thirsty and hoping to cool off when he saw a pleasant spot off the side of the road, lush with trees and shade. Deciding to eat lunch in the shady grove, he was glad his pack was filled with local bread and cheese and glad it held a large bottle of natural spring water. Getting closer, the grove didn't look like it was visited very often. It didn't look like it ever been visited. Shrugging, he felt it would be the perfect spot for inspiration.

Smiling, he drank water, felt a cool breeze, and he was looking forward to thinking of words for the sweet melody he had been working on. All he had written until then was a catchy bridge. He was stuck, singing the one part over and over.

"Da de dah, de da, da. Da de da, de day, de, day..."

Yep, really needs some mystical words people would try to figure out. Obscure. Vague, maybe. And some magical, really awesome sweetie in there. That's what the song needs. Oh yeah, that's what I need.

Finding the lushest spot in the grove, looking around for inspiration he was shocked to find a large, deep hole near a mound of rich black earth.

There was an old spade laying near it. Standing in front of the opening he was fully in awe, staring at a cross looking a lot like an ancient upside-down sword. Studying it, he wondered how anyone could have ever wielded such a giant thing. *Nah, must be from a monument place.* Growing brave, he forced himself to the edge of the hole, glad he hadn't fallen in while distracted as he pondered his new song. At the edge he was greeted by the fossil remains of two giant dogs, laying there at rest and guarding the hole. *Good doggies. I'm a friend. No biting...* He could only smile at such loving pets.

Eyes widening, he gathered his courage then took a quick look in the hole. *Yep, I knew it. A grave, uncovered. Oh, how sad. Wow!* That was his first reaction. Then, as he stood thinking, looking down into it for a long time, it became incredibly beautiful. He stood looking, his mind filled with feelings.

The grave held two people. A man and woman. Having no way of knowing exactly what happened he could only guess one had died, the other dug the grave for them both then joined the other one in death. *Whoa! Yeah, the kind of thing you read about now and then. Some murder/ suicide thing, or maybe a really awesome true love story.* That notion hit him hard, and he became sure of it. *Yep, they wanted to tell the story of their love. There they are. Together in love, with each other forever.* The tale would have its ending when he covered them with earth. He would honor their love by writing the final chapter in their story that way. It would be a defining moment in his life too.

Looking at the spade, he spied some white blossoms nearby. Putting the spade upright in the ground, he fetched the blooms and decided to lay half on the lovers, then put the rest on top of the grave. He nodded. *I'll take a picture of the flowers in front of the cross headstone thing. Post it later, awesome optics.* He grew determined they would have a righteous burial, then nodding to himself, was sure he would write a song about their true love once they were covered. *An original. Post my tune with the picture. Hope it goes viral… This is legend. Epic!*

Before starting to fill the grave, he took a long last look. The man wore leather pants and a decent wool shirt very much in style. He was really large. A genuinely big man. The woman was the opposite. He gazed at her, wondering what she was like. Wondering if the man truly knew and understood her. She was very petite. Wonderfully delicate from the size of her frame, wearing a very pretty floral dress with delicate embroidery. The clothes all looked brand new. Rubbing his beard, he wondered how the clothes could look so good, yet be on two skeletons? But, they were wearing them. It was hard to guess how long they'd been laying there. *But, wow, no flesh at all, just white bones? It must have been a really long time ago when they died.* He would never know. *If anyone knew, hey, the grave would have been covered up long ago.*

He took the flowers, smelled them, sprinkled them on the two lovers, then said a prayer for them. He became emotional. Just as they must have wanted to be together in life, they chose to be together in death. A love eternal. That made him feel so alone. He longed to be on the road with his own petite love. *Whoa. Yeah. My own little Angel. Total awesome love, yeah, and petite like that, for sure. Then wearing a dress just like that? Wow. That had to be one hot romance.* It gave him inspiration. He spoke to them.

"Hey, I'm going to fill you in, okay? I feel so much right now. All kinds of thoughts and feelings. To get here, I know you each must have gone through a lot for each other. A whole lot, I am sure of it. I feel it. I'm glad you're together. And now you'll be safe. I'll do the rest."

Not even thinking why, he suddenly knew it would be fitting to sing a very old song as he laid the dirt over them. His mind kept going to an old ballad he learned when first playing guitar in a coffee shop a few years back from a customer as they shared old songs. Stopping, looking back to the road that led to a village he learned about in his hiking guidebook, the song came to mind as he once read the song originated a very long time ago in the same village nearby. He thought the name sounded familiar, so the bustling village must have had a very drama-filled past given the words to the song. He stopped again, knowing it was not a song he would sing after the dirt was fully laid over them. *Too much doom and gloom, but what a great melody...* It seemed fitting as it was a somber song for his very somber task. And, as it was a local song filled with tradition, it seemed fitting in that way too.

Starting to shovel dirt slowly, he thought how all such songs had some kind of interesting story behind them. Perhaps embellished a bit over hundreds of years, but the story was usually still there. He was sure even new renditions were faithful, building on the words and story the song was inspired by. He believed old ballads were about real people. They were all stories that needed to be remembered. *If I could write something still played after 800 years like this one, wow, I'd jump in that hole right now if that's what it would take.*

He decided to tell the two loves down in the ground not to fret. It was only an old song. Nothing more.

"Hey. It's all good. Just an old folk tale some old geezer put to an even older tune. Hey. Really, don't worry. Just a classic old song from town to help me get this all straight in my head so I do your burial right. You'll dig it. Nothing at all to do with you two love birds."

He smiled at that. *Yeah. Love birds. Flying away to hold each other for all eternity. I wish I had known you...* Stopping a minute to remember all the words, he shoveled away, singing the old song as they faded into the earth.

About the Author

Author, publisher, photographer and designer, Terry Ulick created the *T: Demonic Investigator Series*, and *Folk Ballads Realized* series of novels for Wherever Books. Recent works include *Angel* and *Colorado Dreamin'*.

Publisher of underground newspapers, consumer magazines, books and a glamour photographer, Terry has a career spanning 50 years of creative works including self-help and empowerment books. When covering rock music in the late 60s and early 70s he interviewed famous rock artists, learning their music was often influenced by folk ballads hundreds of years old. That inspired the *Folk Ballads Realized* series. His life experiences shaped his books about Angels and demons.

"In my books I take all my life events, which are not typical of most people, and reflect on how I've come face-to-face with evil many times. How many people can hitchhike, get picked up by John Wayne Gacy and live to tell the tale? That was meeting a true demon. Evil exists. I had a near-death experience that was beyond imagination. I have experienced the Divine... and a very beautiful Angel who can't be described in human concepts. In my latest book, Angel, *I wished to show how we are capable of beautiful love, understanding, and kindness... and smart enough to not fall for evil disguised as attraction. We all have free will. We all need to use it and walk away from evil."*

By Terry Ulick

www.ingramcontent.com/pod-product-compliance
Lightning Source LLC
Chambersburg PA
CBHW010448310726

48979CB00018B/2862/J